LYONS PUMPED A SINGLE ROUND INTO THE FALLEN ATTACKER'S SKULL

The man at the end of the hallway paused and turned at the sound of the finishing shot. He had one more round in his big revolver, and he raised it toward Lyons. The Ironman wasn't risking the spread of buckshot reaching him. He pumped three rounds into the outlaw biker, catching him in the upper chest.

The gunman's revolver blasted a storm of lead into the ceiling above him as he crashed backward, ribs broken, lungs torn apart by the fat 230-grain mushrooms of lead and copper.

Lyons swept closer, his Colt leveled at the man's head.

In an instant, guards were running everywhere. Lyons lowered the pistol, muzzle aimed at the carpet. The uniformed men regarded him cautiously, then looked at the body on the ground.

"Try not to get any more blood on the walls," one guard grumbled. "We'll send up someone from maintenance to fix whatever they shot up."

Lyons took a deep breath, then nodded.

Their first r_____ ___ ___ weapons auction, and someone had alread_

DON PENDLETON'S

STONY

AMERICA'S ULTRA-COVERT INTELLIGENCE AGENCY

MAN ®

DEATH DEALERS

A GOLD EAGLE BOOK FROM

W✪RLDWIDE ®

TORONTO • NEW YORK • LONDON
AMSTERDAM • PARIS • SYDNEY • HAMBURG
STOCKHOLM • ATHENS • TOKYO • MILAN
MADRID • WARSAW • BUDAPEST • AUCKLAND

Recycling programs
for this product may
not exist in your area.

First edition December 2014

ISBN-13: 978-0-373-80448-1

Death Dealers

Special thanks and acknowledgment to
Douglas P. Wojtowicz for his contribution to this work.

Printed in U.S.A.

DEATH DEALERS

CHAPTER ONE

Blackness engulfed Dr. Robert Baxter's vision as what felt like the weight of a mountain range lay upon his back. He tried to shift himself, squirming his way through the cracks that surrounded him. It was midnight-black in there, and as he tried to take a breath, he could feel the pressure of the rubble around him. Fear gripped him, but he flexed his fingers, dug his toes in and inched along.

He could feel the scrape of pebbles and dust against his bare chest. Somewhere in the explosions that had rocked him and the rest of the Naval Weapons Testing Ground, he'd lost his shirt and laboratory coat. His glasses were gone, so even if there were light, he couldn't have seen much farther than the crook of his elbow.

He was forced to stop when he encountered a hunk of reinforced concrete that was far too big to move. Baxter wished that he had the strength to shove such things aside or to flatten himself like putty and slip between the gaps. Hell, at this point, he would have been happy just to be able to see anything

Come on, Baxter, you're a rocket scientist. Use your goddamn brain.

The trapped man ran his fingers along the flat surface, testing and touching it. He reached up, following the face of what seemed to be a wall. Fingertips jammed into the corner and Baxter winced as he pulled his hand back across the slope, feeling his knuckles scoured and abraded by whatever was there. However he could tell that there was at least a few inches more room in that gap. There was a section of rebar exposed on the ground, so he clamped both fists around it, pulling himself out of the crevice holding him tightly.

Tugging himself out was arduous and he could feel his slacks tugged, snagged. His back and shoulders, his stomach and chest, all felt the snarled hooks, the poking and gripping talons of what must have been a million little nails gouging at his naked skin. Finally he was loose. He slumped into the rut next to the flat slab.

It must have been a column. If it were wall, he'd have felt the seams between the cinder blocks.

If something could knock down a column that thick, then whatever had struck the building must have been incredibly powerful. He started pulling himself farther along. His legs were still in the crack behind him. Baxter had turned enough that his shoulders could get to their full breadth, his back pressed against the flat, smooth concrete behind him. He had to get his feet loose, and the snarls and splinters that bedeviled his chest and back were now ripping his slacks. One shoe was already gone and the other now popped off, snagged on some outcropping.

Baxter folded his knees to his chest, feet finally freed from the sandwiching weight he'd slithered away from. He let his legs extend beneath him, enjoying the relative roominess of his new prison. Here, he was able to breathe; he could reach down and up.

The space ahead seemed to tilt slightly higher, broadening, giving him more than sufficient room to begin crawling anew, but Baxter wanted to wait, to catch his breath.

However he knew that waiting here until he gathered up more of his strength was just him not wanting to make the effort. This place was safe, it was cozy, but it was merely the illusion of comfort. He needed to get out into the open air.

Baxter rested his forehead against his wrist, swallowing. The rocket scientist was not a people person, living inside his skull most of the time, applying his formidable intellect to the calculations necessary to produce the kind of high-efficiency engines that would make the U.S. Navy's missiles into the fastest things in the air. His latest effort had broken Mach 10 with a simulated 235-kilogram military-grade Pentolite warhead. At 7000 miles per hour, there were few things that could intercept such a projectile, especially given his comrade's work on computer guidance and threat-avoidance algorithms.

Since Exocets had proved capable of devastating warships with warheads lighter by 70 pounds, the new design would be more than adequate to take on an enemy navy, everything up to an aircraft carrier.

That kind of math was a deeply internal thing; it was his haven, his safety. It was akin to this little slot underneath tons of rubble, a concrete shell that cradled and sheltered him in blissful darkness and silence. When dealing with other humans, he was much more at the mercy of prejudices, biases, illogic. The variables introduced in such interactions were not neat, tidy, like physics and mathematics. The laws of Newton were something he turned back to when the concept of networking was simply controlled madness and appeasing those without vision that penetrated down into the truth of reality.

Baxter couldn't help but think of how he looked right now. Reduced to slacks that were shredded and torn, totally distressed, he looked like one of his childhood heroes. Disheveled, mousy-brown hair, long, scrawny limbs, barefoot and shirtless, Baxter was likely a dead ringer for a certain purple-trousered nuclear scientist, freshly awoken from his alter ego's gamma-powered rampages. The rocket scientist regretted having gotten so far into science, though.

"Get moving," Baxter barked to himself. He began squirming along. He set rocks to mark the distance he moved through the crawl space, measuring his height against the distance he moved, counting the seconds necessary to make such a journey. It took twenty seconds to crawl five feet, the distance from his shoulder to his foot, so he estimated his approximate position in the base.

Math was his refuge. He wished that he could rely on something more, something better, actual sight with which to measure, but at least the counting of seconds, the counting of lengths of his body, kept his mind occupied. With focus, he would not give in to fear and despair. Baxter knew that the best means of coping was to concentrate on what could be changed.

Slowly, surely, the space he crawled through grew larger, roomier. He laid himself flat on his belly, pausing and cradling his head between his forearms. Baxter let his thoughts drift to the sight of a man walking on coals of flame, with the caption "doable." A contrasting image, another man walking on strewed children's building blocks, was captioned "impossible."

"Great," he murmured. He rolled onto his side, finding all new misshapen rocks that poked and prodded his ribs. He grit his teeth, wishing for release.

Just one moment. I don't care that the science sucks. Just one instance of gamma strength.

He pushed against the roof above him. Suddenly it began to shift and his heart rate shot into high gear. This wasn't a delusion that he was somehow hefting the weight of the rubble atop him; it was panic in the horror that somehow he'd upset a delicate balance and was now going to crush himself into a fine paste.

"No!" Baxter screamed.

Light streamed down, burning his unaccustomed eyes. He folded up, waiting for the irresistible, implacable weight crushing his bones, squeezing the juices from him. Nothing came through, though. No pressure increased upon him; even through clenched eyelids, he could see the gleaming light of midday.

"We found him!" a voice shouted.

Baxter tried to open his eyes, but the sun was too bright. He could only squint, but gloved hands hooked under one of his arms, dragging him to his feet.

"Dr. Baxter?" He heard the voice in his left ear.

"Yes," he answered, coughing. The ground felt wobbly beneath him. "Yes, I'm Robert Baxter."

"We found him!" someone shouted again.

"You'll be all right," the man told him, draping something over his shoulders. The ravages upon his back and shoulders were not too rough that he couldn't tell a blanket. It was unusual to feel so bare and cold in the desert, but it was winter. The winds were brisk, whipping around him.

"We're getting you on a helicopter, sir," the man added, guiding him along. He tried to get a better look at the soldier helping him out. Stark shadows showed over the man's face, down the length of his body. This wasn't the light of the sun and he remembered, before the churning darkness, that it was night when the explosions rocked the testing facility. Even so, he kept walking.

This was a nighttime rescue.

"How did you find me?" Baxter asked.

"You have a subcutaneous RFID chip embedded in your skin," the soldier told him, helping him step up and onto a helicopter. Baxter felt the cushions compress beneath him and he leaned against the back of his seat. The knowledge of a chip in his body stunned him, he couldn't remember when he would have had such a device introduced, unless it was part of the physical he'd had.

"Rob?"

Baxter could barely make out the sound of his name being spoken, had only a hint of what the voice sounded like, but even through the rumble of the helicopter's engines and the slap of rotors against the air, he could tell it was a woman speaking to him. He forced his eyes open wider, looking to see another bundled figure sitting across from him inside the cabin of the aircraft.

Her normal flip now hung down, stringy and matted, from sweat and distress. Her blue eyes were veined in red, bags hanging beneath them. And yet the sight of Beatrice Chandler, the computer wizard whose guidance systems were the other vital ingredient in the Mach 10 missile prototype, still stirred Baxter's feelings. As worn out, as out of sorts as she was, she was a beautiful, wonderful sight. His heart tripped, skipping a beat, and he reached out a hand to hers. She wrapped her delicate fingers around his. "Bea!"

Baxter turned to the soldier who'd guided him into the helicopter, then nodded toward the seat next to the woman.

"Go ahead!" the soldier shouted over the din of the chopper.

Baxter switched seats and snuggled against her. He lifted a part of his blanket, like a mother bird extending her wing, and enclosed Chandler's shoulders, pulling her closer to him. Her hair was stiff and salty with sweat, but he still kissed the dome of her head, still pressed his cheek against her greasy locks. She slid one arm around his waist, laid one hand on his chest.

For a man who didn't have much in terms of people skills, the contact between his body and hers was a godsend. Beatrice was a fellow scientist. She, too, lived a life of order, of logic and reason, and for that very reason, he could never feel alienated by her, never be betrayed by a sudden shift of whimsy.

"What happened?" Beatrice asked into his ear, the caress of her lips so close and intimate it distracted him from the situation at hand. Chandler had asked him a question, though, and as a scientist it was Baxter's duty, his drive in life, to provide an answer to any question to which he could respond.

"The base was attacked. Something moving at a similar velocity to our prototype design, perhaps several, penetrated the testing center's antiballistic defenses,"

Baxter replied. "I was in Radar Twelve, calculating the velocity and course of our test motor when one of the first struck."

Chandler looked up at him, her blue eyes wet and welling with tears. "You're hurt."

Baxter looked down at his chest, noting the crisscrosses of crimson lines, as if some inept, maddened artist had tried to add detail to him with a red marker. "Fortunately when the roof came down, I was placed such that I would not be crushed. Unfortunately conditions conspired so that any passage I made necessitated the shedding of clothing."

Chandler managed a weak smile and then rested her head against the crook of his neck.

It was so comfortable with her this way, Baxter almost didn't notice the soldier's movements across from him. The man pulled a hypodermic needle from a small box in his lap.

Now, inside the chopper, with the interior lights of the aircraft providing clearer illumination, he was able to ascertain the appearance of the man. The attention to detail that grew from his intellect and aspirations to being a rocket scientist showed him that the camouflage pattern worn by this infantryman was all wrong for the Naval Weapons Testing Institute's uniforms. If this was someone from outside the Navy, perhaps an Air Force pararescue team, then why were the patches on the man's sleeves so studiously identical to the normal naval infantry assigned to the base?

Also, he noted, the features of the man were Chinese, not Caucasian. Baxter thought back, trying to recall inflections of the soldier's English, seeking out further incongruities.

"Who are you?" Baxter asked, stiffening. He was now on full alert. Though he sat straighter, he knew it was nothing more than the bluff of an animal making itself seem larger to deter predators from attacking. Strength ebbed from his limbs, what musculature there had been already strained to the limits by crawling through the cracks in the rubble of the collapsed Radar Twelve center.

"We're taking you somewhere safe," the soldier with the hypo stated. "Now, I'll be putting this in you just to keep you calm. There's no point in allowing you to be distressed for the upcoming journey."

"To where? China?" Baxter asked.

The soldier smirked. "What gave it away?"

"The digital camouflage," Baxter said.

Chandler stirred at his side, looking back and forth between Baxter and the soldier.

Another pair of men stepped through the side doors of the helicopter, effectively bracketing them in.

"Rob, what are you talking about?" she asked.

"We're being kidnapped," Baxter told her.

Chandler's eyes went to the faces of all three of their rescuers.

Ethnic diversity in the United States' military was one thing, but with each of these men being Asian and wearing the wrong digital camouflage patterns, Baxter's mind was now clearly focused. He tried to assemble plans of escape, but none of them would work without a sudden infusion of at least fifty pounds of muscle mass; even then, most of them would also entail gunfire chasing him and likely striking Chandler.

Baxter extended his arm, lowering his gaze. Chandler straightened in her seat. "Can't we do anything?"

"They're trained and they're armed," Baxter told her. "We're both defenseless, thanks to military protocol regarding civilian contractors on government premises. Even if I had enough energy in me left to disarm one of these men, the others would stop me. And harm would likely come to you, as well."

"So what do we do?" Chandler asked.

"Submit. And hope someone comes to search for us," Baxter said.

He felt the bite of the hypodermic needle press into his arm. Waves of numbness emanated from that epicenter, spreading up to his shoulder then splaying out. His heartbeat calmed, slowed, and his head grew fuzzy, the world around him more and more indistinct.

They'll try to get the engine designs out of you. That was his first thought as his consciousness slithered along the slope of oblivion that engulfed him, tugging him back down into the darkness he'd only escaped minutes ago.

Why would they need our designs? Baxter's mind, even in the last stages, the final throes of consciousness, was sharp and keen as ever. The attackers on the base would not need to utilize his engine designs because the missiles that had struck the base were approximately two-thirds the velocity of the ones he'd worked on. It was under Mach 7, still slower than a thirty-four-foot mammoth such as the Indian Shaurya missile, which could blow past 5700 miles an hour. There would be no doubt that such a weapon, with a payload of more than one ton of explosives, would easily devastate anything on the sea or land using a conventional warhead. There was also the ability to carry small nuclear tips.

The only problem with the Shaurya-size missile was the launch. It required either a transporter erector launcher such as the Soviet MAZ 7917—a truck whose civilian nickname was "Volat" or "Giant" in Belorusian—or an underground silo.

The one the U.S. Navy was working on was to be, at most, two-thirds the length and weight, and transportable on the decks of fast-attack boats as small as 200 tons.

Baxter's thoughts turned toward the Chinese and their proposed super ship killer, and that these soldiers were Chinese.

Questions about the Asian kidnappers wisped away like smoke. There was nothing left to come to mind as he blanked into unconsciousness, hefted into the night sky on a helicopter.

CHAPTER TWO

The ceiling fan rotated slowly and Carl Lyons's night vision had accustomed to the shadows so that he could even make out the wicker patterns inlaid into the paddles as he lay on his back. The Hawaiian night was full of the songs of insects and birds outside the open windows, but their tunes carried from the surrounding jungle, making this calm, warm night, silvery-blue moonlight cascading through gossamer drapes, seem far more warm and welcoming than it had any right to be. He was in this hotel under the name of Karl Long, also known as Stone among the Heathens Motorcycle Club of California.

This was an undercover operation for Stony Man Farm, and Lyons wasn't here solo. In other hotel rooms were his two partners: fellow Able Team member Hermann Schwarz and Phoenix Force's Thomas Jefferson Hawkins. Lyons would have felt more comfortable here in Hawaii with Able Team as a whole, cohesive unit, with the third member of the squad, Rosario Blancanales, as part of this deception. However, as Lyons was supposed to be a former member of the Heathens, and an up-and-coming bit of new blood in the Arrangement, hanging out with a Hispanic man, even if he was a blue-eyed "true Spaniard," would have been suspicious. So Able Team had brought in Hawkins as a replacement.

All three men would be quite passable as members of a white supremacist movement. Lyons was tall, blond and Nordic. A twenty-first-century Viking warrior with a day's worth of rough stubble on his chin and the faded tattoos running down his neck, arms and chest proclaiming his allegiance to the white race. The tattoos were fake, etched into his skin with a biological dye that would fade to nothingness after a month. Until then, the big blond ex-cop would have to endure the presence of obscene hatred and twisted, almost-blasphemous religious symbolism scoured across his skin.

That was part of why he couldn't sleep tonight, why he allowed himself to be absorbed into the slowly rotating fan blades as they barely churned the night air in his room.

This was far from the first time Lyons had gone undercover, and also far from the only time he'd ever had to don the hideous mannerisms of a bigot to do his job. What kept him awake was more than disgust for the identity he'd slipped into, and more than paranoia that made him keep a Colt Python under his pillow, within easy reach of his right hand.

It wasn't paranoia if you were surrounded by representatives from dozens of gangs around the world, all assembled for a global auction by handwritten invitation—one that Able Team had uncovered while cleaning up loose ends from a prior crisis. It had looked handwritten but in truth had been merely printed, the cursive script the product of a font. No one would be able to perform a handwriting analysis on the mechanized scribbling on paper, and there were also no fingerprints except for those of Kevin Reising, the man who'd received the letter.

Reising was currently still listed among the living, but in hiding. The truth of the matter was that his corpse was nothing but charred ashes, with a .45-caliber slug where the brainpan should have been. The announcement of the man's death would not be released until after there was no longer a need for the current undercover identities of Karl Long, Herman Shore and Thomas Presley.

By then the organizers of this event, a sale for everything from handguns to long-range missiles, would be dead and gone. The host organization of this auction went by the name of Abalisah, and this hotel was far from the beaten trail, on a small island of the archipelago. With a title that was Arabic for *devils,* it was a sure sign that things were not going to be safe and calm. The man who was the face of the auction was a tall man who could have been anything from European to Middle Eastern. His skin was well tanned, but he had no accent, no truly identifiable features. He was called Jinan.

"Do what you will," Jinan had said over a loudspeaker, his voice distorted by a modulator. At least it might have been, but it also could have been a simple computer program or just a schmuck hired to read a sheet of paper put before him. "You have been allowed to keep your sidearms, your knives, your poisons. I merely wish your money, so if you cannot outbid your enemy, perhaps you can steal from him or perhaps murder him. The only things that I forbid are attempts to steal my property or attacks upon my personal staff."

Anything goes, Lyons thought, sliding his fingers under his pillow and around the handle of Colt Python, feeling the diamond-checkered grips against the palm of his hand. Surrounded by enemies, dozens of whom Lyons recognized from their Interpol profiles accessed at Stony Man Farm, he and his partners were in deep.

There was a rap at the door and Lyons sat up. He looked over and saw that it was closing in on three in the morning. He hadn't placed any orders with room service. By the same token, he couldn't imagine why someone out to blow him away would knock politely at his door. Out in the hall, he heard more knocks on different doors and softly spoken words even as they were opened.

Lyons got out of bed, not bothering to put on pants or underwear. It was perfect weather for lying in bed, no covers, naked and enjoying the sea breeze wafting through the window. A pair of undershorts wouldn't make him any less vulnerable to gunfire or a knife. Still, his cop training took hold as he stood behind the doorjamb while he turned the knob to his door. If a bullet were to cut through the door at his moment, it would slice into empty air, not his chest.

The door swung open, silent on well-oiled hinges, and Lyons caught a hint of jasmine in the air as he looked into the hall. It was lit, but not so bright that it made his eyes hurt as they adjusted. Instead of a killer in the hall, there was a woman standing there. He couldn't tell her age as she stood in front of him in the doorway.

Her skin was deeply bronzed, bare shoulders in sharp contrast to the cream-hued cloth that looped around her neck and then came down to cradle her full, soft breasts. The fabric draped to one side and knotted over her hip, exposing the curve of silken flesh beneath. The light caught a glint of gold from a small ring that adorned her navel while that same light cast an undeniable silhouette, leaving no doubt that the filmy fabric was the only thing between her bare skin and the sultry evening air.

Once more, Lyons hated the skin he was forced to wear, the tattoos of white power with hateful slurs branded, if only for a month, on his flesh. However, as he returned his gaze to her face, he saw that she wasn't a black woman. He tried to place her, either as Hispanic, or perhaps a Pacific Islander, but her large brown eyes and full sensual mouth were most definitely not Asian or Caucasian.

"Mr. Long, my name is Sanay," she said. Her accent was as unidentifiable as her features, and Lyons couldn't help but think that the branches of her family tree had roots in different parts of the forest. There was a hint of British in it, but her voice was as elusive in its origins as her appearance. "I am your gift for tonight from Master Jinan."

"Master Jinan," Lyons repeated, looking her up and down. Was this some kind of test? After all, Karl Long was an Aryan thug, an outlaw motorcyclist whose racist pedigree had been cemented with a violent assault on a La Sombra prisoner that had left him brain damaged and with an amputated arm. It wasn't murder, which would have meant that Long could never leave prison, but it was a show of strength and unity among the Arrangement. "What makes your boss think that I'd have interest in a little brown thing like you?"

Lyons smirked, hating the words that poured from

his lips but also knowing full well that Long was spending prison time for the assault and rapes of Filipino, Polynesian and Hispanic women. Even her age, a little north of thirty, and her diminutive five-foot height, matched Long's taste in victims.

Abalisah's researchers were good, uncannily so, to have pulled up those kinds of facts about him. So even as Lyons made his dismissive challenge to the girl, Sanay stepped into the room and closed the door behind her. She glanced down to the cocked pistol in Lyons's hand and then to the growing arousal obstinately making itself known despite his bravado. Her dark, slender fingers gave him a light brush, the tips of her nails tracing lines over his tightly packed abs before she cupped her palm over his pectoral muscle.

"Abalisah knows all the darkness in this hotel. Yours. Mine. Everyone's," Sanay whispered, pressing closer to him. Her other hand glided over Lyons's hip and she explored his body in the darkness.

She was barefoot and she rose to the tips of her toes, lips barely able to press against his collarbone, brushing lightly, tongue darting out to taste his skin.

Lyons hooked his arm under hers, and he flexed, lifting her higher. He was able to hold her up with only one arm, bring her mouth to his, lips so soft and inviting that Lyons could easily forget himself as he carried her toward the bed. Sanay helped Lyons, bracing her thighs against his hips, her slender arms draped around his neck.

The Able Team commander still couldn't get rid of a knot of dread in his stomach, even as he joined with Sanay, exploring her wonderful caramel skin, her dark, firm nipples, velvety soft lips and warm, tender tongue in her mouth.

THE LIGHT OF dawn would not pour through Lyons's westward-facing balcony, but he did notice the graying skies as sunrise approached.

He lay still, Sanay, the exotic, beautiful woman entangled around him, a trickle of wet drool having dried and crusted on his chest. He couldn't see her; his eyes were mere slits, only open enough to register the increasing light of day.

Lyons could feel her moving, stirring from his chest and crawling off him. He continued breathing deeply, as if asleep.

Maybe the women were sent to these rooms as spies.

Sanay quietly moved to the nightstand, where he'd placed his pistol the night before, and lifted the revolver. When Lyons heard her check to see if the weapon was loaded, he acted without thinking. He clamped his hand down hard over hers, pinning her finger inside the trigger guard. He heard the ugly pop of her index finger, but even as that happened, he drove the heel of his palm against her jaw in a Shotokan karate stroke.

The blow knocked her to the hardwood floor with a sharp crack. The revolver was locked now in Lyons's left fist, and he watched as a trickle of blood seeped from her cheek onto the rug. Even as he looked down at the grisly damage he'd wrought in the space of a few moments, he noticed something else on the rug at his feet.

Sanay had removed the rounds from the revolver, rendering it useless even before she'd pointed it at him.

Lyons did a press check; the weapon's barrel was

empty. She'd made it seem as if she were about to attack him, but it had been a ruse. Once more, he had an uneasy feeling wash over him. The tattoos on his flesh seemed to come alive, their hints and promises of intolerance and rot audible in their gnawing on his soul.

"Why'd you let me almost kill you?" Lyons growled, taking her by the wrist and pulling her into a sitting position. His cold blue eyes must have flashed with lightning-bright anger because she winced, recoiling at his touch.

"Because…Jinan would not believe your story…" Sanay whispered. Blood now stained the side of her neck; there was a gash down one cheek. Her big brown eyes were glimmering with tears. "He would kill you."

Lyons loosened his iron grasp on her wrist.

"No…don't stop. He'll kill you," she whispered.

Lyons sat on the mattress. Karl Long was a rapist. He wouldn't make gentle love to the kind of women he'd been in prison for violating. The Able Team commander had stumbled dead into a trap, dropping evidence that he was not the sexual predator, the destroying creature, whose identity he'd assumed.

Too many years on the LAPD had taught him that rape had very little to do with sex, with sensuality, with lovemaking. And yet, that tiny bit of information had failed him as he'd given in to his body's normal, human sexual desires, bonding with Sanay, tending to her tender little form the way she'd explored his hard physique. Already, the lips of the laceration on her cheek puffed up, darkening. Her jaw was also deepening its hue, red and raw from where he'd punched her.

"I needed you to do that," Sanay repeated softly. "He'll kill you if you don't."

Lyons cupped the tip of her chin, looking into her eyes. "Why would you do this?"

"Because you're kind. You're a good man," Sanay answered. She lowered her head, scrunching her shoulders up around her neck. "A man like that doesn't deserve to be treated like…"

Lyons bit his lower lip. At once, he was ashamed of his violent reflexes, but at the same time, they'd intervened and protected him despite himself. The girl had leveled a gun at him.

"You took a damn chance," Lyons growled. He helped her up, a hand under each armpit, then sat her beside him on the mattress. "What if I'd shot you? What if I beat you to death?"

"Then this would be over," Sanay answered.

In the ever-growing light, Lyons could see that Sanay's skin wore her years with nearly as much character as he'd earned in his years of battle. Cigarette burns, healed cuts and freckles were now visible as the concealer makeup she'd worn had been scrubbed away by their vigorous lovemaking. Her whole life was a wrought tale carved into her flesh, hidden by that caramel coating.

And Lyons hated himself for having gone full karate on her. He knew that his palm-heel stroke would leave hairline fractures along Sanay's mandible, and she was still in pain right now. It would stay with her as a constant, sharp ache for months, acting up every time she bit down hard. He just knew that she'd be taking an extra painkiller or two to numb herself further against the lifetime of punishment she'd received.

Lyons gently dabbed the blood from her cheek, careful not to apply pressure to the swollen edges of her laceration. Sanay's welling tears didn't fill her eyes quite enough to trickle down her face, but Lyons could see into her dark, soulful eyes, spotting a small spark. A tint of hope gleamed in them. He could see that he was the first in a long time who had treated her like a human.

"Don't," Lyons told her, his deep voice having a slight crack in it. He'd been here before, with brave women, those who knew how to fight and survive.

"Don't what?" Sanay asked.

"Don't risk yourself for me," Lyons ordered.

"Jinan said to expect to be raped, to be hurt, to be destroyed," Sanay whispered. "But he said that if I made it, he would give me all the opium I needed. Enough to ride away into eternity."

She looked down at herself, sinking her upper teeth into her soft, cushiony lower lip. "This…this isn't enough. You'll—"

A knock at the door cut her off. Sanay froze, her sadness-brimming eyes finally bursting like a dam as she shot a glance at the door. Lyons moved with the speed of a cobra, scooping up his Colt Python and readying it for action.

Still standing at the jamb, using it as a shield, he tore open the door. "What the hell do you want?"

Lyons was eye to eye with a man who looked too wide to even step through the hotel doorway. He could see brawny muscles rippling in the newcomer's neck, shoulders, upper arms and chest. However the farther down he looked on the ever-broadening form, those muscles ebbed, slipping under a layer of fat that, at a distance, would have most fools thinking him to be a ball of blubber. Fortunately, Lyons had run into many of this type of man, as well. He called them "hard fat," men who would never display a set of washboard abs, but had endless reserves of strength and endurance, capable of tossing around throngs of bodybuilders as if they were rag dolls. The Lump, as Lyons named the man, glowered in reaction to Lyons's hostility.

"Picking up the bitches. Or what's left of them."

The man had no accent, though his features were solidly Polynesian. He also didn't show the slightest bit of intimidation at the sight of the Colt in Lyons's fist. He turned to Sanay and barked. "Here! Now!"

Sanay sprung to her tiny feet and darted from the bed to the doorway. She hadn't bothered to pick up the folds of flimsy cloth that Lyons had torn off her the night before.

"Was expecting you a little more ripped up," the Lump said.

Lyons glowered at him. "Jinan said not to kill the staff."

The round ball of disguised muscle tugged Sanay into the hallway, looking at her closer, his gaze falling on the darkening bruises of her face.

"Well…" Lyons added, letting a little sheepishness creep into his voice. "I remembered that eventually."

The Lump swiveled his head atop that tree trunk of a neck, ropes of tendon and sinew stretching from it and into his shoulders like the gnarled roots of a hideous tree. "She ain't staff. She's party favors."

The Lump pulled on Sanay's wrist. "Come on. I'll get you some fresh…"

Lyons growled, cutting off the slab of humanity in the hallway. "Screw that. I want her back. The bitch sits up and begs when I cough. Don't want to have to train something else like that."

Lump glanced from Lyons to the frightened girl. Sanay looked like a rabbit caught between a wolf and a mountain lion. The slab glanced back to Lyons, standing there naked—the only thing he wore was a scowl of annoyance—accessorized with a menacing Colt.

"I'll have her cleaned up, just like last night," Lump told him.

Lyons nodded, standing by helplessly as Lump tugged Sanay after him. She looked at him, confused.

Lyons slammed the door shut, resting his head against the doorjamb. He looked at the reflection of his face in the chrome of the door chain's slot.

He hated what he saw.

CHAPTER THREE

Barbara Price stood in the center of the Stony Man Farm Computer Room, looking between the touchscreen tablet device in her hand and the gigantic global map stretched out on the wall. Around her were the computer workstations of the four technological geniuses of the cyber crew: Aaron Kurtzman, Carmen Delahunt, Huntington Wethers and Akira Tokaido.

As mission controller, Price was staying on top of all open correspondence channels and keeping track of her field operations. Currently the cyber team was trying to locate Robert Baxter and Beatrice Chandler, scanning the world for their RFID chips. Given the ferocity of the attack, most people would have considered both scientists dead, but there had been a passive signal as leaving the perimeter of the base.

A global search would be much more difficult. One intruder had been located on the base, a disguised commando, Chinese in ethnicity, with forged identification papers, unit patches and dog tags that, if Stony Man looked really hard, could be traced back to Shanghai and the Ministry of State Security. This would have proved to be convincing evidence, if only for the fact that the intruder had been killed with the same U.S.-issue weapons and ammunition as the attacking commandos had likely carried. Indeed, that the man's

Beretta and rifle were found—and had been traced to stolen American arms lost in the Gulf War—only made Price more suspicious about the red herring dropped in the desert.

That was why Akira Tokaido was currently checking every ounce of digital traffic coming out of the People's Republic of China, looking for incidents of a similar attack in-country. She didn't know if there would have been enough coordination for two teams to make concurrent attacks, but there were signs that four days prior to the attack in the American Southwest there had been a similar missile misfire on a base in the Gobi Desert, 275 miles northwest of Beijing, 20 miles north of Hohhot. The detonation of a missile that should have been deactivated was given as the reason for the catastrophe that had left dozens dead and a hundred more injured.

Of course, that was merely the official story out of China. The truth, however, would be much more arcane, and naturally that is what Price assumed happened. Right now, the real facts were sketchy, which was why Tokaido was busy raiding PRC military databases.

Price turned her attention to her tablet, pulling up the information on the missing scientists, Baxter and Chandler. The Stony Man mission controller made careful note that there was evidence of a more than genial relationship between the two, and that it was likely that any effort at taking one might have been a guarantee of capturing the other. Price was well aware of the kind of emotional manipulation the peril to a loved one could hold over a person. Right now, there was an excellent chance of recovering the pair.

Baxter and Chandler were the only two missing from the base; other bodies had been uncovered, accounting for nearly a hundred murdered victims. Most had died at ground zero of one-thousand-kilogram-warhead detonations; others were simply in the wrong place at the wrong time, shot through the head while wounded. Even so, the commandos who'd made the attack had been careful not to damage still-operating security cameras, so that the U.S. government would get a good look at what appeared to be PRC soldiers disguised as Americans attacking a base in New Mexico.

Tokaido quickly sent a note to her tablet, the information showing up in a new panel.

Air Force dispatched, seeking out attackers. Searched one-thousand-mile radius utilizing AWACS, found no sign of assaulters' helicopters. Missiles showed up on radar only moments before attack, again, launched from location unknown.

Price nodded to Tokaido, acknowledging the preliminary information. The youngest member of the cyber crew wouldn't stop until he could deliver every detail necessary so the skills of the Stony Man action team could be applied with deadly laser focus. Indeed, though the cyber team was merely a support to the commandos in the field, it was with these keyboard rangers that Able Team and Phoenix Force could be deployed to locate and destroy threats to innocent lives and world peace.

It had been three days since the first incident in China, and only by the sheerest of luck had Able Team come across Kevin Reising and his compatriots. They'd been based in Los Angeles awaiting a message and a destination. This was the day before the American incident.

Hunt Wethers fired a report to Price's tablet. It was from one of the Navy AWACS birds that regularly patrolled just outside Chinese airspace and over international waters. The craft had timed its patrol and observation of the Leizhou Peninsula specifically, knowing there was going to be a test firing of a new genus of the Dong-Feng 21 antiship ballistic missile.

Not coincidentally, the DF-21 variant was purported to possess a maximum velocity of Mach 10. At 35 feet long and 16 tons in weight, not only could it carry enough explosives to kill an aircraft carrier in one shot, it also had nuclear warhead capabilities and a range of 1100 miles.

Of course, the difference between a silo-launched ballistic missile and a more portable option such as the American design was phenomenal. Huge warhead capacities and high speeds were vital ingredients to altering a military balance. The Dong-Feng antiship variants were meant to provide the Chinese navy with utter superiority when it came time to reclaim the island nation of Taiwan. One missile could break an allied carrier apart; its nuclear variant could flash fry an entire carrier group.

Both ways were means of overwhelming any defense against Chinese military expansion.

The American missile system could be mounted on cruisers and fast-attack crafts, land-launched or carried on fighter-bombers. Just because both weapons systems had the ability to break Mach 10 was no reason to try to combine them. DF-2Xs reached Mach 10 because they rode on midrange ballistic missiles, rocket engines that were more than capable of launching satellites into orbit or delivering an MRV warhead. The American design was meant to deliver its warhead at such a high speed, and with such agility and accuracy, that the mass of the missile would provide penetration through even the thickest of hulls.

Of course, with the presence of an auction promising the latest and deadliest hardware, including just the things necessary to take out enemy fleets, Price couldn't help but feel that more than coincidence was at work here. "Once is happenstance. Twice is coincidence. Three times is enemy action."

"Quoting Ian Fleming?" Aaron Kurtzman mused.

"Just trying to make certain I did the right thing allotting a Stony Man crew to this auction," Price said.

"Two separate styles of carrier-killer test programs are attacked, and then someone advertises it?" Kurtzman asked. "You've got good instincts on this, Barb."

She nodded, looking down at the screen of her tablet. So far, Stony Man had been fully capable of gathering all the information they could about the New Mexico attack, if only because the Sensitive Operations Group had many federal connections, both inside and outside conventional channels. China, however, was a very different situation, and tapping into their information had taken effort and penetration of high-security government systems. That Tokaido had located so much thus far was a sign of his skill and the power of the Farm's cyber systems.

The auction had been confirmed through multiple sources, as well. Not only did Kevin Reising have his invitation, but there had been a rise in digital currency exchanges—peer-to-peer payments that didn't pass through legitimate banking functions. That data-cash was being funneled to a website called the Arsenal Europa, which had been touting the auction. Discovering the auction had been the combined efforts of Wethers and Delahunt, both of whom utilized their particular, individual instincts to narrow the search to its confirmed presence.

They'd also managed to home in on a large supply of data-cash in storage under Reising's accounts. The sums were substantial, well over fifty million dollars, allowing for more than a few high-tech, high-impact weapons. What a soldier for the Heathens outlaw motorcycle club would do with such a supply of cash made Price shudder.

Of course, a previous Able Team operation had established links between the Heathens and the Aryan Right Coalition, a white supremacist group that was actually the action arm of an even more shadowed organization that called itself the Arrangement.

The Arrangement had lost scores of men and millions of dollars in that conflict, but apparently that hadn't been enough to set back the mystery group. Not if they could pony up that amount of funding to rearm and rebuild their shattered army.

"Hunt, do you have any more information about where Reising's money came from or where it's sitting right now?" Price asked.

The tall, slender, black professor looked up from his workstation. "Negative. Trying to dig into this data-cash network utilized by Reising is difficult, which is precisely why he chose it."

"How so?" Price asked.

"Normally, I'd hope to find a centralized store of information, but the network itself is decentralized. It's a mobile, mercurial entity. You need to have proper keys to locate your own money and allow transfer of funds. However, even going through those particular encryptions, you cannot access anything else. It's like sticking your head into a disconnected pond and hoping to find a river to the nearest ocean," Wethers explained.

"So, we're up against, essentially, the Mississippi River Delta rather than looking for Lake Michigan," Price said. "Instead of a box, we're stuck with just a tube, which in itself doesn't necessarily lead to another tube, even though it's all one ever-increasing, ever-branching main artery."

"Correct. This is the capillary system, which is useless without the arteries and veins, but while we can see an individual capillary, there's no direct link, so we're not even certain there is a heart. We could be in any organism," Wethers explained.

Price winced. "Keep trying. This is the best we've got. I want to be able to figure out who Reising wanted to pay, but I also want to know where the money came from."

"You will find no more tireless crusader and seeker of this information than I," Wethers told Price.

Price looked at the clock in the corner of her tablet display. It was almost time to talk to Hal Brognola, the big Fed who'd helped to assemble the Sensitive Operations Group, alongside Mack Bolan, and who gave the Farm its legitimacy thanks to his high rank at the Department of Justice. Though not a cabinet secretary, Brognola often had the advantage of the President's ear.

With that knowledge, she gave her cybernetic crew a quick goodbye and exited the Computer Room.

She opened the encryption on her tablet, clearing the rest of the data from both the screen and its random access memory. It was a paranoid habit, sterilizing the device of the full data she'd been accessing just for a telephone call, but the Farm had battled against major intelligence agencies and conspiracies with considerable hacking abilities.

"Barb," Brognola said as his video call came through on her tablet.

"Hal.... So far, the capsules inside Carl, Gadgets and T.J. are still reporting normal vital signs," Price informed him right off the bat.

Brognola had known Lyons and Schwarz for a long time, since even before the founding of the Sensitive Operations Group.

"These are the passive sensors, correct?" Brognola asked.

Price nodded. "We've got their location, as well. They simply can't talk to us and we cannot warn them. Other than that—"

"Remember." Brognola cut her off. "If things go to hell, you just have to remember, that's Able Team and Phoenix Force already on the ground. To them, being surrounded just means they don't have to watch their fire."

Price smirked. "That's one positive way of looking at it."

"What about Blancanales and the rest of Phoenix?" Brognola asked.

"They're currently in Hong Kong, checking in with David's old girlfriend, Mei Anna," Price said.

"Which is very iffy, considering China is an enemy state," Brognola mused. "Though, technically, we're working alongside them here."

"The Ministry of State Security doesn't know that, and even if they did, there's still going to be a bit of bad blood between our two agencies if they figure out who McCarter and company are," Price said. "Just a couple of weeks ago, Phoenix intercepted an MSS 'fund-raising shipment' of heroin and destroyed it."

"If the MSS has more than a rumor of Phoenix Force's existence, that would be bad. Very bad," Brognola stated. "But there was no evidence of whom and what attacked that shipment, correct?"

"Correct," Price returned. "It's my job to see the worst-case scenario, however. So forgive me if I give you these kinds of cues."

"It's a shame that both teams are already deployed. I'd have loved to have someone on the ground in New Mexico just to get some hard data on the actual raid," Brognola said.

Price could imagine Brognola's jowled face turning into a grim frown. "So far, the Department of Defense investigators seem to be doing quite well on their own. We're monitoring evidentiary data and field reports, and doing what we can to track down leads based on that data and feeding it back into the investigation. If something requires a ground response, we can always pull Phoenix off the current operation, or we can see if Striker is available."

"We don't usually get that opportunity," Brognola returned. "But it's worth a try. Anything on the China attacks?"

"The Gobi desert facility that was struck was the

same one that test-fired the Dong-Feng-21 variant in 2013," Price told him. "So we're currently operating on the idea that the attackers were after the experimental ballistic missile designs. There's a bit of disjoint, however."

"The DF-21 and the American engine prototypes are incompatible," Brognola concluded.

"Right. The DF gets so fast because it is riding atop an engine that can reach low orbit, while the American design is intended for nap-of-the-earth or wave-lapping altitude at Mach 10, necessitating the complex guidance systems," Price affirmed. "The cybernetic team is currently aware of this disparity and is looking to see what else might have been there."

Brognola grunted his receipt of the message. "I hope it's just a missile system."

"Just a missile system? The Dong-Fengs are nuclear capable," Price stated.

Brognola's grumble of worry was deeper now. "It's not nuclear warheads that concern me. It's something that sounds like it's out of a James Bond novel."

Price narrowed her eyes for a moment, trying to think of what Brognola was referring to. Then it hit her. "The BWMO—Beijing Weather Modification Office? That *does* sound like something out of the movies."

"Like it or not, however, they've gotten very good at seeding clouds to produce rainfall," Brognola stated. "All for the purposes of dispelling hailstorms and counteracting the advent of dust storms that affect Beijing itself."

Price resisted the urge to open the Stony Man databases while on an outside call. What she did recall from the facts she knew, was that the BWMO utilized missile systems and cannons to seed clouds. With those shells and warheads, they'd been able to irrigate miles of arable land and protect it from hail damage utilizing materials such as aluminum oxide, barium or silver iodide.

Barium—that locked in Price's mind. The material was naturally radioactive and, while it generally was not hazardous in a radiological manner or carcinogenic in water-soluble form, it was potentially poisonous. Its effects on the nervous system and muscle fibers were well documented, but as a serious weapon, the barium in even a concentration of seeder missiles or shells would prove wanting.

Seeded clouds could also be loaded with other hazardous materials, however. Price also couldn't help but think that much of the concern over man-made climate change had no better source than manipulation of the weather of a half-million-square-mile area, barring pollution and natural volcanic ejecta.

"When I get in touch with David, I'll have him check on that factor," Price stated. "Either way, be it a MaRV warhead or weather manipulation, the potential for damage for each can be huge."

"We're not sure what was taken in China. Just that they released the cover story of a misfired missile," Brognola reminded her. "It could have been something akin to what happened in New Mexico, where the inventors were taken. The wreckage is still being sorted through, isn't it?"

"No assumptions are being made. Just keeping an eye on what could be coming down the pipe."

"Let me know if anything pops up with Anna," Brognola reminded her.

Price killed the connection and returned to the Computer Room. "Guys, one of you take a look into the Beijing Weather Modification Office to see what kind of materials and munitions they have on hand. Things might just get a lot more complicated now."

"Weather modification," Wethers mused out loud. "No stranger than Frankenstein-like organ hijacking, various forms of zombies and cannibal-psychosis-producing fungi."

Tokaido cleared his throat. "Remember the time we saved the world from that weird shit?"

Delahunt smirked. "Remember? We call that Wednesday morning."

"Enough shots from the peanut gallery. Carmen, you got the weird detail," Kurtzman called out. "Barb, Phoenix is making contact now."

Price nodded.

Hong Kong appeared on their computer screens. Kurtzman was watching local law-enforcement communications and Tokaido was checking for signal chatter among the more secretive groups. If things went to hell, Stony Man could watch. But only Phoenix Force could fight its own way out.

CHAPTER FOUR

David McCarter was alone on the streets of Hong Kong. While the initial plan was to have Phoenix Force act as cover and overwatch, that plan was not going to come to fruition. Five men, moving in a coordinated manner, would simply attract too much attention. Encizo and Blancanales were traveling as Argentine businessmen on a "busman's holiday." Manning and James were also in the role of tourist, this time both of them acting as Canadians.

Phoenix Force's presence in the city was to be kept as low profile as anything, especially in regard to their operation on the Hong Kong docks, intercepting a shipment of heroin intended for American shores. Though the Stony Man computer crew looked for signs that the team had been recognized and was on watch lists, McCarter was still in a paranoid mood. It had been a classic Phoenix Force raid, full of fire and thunder, ending with his team disappearing into the shadows like smoke.

The Ministry of State Security had been both ally and enemy in the past, as corrupt entities within the agency had been keen on getting funding that didn't tie directly to Chinese taxpayers. The destruction in society caused by drug-related crime was merely a side benefit. As Phoenix Force's leader, McCarter had encountered enough American and British-run rogue operations to know that "his side" was no more innocent than the Red Chinese. Even so, the MSS was primarily concerned with the state, not the countries in competition with them, and certainly not foreign citizens.

McCarter finally reached the bar where he planned to meet Mei Anna. Ever since first working together in a mission to Hong Kong a few years ago, McCarter and Mei had been attracted to each other and had maintained a long-distance romance. It was one of the longer intimate relationships the Briton had engaged in, made slightly more difficult because of Mei's professional obligations, not to mention McCarter's constant vigilance and need as a member of Phoenix Force. Even so, Mei proved to be invaluable in dealing with Chinese situations; her linguistic skills were, naturally, better than McCarter's own smattering of understanding.

He sidled up to the bar and ordered a bottle of Tsingtao for himself. While on the scene in Hong Kong, none of the team was armed, at least in terms of firearms. McCarter still had a folding pocket knife, as well as various flat, polycarbonate utensils. One was a D-shaped hand device that had a smaller projection straight out the back of the D. When McCarter wrapped his hand around it, a short cylindrical point jutted between his middle and ring fingers. That tip would concentrate the force of the Briton's punch to the point where it could shatter bone. Neither it nor his concealed knife would be a match for an AK-47 blazing away at him, but if McCarter couldn't go toe to toe, he'd fight from ambush and concealment. One broken trachea could equal a rifle and thirty rounds in his hands to even up the odds.

It was an absolute worst-case scenario, but Phoenix

Force was always called in when the worst went down anyway. It was intellect, preparation and prowess that made up for lack of manpower and firepower in these desperate instances.

"Hey, stranger." A soft, gentle voice spoke to his right.

McCarter swiveled on his seat, broadly grinning, his smile a beam as he beheld Mei Anna. She was deceptively small and sweet-looking, her hair in a pixie cut, a shoulder-padded jacket hanging open to reveal the silk slip that displayed her décolletage and would likely draw eyes away from what surprises she had on hand for an emergency. He slipped off the stool and slid his arms under hers, stooping so that their lips met, briefly yet intensely.

McCarter rose from the kiss and she followed it with a tight hug. In an instant his jacket pocket grew heavier and Mei gave him a quick wink.

"What's new, Tiger Lily?" McCarter asked with a grin. On the few moments when they either weren't working together or lost in the throes of intimacy, Mei and the Briton took a little time together to watch favorite movies. The rewritten espionage thriller redubbed as a comedy that McCarter referenced was one of those. So much so, it had become their unofficial greeting.

Mei climbed onto the stool next to McCarter, raised two fingers and didn't even have to voice her order. McCarter returned to sitting, as well, taking a sip from his beer. The bartender returned with a pair of cocktails and an extra bottle of beer.

"You know these are delicious, so I can't tell you they are new," Mei said, lifting her cocktails. "Bring your beer, we'll head to a booth."

The bar itself was active but not crowded. There was certainly a good screen of background noise, but with no throng of bodies pressed together, the two of them could move easily to a quiet booth and not fear that the press of humanity could listen in on them.

As soon as they scuttled into the booth, side by side so that McCarter could wrap his arm around her shoulders, so he could feel the warmth of her against him, he set a quick kiss on the top of her head, enjoying the smell of her hair. She looked up at him, almond-shaped, deep brown eyes regarding him with affection. He could also feel a tension in her.

"What's new is some seriously screwed-up stuff," Mei said softly. "I'm assuming this sudden date is because of the troubles near Beijing?"

"Gobi Desert testing institute," McCarter said. He reached into the pocket that Mei had filled and felt the outline of a small revolver, already snugged into a pocket holster. Hook and loop material clutched the inside of the jacket pocket so he couldn't draw the revolver and look like an idiot pulling the leather sheath with it. "Thanks, by the way."

Mei wrinkled her nose. "I couldn't bring a Hi-Power...couldn't fit it in my clutch."

"So what happened up north?" McCarter asked.

Mei held her tongue for a moment, looking as if she didn't want to say exactly. "Have you heard of the Beijing Weather Modification Office?"

"Yup," McCarter answered. He didn't say that Price had thrown him an encrypted text mentioning the possible involvement of the agency before he arrived at the bar. "Personally, I always wondered why they assigned almost forty thousand blokes to a rainmaking operation."

"They are effective," Mei returned. "They've done a hell of a lot of work."

"And some of it might just be weaponized weather?" McCarter asked.

Mei nodded.

"Far be it from me to be skeptical, especially in the wake of taking out the Dragon's Eye, a laser that could have leveled Taiwan, but how can cloud seeding and hailstorm busting be that much of a threat?" McCarter asked. "I realize that playing around with the climate on the scale of the nation of China could affect world climate patterns, but no rainstorm is going to take out an aircraft carrier group."

"No, you would need something along the lines of a hurricane," Mei returned.

That hit McCarter like a lump of iron slag in the stomach. "Hurricane? How?"

"In Taiwan, we were aware of the possibilities that China was working on a Massive Ordnance Air Burst explosive as a possible aircraft-carrier-killing missile. Enough to destroy the ship and perhaps cripple the support craft around it, without being an actual nuclear attack," Mei said.

McCarter was familiar with the MOAB, a thermobaric explosive that came in two parts. One being a burst that diffused inflammable fuel or explosive dust over a large area, while the second ignited the aerosolized cloud, which itself would detonate. With a large dome of fire detonating, it would produce enormous pressure. In the twentieth century, they'd called the bomb a Daisy Cutter, since the detonation would cut every living thing down in the area, all the way down to the daisies. "I've had Gary make one or two of those."

"I figured," Mei responded. "Are you here alone?"

"I left them behind. I don't need a bloody set of chaperones for a date with my girl," McCarter answered.

Mei smiled. "You know that I have my own support crew around the place."

"Especially the bartender," McCarter noted. "Unless Taiwan took over the Russians' telepathic research."

Mei stuck out her tongue. It was meant to be a defiant gesture, but to David it was just unbearably cute. He leaned in and took a quick taste, lips crushed against hers. He didn't want to break the kiss, but there was still business to attend to.

Mei cleared her throat. "The Dong-Feng can carry Multiple Individual Reentry Vehicles—I'm sure you remember MIRVs from the days when the USSR and dinosaurs roamed the Earth."

McCarter gave her a poke in her stomach. "Was that an age joke?"

Mei chuckled. "Just making certain you're paying attention and not undressing me with your eyes."

"My eyes and ears can work independently, love," McCarter said. "Right now, my eyes are snogging the hell out of your naked self."

Mei smiled, then poked him in the center of the forehead. "Well, ears, pick this up. MIRVs can have any sort of warhead. Nuclear. Conventional. MOAB. Cloud seeder."

McCarter suddenly felt himself focus, sitting a little straighter. "Seed the clouds over the ocean. And then do something that could increase the water temperature over a vast area."

"Like, say, the thermobaric cloud from a MOAB," Mei said. "What isn't superheated gets vaporized by the blast, adding to the humidity. The sudden lack of air pressure sucks in more air…"

McCarter frowned. "Boom! One hurricane bomb."

"Made from readily available materials, not just the Dong-Feng family of missiles," Mei said. "The mathematics and physics of it are just way outside of my limits."

"But if you hire thirty-seven thousand weather scientists and mathematicians, they could do the grunt work," McCarter returned. "Damn."

He started thinking about why the marauders would have wanted a Mach 10–capable engine and a guidance system meant to defeat radar when it clicked with him.

If you fired a ballistic missile, it would definitely show up on radars around the world. But, if you could take the individual components of different warheads and put *those* on the ends of the rockets, you could deliver all that firepower without giving away the fact that an ICBM was launched toward you to drop a hurricane on your doorstep, or let your original location be known. That had been one of the most troublesome contentions of tracking the origin of the two different attacks, as the missile blasts preceding them had followed a nap-of-the-earth course.

He'd have to run the general idea past people who were far smarter than him. McCarter was smart, but he was far from being a rocket scientist. These things sounded possible, and there was a United Nations resolution and treaty to prevent the weaponization of weather. Unfortunately, the United States was not a signatory, and neither were many other countries.

While all of this ran through his mind, he finished the cocktail that Mei had bought for him—his taste buds agreeing with her that it was delicious. He stroked her hair, squeezed her hand and hugged her tighter off and on. The time he put into thinking about the possibilities of the Chinese and American weapons systems combined felt all too long, and he was coming nowhere close to a solution, while the time he spent reveling in the warmth and human contact he shared with Mei was like the flicker of an instant.

He recalled what Gary Manning had said about Einstein and time relativity. "A second with your hand on a hot stove is like an eternity. A day with a girl you love is like a fleeting instant."

Of course, McCarter liked the pool-table description of time and space interacting, too.

"So, why did you give me the pocket rocket?" McCarter asked.

Mei smirked. "Don't I always... Oh, the revolver."

"Cheeky girl," McCarter chuckled.

"The informant who relayed the tidbits about the 'hurricane' missile was reported as having committed suicide," Mei said. "He threw himself out of a fourth-story window. And when that didn't work, he curb-stomped himself."

"Curb-stomped. Figuratively?"

"Literally," Mei answered.

McCarter wrinkled his nose. The literal act of a curb stomp was to set someone's head and upper jaw against a hard, raised surface. Then, the person was either kicked in the neck, or a foot was brought heavily down.

The result ended with torn cheeks, a crushed lower jaw and a skull messily separated from neck vertebrae. It was one of the most brutal means of murder McCarter had ever seen, one that even he hadn't used in battle.

"You're covered, right?" McCarter asked.

Mei nodded. "I'm paranoid as hell. And I'm surrounded by my people."

McCarter could see the flicker of fear in those dark, almond eyes. He knew from personal experience that only the most brash of fools was never afraid.

"I'll do you a solid, love," McCarter murmured, lips close and brushing her ear.

"You're not going to make yourself bait," Mei said. "That's insane."

"Insane is my middle name," McCarter countered. "Besides, if I can find the bastards who killed that informant, I could get a better handle on who made the theft."

"And what if it's MSS plugging a leak?" Mei asked.

"Then the Commie buggers have it coming for building a goddamn fleet-killing hurricane bomb."

McCarter took out his phone and transmitted a file to her device.

"Call my lads," McCarter told her.

"And what do I say?" she asked.

McCarter stood and adjusted his jacket, making certain the revolver was still firmly in its pocket holster. "Hunting season is open."

ROSARIO BLANCANALES leaned on his cane, standing and admiring the Cenotaph, a memorial to the honored dead of both World War I and World War II. The 1940s had been a vastly different time, when Hong

Kong was more or less homogeneous and still clung to a mix of old ways and new British fads that filtered in with Great Britain's protection as a colony in Her Majesty's empire. During the second conflict that the Cenotaph commemorated, Hong Kong had suffered greatly from Japanese incursion. Citizens starved, medics even under the neutral protection of the Red Cross had been murdered, and more than ten thousand women and girls had been brutally raped. Those names were not carved into this tower of stone, but there was still a brief, powerful prayer for them.

"May their martyred souls be immortal and their immortal spirits endure."

He could not read the Chinese characters in which the inscription were made, but he knew the meaning. Standing there, he could see that spirits did endure.

Because of all the corporations that called Hong Kong home, because of the cultural impact that it had on the world, even the 1997 transfer of sovereignty to the People's Republic of China had done little to dim the neon, the glory and the wild mayhem that was this grand old city. On every level, from the lowest of underground crime to the peaks of wealth and power, the city was simply too vibrant, too energetic, to have been tamped down by Communist rule, to the point where fried chicken and pizza had infiltrated the mainland.

Blancanales's phone came to life. He answered it. *"Hola, amigo!"*

"What've you got for me?" He heard McCarter on the other end.

"Just a bit more news about the weather," Blancanales replied. Over their secure, encrypted devices, the two had mapped out the way this conversation had to go. They then switched to disposable cell phones for the sake of seeming secure, all the while leaving their conversation open to prying ears.

The two were acting as bait, especially since Mc-Carter had told him of the efforts to silence those in the know about the raid on the Weather Modification Office's technology test area along the Gobi Desert.

There was a good chance it might have been the government who killed the man, but his manner of death was brutal and hand-to-hand, the work of someone who knew better than to pack firepower in this country. Someone who did not want the handiwork traced back to them. That didn't make sense, even for the Ministry of State Security, who would have no problem shooting someone for the crime of treason.

No, crushing someone's skull with a boot stomp was the act of their enemy, killing without leaving signs of weapons or nationality.

So Blancanales and McCarter traded discussion. The Phoenix Force leader had been seen leaving the contact of the murdered man: Mei Anna. They were hoping that someone would be on his scent, listening to his phone calls, something that could be done with a phone-cloner unit, a device small enough to slide into a pocket.

Right now McCarter was approximately ten blocks away, walking in Blancanales's direction.

And Blancanales, despite his salt-and-pepper hair and the cane he leaned on, looked good playing the part of an old man. The cane was a martial arts weapon. Blancanales was an experienced practitioner of bojutsu—not *jitsu* but *jutsu*—the practice of the use of the short staff or cane in actual combat, not the art.

To be certain, Blancanales did have a firearm on his person, but a very flat, concealed weapon. He didn't relish getting into a gunfight in Hong Kong, not when the police would fall upon him armed to the teeth.

They kept talking, trading vague references about missile technology and the weather manipulation systems, going for length of call, making certain their opposition could home in on them.

It was a risky gambit. Blancanales kept tensing at the sight of official-looking cars, glad that they were mostly the same Hong Kong park maintenance vehicle, and the occasional passing police car. This kind of loose talk could drop a lot of heat on them.

Blancanales recalled the motto of David McCarter's old unit, the British Special Air Service: Who Dares, Wins.

That's when Blancanales noticed a van pull to a stop and disgorge two tall men dressed in black. They didn't appear to be armed, but they didn't need to be. They were both taller than Blancanales, and the leather gloves they wore over their ham-size fists were quiet proof that this dare had drawn a response.

Blancanales leaned a little harder against his cane.

Let the hunt begin.

CHAPTER FIVE

David McCarter walked at a brisk pace, the disposable cell phone to his ear, continuing his conversation with Rosario Blancanales, letting the words come out as something only slightly above gibberish. Luckily, he and the other man were working from a script they'd memorized. They needed only to hit proper keywords to attract attention, and the use of a prepared script allowed them to concentrate on their surroundings. The trouble with playing bait was not that they were consciously in the line of fire, but that they had to be aware where that line started. He heard Blancanales's tone change.

"Hunt," the Able Team veteran said, and the phone clicked off.

The word "hunt" was not in reference to Huntington Wethers back at Stony Man Farm, but that their objective as bait had succeeded. Someone had showed up. McCarter's eyes kept sweeping the street and sidewalk around him. No one had come toward him yet, though he had an itch at the base of his neck, a tingle of danger that wasn't exactly on a conscious level. McCarter had survived enough operations to realize that the unfocused discomfort was not a sign of his instincts misfiring, but actually picking up on some subtle hints that he was being stalked.

McCarter had his hands in his jacket pockets, his right hand's fingers wrapped around the handle of a .22 Magnum Taurus. Even out of a short barrel like the snubby, it had nearly the energy of a 9 mm bullet, and there were eight of them in the cylinder. McCarter also had his knuckle load, the deadly spike capable of killing, though in this instance, he was more interested in stunning his foe.

Questioning a corpse would not be the easiest of things, but if worse came to worst, McCarter could at least rifle through a dead man's pockets and make observations about the state of his body. He'd also get photographs and fingerprints of the dead man, but right now, he wanted someone who could speak.

Even as he dangled himself as bait, there was also a section of him worried about Mei Anna and her people back at the bar. That tingle of warning at the base of his skull told him that it was likely he had drawn the wolves away from her door. As it was, the bar was on a tight lockdown, to the point where Mei had literally stuffed the revolver into McCarter's pocket the minute they saw each other. Attacking her now to cut off the seep of information would be too risky and foolhardy. Even if they somehow succeeded in attacking her in her own headquarters, the cost in manpower and the attention the violence would bring would undo any efforts at cover-up.

There. McCarter's instincts rose in reaction to a sight out of the corner of his eye. As was the case with most instinctual responses, McCarter's conscious mind wasn't quite certain of what had popped up on his radar, but he knew where the threat was. He knew the distance to what triggered his surge of fight or flight.

The sidewalks around him were packed with people, all of varying heights, even though the six-foot Mc-Carter loomed over many of the Chinese in the crowds.

There were other six-footers sprinkled here and there, but none of them appeared to be trailing him nor showing aggression. Then again, McCarter was keener to stay low profile when trailing someone, and if their enemy was assassins out to protect their conspiracy, they would not make a lot of noise, not until they were within striking distance.

No, McCarter's opponent was quiet and had only betrayed something small that tripped his instincts, but had kept him from actually noticing the attacker. He fought against the urge to concentrate on memories and input. The best result he had in reaction to ambush was not to concentrate on what could be wrong; instead, he should just look for the whole picture. His reflexes worked finely because he didn't distract himself from the totality of input being picked up by sight, sound and touch.

And that was when McCarter saw the person shoved out of the way, just out of the corner of his eye, an instant before he whirled in swift, certain response. McCarter folded his arm and brought the "chicken wing" down tight against his side, suddenly blocking the punch that swung at him, low and aiming at his kidney. Britain's Special Air Service taught that an attack on an opponent's kidneys was the surest path to incapacitating them with a minimum of fuss. A knife would cause instantly lethal renal shock, but a punch would crumple a man like a discarded newspaper.

McCarter's elbow took the force of the stunning punch, pain jolting up through his shoulder. But the pain was not indicative of broken bone or dislocated joint because his fist still remained clenched and ready. McCarter extended his arm, snapping his fist at the foe who struck at him, but the enemy was swift. Knuckles scraped the nearly bald head of the compact fireplug of a man, but the brunt of his punch was slipped by a quick movement of his head.

The bald attacker whipped out his other fist, a punch that should have hooked around to strike McCarter at the base of his spine, but the Briton was also moving, turning to bring his other arm in front of him as a means of shielding himself. That left hook from the bulldoglike man snapped into McCarter's own arm, blunting that strike. The ex-SAS commando lashed out with his left boot, striking toward the ambusher's knees, but the enemy's footwork was swift and he seemingly danced away from the initial assault.

Now that they were face-to-face, McCarter could see that this guy was some form of European, though matching the diminutive height of the rest of the Chinese populace average around him. What he lacked in height, he made up for in bulk, arms sausaged into windbreaker sleeves with big fists poking out. The Phoenix Force commander could see the deformation of his foe's knuckles, showing that this guy had trained long and laboriously to make his hands hardened clubs devoted to pain.

The squat killer moved in again, and McCarter switched feet, stabbing out with his right to try to catch the man under his sternum. Those meaty cudgels crossed, blocking the attack, and the Briton retracted his kick even as blunt fingertips clawed at the slack around his shin. That didn't slow the bald assassin's onrush. McCarter kept his feet at right angles to each other, forming the tactical T that ensured it would be difficult to push him off balance. It was ingrained into his reflexes, so that even as he backed away from another snapping fist, the Briton's footing was certain.

The sudden eruption of martial arts combat on the sidewalk made people scatter, which thankfully allowed McCarter some breathing room. He didn't have to worry about bystanders wandering into the melee and becoming injured. McCarter slap-deflected another assault, and went on the attack, whipping his elbow around to catch his foe in the face. With both of their forward momentum combined, McCarter felt his humerus spark with the jolt of "funny bone" reactions, but was rewarded with his opponent staggering backward.

McCarter kept on the attack, only to catch a snap kick that barked off his shin, knocking the support from beneath him. The Briton staggered to his other foot to maintain his balance, spearing at the attacker with a knife hand. Fingernails gouged at forehead, bushy eyebrows and down into the enemy's eye, McCarter making as much use of his increased reach as he could. Even as that raking slash connected, a powerful hammer struck him in his exposed side.

In his lunge, McCarter had left himself open. Ordinarily such a mistake would have come and gone too quickly for an opponent to take advantage. This time, however, the punch knocked the wind from the Phoenix Force commander and he stumbled to one knee. The squat attacker rubbed his eyes across his forearm, blinking blood away that seeped from his torn skin. The club-fisted warrior lunged in, but McCarter kicked off with all of his strength, lunging headfirst into his foe's stomach. Fists that had been aimed for his head or neck instead fell upon his heavily muscled back and ribs. The impacts were painful, but not fatal, while McCarter lifted the killer off his stubby legs.

The Briton hooked the back of his foe's thighs and then allowed himself to topple forward, wrenching the assassin down to the sidewalk. The man released a pained grunt before his knees wrenched upward, dislodging McCarter from his position. The Phoenix commander hammered off a side punch, unable to target his foe's kidneys, but the body blow went further toward emptying the bald attacker's lungs.

McCarter fired off a second punch, striking below his enemy's belt buckle, the blow stabbing deep into the man's groin muscles. He cupped his hand over the assassin's knee and pushed it out hard to the side, exposing the soft inner crease that McCarter wailed a second punch into, this time aiming for the inner thigh to disrupt the femoral artery. His foe wailed in pain when that blow connected, but McCarter was not through. The Briton tangled his arm with the attacker's lower leg, then wrenched hard.

The bald little fighter's knee popped with an ugly sound, driving his voice into a higher octave of pain. Twisting his ankle forced the guy to flop to his stomach. This wasn't a mixed martial arts ring fight. There would be no tapping out. McCarter slammed the guy in the kidney with everything he still had in the tank. With that final chop, there wasn't any sign of further violence from his foe.

McCarter tested his weight on the kicked leg and felt lucky that it had merely been a glancing kick. There was no seeming fracture, and he could move his foot. That was more than his ambusher could say.

The Phoenix leader grabbed him up by his collar. As soon as McCarter had him ready to move, Gary Manning brought his minivan to the curb, honking the horn.

With a hearty heave, he slammed the bald, club-fisted assassin into the back of the van, then climbed in and slid the side door shut.

"I thought you would have had this one done long before I got here," Manning quipped.

McCarter shrugged. "I played it out because I know how much of a bitch Hong Kong traffic is."

Manning looked over his shoulder at McCarter. Even in the dim interior of the van, he could see the Briton had been through a hell of a fight. The Phoenix commander cinched the guy's wrists together behind his back with cable ties, more than one just to make certain the restraints would hold the thick-shouldered killer.

The thug looked up from the floor at the two men, and McCarter rested the sole of his boot against his throat.

"Gettin' yer throat stepped on is a slow, ugly way to die," McCarter growled. "You might have a chance not to die if you sit still."

"Leg." The man spoke. The word was too short for any hint of accent to arise, but McCarter looked more closely at his appearance, pulling out his pocket flashlight and his personal cell device. With a click of the button, the commander had his prisoner's photograph taken. A few motions with his thumb and the photograph was on its way to Stony Man Farm.

"I know your pin took a twistin'. I did it, mate," Mc-

Carter told the prisoner. "You going to tell me who you are or where you came from?"

"Eat the dicks." The attacker spit.

McCarter sighed. "Then just lay there and shut up." To emphasize his point, the Phoenix Force leader pulled the revolver from his jacket pocket and leveled it at the man's face.

"Only a .22," the prisoner said. "It'll roll right off my skull."

McCarter smirked. "But it'll take out both of your eyes and mutilate your face. I'll leave plenty for you to talk with, but you'll be blind and hideous for the rest of your miserable existence."

That quieted the assassin.

Now to find out how Blancanales was doing with his hunt.

THE BRUISERS GREW closer to Rosario Blancanales as he leaned heavily on his cane. They regarded him with stony, hate-filled glares. Both were taller than Blancanales, and seemed to have been chosen for the sake of the width of their shoulders and thickness of their limbs. That didn't mean they didn't possess skill, but Blancanales was hedging his bets on keeping them mentally disarmed. As he stood, using the cane as a crutch, and dressed in loose, baggy clothing, he tried to cast the image of an old man trying to play a young man's game.

Both of them were European, possessing Slavic features. At least they were smart enough not to wear sunglasses at night, but now, the Able Team veteran was on the alert that these two guys could be so much more than just bags of cement with fists.

"Gentlemen?" Blancanales greeted them as they got within a few yards of him. "I'm afraid you found me out."

Neither spoke as he scanned Statue Square, the park where Blancanales had been observing the Hong Kong cenotaph. They were making certain they hadn't been drawn into a trap with human bait. This spread-out tourist attraction would provide plenty of places for Blancanales's backup to hide and there were rooftops that could be used for sniper overwatch.

One of the men had yellow scrub for hair. The other, with a rust-colored scouring pad for his top, Blancanales noted, stepped right up to him and looked down upon him.

"Your friend, he will not be speaking to you again," Blondie said.

Blancanales looked down, sighing. "He was a good man."

"We will need to ask you some questions." Blondie's big hand wrapped around Blancanales's shoulder and squeezed hard. Those fingers, thick as sausages, clamped down with painful precision, making Blancanales stand straighter, no acting required to twist his features into agony. The blond Russian reached down to take away Blancanales's fighting cane.

You underestimated them, Blancanales thought the moment before he slashed the hardwood cane against the side of his oppressor's knee. Through his knowledge of human anatomy and his years of not only training but field experience with the fighting stick, the simple slice suddenly toppled the brawny Russian, forcing him to release the Able Team veteran's shoulder.

Blancanales stepped back, already feeling the bruises

forming from the monstrous claw that had threatened to crush his shoulder joint. He whipped the cane up and was ready to destroy the blond man's face when Red lurched toward him, moving with all the power and speed of a charging buffalo.

Blancanales threw himself aside as 250 pounds of freckled muscle surged past him, breaths and ponderous footfalls making him sound like a locomotive. The hurt Russian grit his teeth and sprung off his remaining leg, fingers hooked like talons to tear at Blancanales's flesh. The Able Team warrior speared out, the brass tip of his cane striking the blond in his Adam's apple before sliding down into the notch of his collarbone. The brawny thug gurgled, but Blancanales could feel his opponent altering his course, minimizing the jarring effect of being jammed in the throat.

Even so, Blondie gasped, sliding into the grass and taking a moment to clasp his hands around his dislocated knee.

Blancanales barely had a moment to look for the other man before a thick rope of muscle wrapped in black leather lashed toward his head in his peripheral vision. Blancanales dipped his head. The clothesline maneuver mussing his salt-and-pepper hair. Muscles glancing off his skull informed him that he'd have lost his head to the strike. Blancanales pivoted the cane in his hands, slicing at his foe's hip, but the collision between man and wood spun both combatants.

Blancanales stepped quickly to recover his balance and looked with dismay upon the Red-topped ape that merely dropped one of his meaty paws to rub the sore spot on his side. Green eyes glared from under a beetled brow, and Blancanales couldn't see a hint of humanity in those features now. This thing before him was a raging beast, and somehow those shoulder muscles seemed to spread even wider, like something out of a werewolf movie. Spittle frothed at the corners of the Russian's mouth, and he surged forward at the Able Team warrior.

Blancanales charged, as well, pressing the attack and stabbing forward as if his cane were a sword. The brass cap struck rippling chest muscles and dragged heavily off the Russian's leather jacket. It hit a wrinkle and suddenly it was as if Blancanales rode a tidal wave, being shoved backward off his feet. His red-haired opponent continued steaming toward him, but Blancanales's grasp on his cane kept him just out of reach of a gigantic hand.

Blancanales slammed his feet into the grass behind him, throwing all of his weight and strength into slowing his freight train of an opponent. Sod wrinkled and tore under the soles of his boots, and the Russian let out a bellow of pain as the hardwood cane snapped in two.

Blancanales's only weapon shattered, he lurched aside as the beast stormed past him, striking a cobblestone walkway chin-first. If that brute could snap his battle cane, then there was no way that Red could have come away from that crash without a broken rib or three. Still, Blancanales rushed to the big thug's fallen form and jumped onto his broad back, coming down on both knees. He put all his weight into the attack, hoping to further stagger the man.

Blancanales saw those thick arms lift, hands flattening against the ground to raise his ponderous bulk and return to combat. The Russian's haircut was too short to get a sufficient grasp on it, but there was no trimming his ears. Blancanales grabbed the twin dishes of flesh and cartilage on either side of Red's head and pushed forward hard, mashing the man's face into the sidewalk. With brutish energy, the Russian reared up like an untamed stallion, seeking to wrest Blancanales from his back.

The Able Team warrior slammed his knee between the attacker's shoulder blades and wrenched back hard. Both ears were torn from the sides of his skull, skin ripping away along his scalp, eliciting thunder from deep within the man-beast's breast. Red bent away from Blancanales's knee, giving the wily Able Team fighter enough room to bring up his other leg and push down hard. Bones cracked as the Russian's face struck cobblestone, blood spurting from a burst nose.

The blond was back, gingerly favoring his injured knee, but still on two feet and ready to step in to make up for the loss of his partner in this conflict.

Blancanales was breathing heavily, but he stood his ground, glaring at the blond Russian, standing astride the corpse of his even more brutish partner. Blancanales lifted his hand, borrowing from one of Hong Kong's greatest breakout action heroes, folding his hand toward himself in challenge. The Able veteran figured that he had a good chance if this fight continued, as he still maintained his full mobility, while Blondie was limping. Bulk and power were nothing in comparison to skill and intellect.

In a heartbeat, hands took the blond by either arm, and the twin meaty impacts of knuckles against a leather-clad torso caused the big Slav to collapse to both knees. Between the dual kidney punches and landing so heavily on his injured knee, the Russian folded at the waist and curled into a fetal position on the grass.

Calvin James and Rafael Encizo were breathing deeply, evenly, evidencing their mad rush across Statue Square to Blancanales's aid. On the edge of the park, a minivan screeched to a halt, the side door slamming open.

"Oy! Time to move!" McCarter's bellow crossed the square.

"Want this one?" James asked Blancanales.

"We're not moving fast dragging him along," he returned. "Dump him and let's move!"

As one, the two Phoenix Force commandos and the Able Team warrior raced across the park to Manning and McCarter in the rented van.

Within a few moments the Stony Man operatives would lose themselves in Hong Kong traffic, disappearing from the scenes of battle as far as the police would be concerned.

But they had a prisoner; a skilled killer who was trying to silence information about the attack on the Gobi Desert base.

For Blancanales, it was worth the broken cane and stiff, sore arm.

CHAPTER SIX

Carl Lyons was ready the moment there was a knock at the door, rising to his feet. He'd dressed and had his .357 Magnum Colt Python in its waistband holster. Opening the door, he ushered in Hermann Schwarz and T. J. Hawkins.

"Did you get a party favor last night?" Lyons asked.

Schwarz tilted his head. "What did you get?"

Lyons could see that Schwarz looked tired. He smelled the chemical stink of methamphetamine hovering around him like a fog. "I'm guessing we all got our vices. What did you do?"

"I lit up my shit," Schwarz explained. "So I been tweaking all night."

As he said so, he made a small hand gesture informing Lyons that he hadn't inhaled. Lyons knew that faking smoking was a little bit easier, but even so, he'd exposed himself to the smoke from a neurotoxic drug. Even that seemed to have left Schwarz a little burned out this morning. Hawkins had heavily lidded eyes and looked more than a little sheepish.

"We're here on business," Lyons growled. "You get baked, and you end up tweaking?"

"I turned my radio into a Taser," Schwarz answered with a shrug.

Hawkins frowned. "My mouth is all raw from chip mouth."

Lyons rolled his eyes and then turned away.

He had to act the part, which meant having a razor's edge thin line between temper and control. So far, the bloodied Sanay had proved Lyons's cover, but that had been her playing on his reflexes. Right now, he realized that those blind instincts and reflexes had likely saved his life and those of his friends.

THOMAS JEFFERSON HAWKINS hoped he'd put on a good enough show as the pot-smoking-and-dealing rookie biker for the Reich Low Riders brought up to the big leagues of "the race war." His Texan accent, in most cases, would have been more than sufficient to sell himself as a bigoted thug in some "Left Coast" cities.

Those opinions of his method of speech, his history as an elite Airborne Ranger, just the places of his birth, were merely projections of bigotry from others. Even before he joined the Army, Hawkins hadn't given a damn about race or creed. As with the rest of the world, as with most of America, Texas was a melting pot, and growing up meeting, going to school with and just making friends with a few dozen Hispanics by age ten was easier than tripping over your own feet.

Even more insulting to the Texan was that his military career had ended when he'd disobeyed a United Nations peacekeeping force and superior officer to prevent the massacre of villagers in Somalia. Hawkins came from a long lineage of soldiers, so career and service were a part of his DNA. When Hawkins had taken his oath of service, there'd been nothing about only protecting white Americans from enemies foreign or domestic. When he placed his life on the line across dozens of missions with Phoenix Force, it wasn't just for the sake of one skin or one state over another.

Like Schwarz, he'd taken a few hits off the pot he'd been given. He'd actually imbibed more than Schwarz had, if only because Hawkins knew that there was far less likelihood of negative health effects off marijuana than methamphetamine. The little that Schwarz had smoked showed on the Able Team genius's features, the bags under his eyes, the half step slower in his stride, even the sounds of his words. A minor taste of the meth, and staying up all night duplicating the activities of a tweaker, had left Schwarz looking as though he'd been run over by a truck.

Still, a half step slower for Schwarz was a sight quicker than most other men. Hawkins himself felt a bit more tired, but he was glad he didn't have a background in meth. Munchies and a lowering of his energy this morning was much better than inhaling a neurotoxin and muscle stimulant.

He knocked back some coffee, then checked his watch. According to the agenda, there was going to be a sample mall for this convention of crazies. Tables would be stacked with the smaller, man-portable goods and there would be videos for larger items.

The mall would open in an hour.

In the meantime, Hawkins, like the other members of his undercover team, had been keeping his eyes peeled for what security was around the place. They could never break character, not certain if there were any spaces not covered by security cameras or hidden microphones. Even if Schwarz could use his electronic skills, there was a good chance that interfering with these observations would only draw far more attention. And so, Lyons continued to act like a grouch.

Hawkins stayed on script. He had a job to do, and they could wait until this mission was over to mentally and emotionally unwind. In the meantime, he kept his eyes peeled and ears tuned. Finding electronics was one thing. Sizing up the security and their competition was something very different. Hawkins could already tell that plenty of the guards were professionals of various stripes. The guy who came through and had hung out at Lyons's door, for example, was a Samoan who Hawkins estimated at six foot two inches and 325 pounds. A lot of it looked like fat, but the man moved as if he were easily half that size, with canny, sharp eyes that paid attention like an eagle scanning for prey on a prairie.

Hawkins observed him through the peephole, having spent more than enough time looking through such fish lenses to have a good sense of what was going on even with the curved distortion of the glass aperture. Measuring the Samoan against Lyons provided a good scale to work with.

Hawkins announced that he was leaving the hotel room, going to see what was up and about. It might not have been the best of ideas to wander away alone. Sitting and waiting was fine under the auspices of being immobile and observing enemies, but sitting in a hotel room was something completely different. At least outside, he could observe. He could fill his anxious nerves with input.

Hawkins didn't intend to engage an opponent, though he did have a pair of small Smith & Wesson M&P 360 revolvers, both in .357 Magnum and loaded with 125-grain semijacketed hollowpoints. Out of the stubby 1.9-inch barrels of the lightweight pistols, the high-velocity slugs reached over 1160 feet per second, bringing 375 foot-pounds of energy on a target. Hawkins didn't intend to pull out both revolvers at once, just use one as a swift reload for the other. The 360s were made of an alloy stronger than titanium, making the weapons exceedingly light. That lack of weight meant they would recoil even harder against his hand. He'd tried utilizing one of the little revolvers with its as-issued grips, but the gun had smashed into the web of his hand and the ball of his thumb like a torturer's hammer. Fortunately, changing the grip profile of a revolver was as simple as using a screwdriver.

The little lightweight twins had Pachmeyer Compacs, which had a vital quarter inch of cushioning, recoil-spreading rubber around the back strap of the revolver. Now it was a blunt thump, not a claw-hammer chop. He could burn off five rapid shots into a target, even with the heaviest loaded rounds. With the stubby .357 Magnums, he could more than defend himself if things came to a head in a conflict, but by their very nature, the revolvers were meant for close, nasty work, though he had trained beside Lyons and Manning to be able to hit a man-size target all the way out to 100 yards. It wasn't easy, so that was why Hawkins trained hard and often.

Hawkins returned his attention to the guard force. The Samoan was likely drawn from local resources. The man showed canny situational awareness, as had every other guard on hand. The security force themselves were well equipped.

Those who carried long arms wore body armor, eye

protection and had hearing protection on lanyards dangling from behind their neck. The choice in big guns was between AK-12 assault rifles—some of the newest variants on the classic and proved Kalashnikov line—and Benelli M-4 Super-90 shotguns. Considering that current Russian military issue was still the AN-94, since 1997 in fact, the AKs were not military surplus or "fallen off the truck" to fill the wallets of Russian officers. The Benelli was also standard military issue from the Los Angeles Police Department to the United States military under the classification M-1014.

Judging by the shape of the magazines, the AK-12s were either 7.62 mm or the 5.45 mm replacement. The guards had their spare magazines in pouches on their body armor, and the pouches were kept shut. Either way, these rifles could lay down long streams of lead at 600 rounds per minute, or put out concentrated tribursts at 1000 rounds per minute per pull of the trigger. The Benelli M-4s were equally devastating, chambered for 12-gauge and could hold seven plus one in the chamber. That kind of firepower was meant for keeping the various factions at this auction in line.

No one in their right mind would want to face down either a blast of buckshot or a swarm of 5.45 mm slugs. Hawkins had been on both ends of these particular weapons, and knew they were both quite reliable and devastating in trained hands.

The hard men with the body armor also had sidearms on their hips. From the smooth lines of the grips, Hawkins wasn't quite sure, but they might have been armed with Caracal F service pistols, which were top of the line and current service weapons of the United Arab Emirates and four other Middle Eastern nations.

Again, Hawkins could only make out the model, not the caliber, but since he hadn't seen many in .40 or .357 calibers, he assumed 9 mm, which gave the guards nineteen shots before reloading. In the heavier calibers, there'd still be a full 17 rounds.

Hawkins looked over the gear of one of the men with a Benelli shotgun. He put on his full-on drawl and approached. "Good mornin', hoss."

The man, a white, looked the undercover Phoenix over. "American?"

Those words came with a Slavic accent. Hawkins smirked. "Ayup. Texas."

"Ah. Cowboy. Pew-pew," the Russian said. He had a beard, but it was kept trimmed, and split to reveal a bright white smile.

Hawkins chuckled. "I don't ride no horse unless it's made o' iron."

The Russian nodded, looking at the tattoos that sleeved his arms down to the wrist. Instead of being repulsed by the lightning-bolt-shaped SSs that represented the Reich Low Riders of California, the Russian actually smiled even more broadly. He tugged up the cuff of his uniform sleeve and showed off his own neo-Nazi insignia. "Brothers in arm. Literally."

Hawkins fought the urge to scowl, instead allowing himself a laugh to echo his newfound friend's. In the Russian Federation, the horrors inflicted by Nazi Germany had long been forgotten. With the country receiving huge influxes of immigrants, stealing jobs in an already tight employment market, neo-Nazism had surged. This man was one of them, and suddenly found a comrade. Though the biodegradable ink would fade within a few weeks, Hawkins never wanted to hide his bare arms so much before, as if he were displaying diseased flesh.

"Slap me and call me a groundhog!" Hawkins spoke with a pride and fellowship he didn't feel in his gut. At least he had a means of sparking a conversation with this guy, and now he could see just what local security was like.

He noted that the security force was using 9 mm autoloaders and 5.45 mm rifles. He watched Yuri's eyes widen at the sight of a "high-tech" American Magnum as small as a Makarov. Hawkins also learned that Yuri wasn't the only member of his militia present here in Hawaii, but the Russian was smart enough not to mention numbers, which in itself was informative to the Phoenix Force pro.

Hawkins did know that there were three shifts of guards, meaning that even if he counted every one of them, he'd still need to do some math, especially since it didn't look as though they would all take off from their shifts at the same time. A smart leader would stagger who went off duty and who came on duty at varying segments, so that there was always the same number on the field, even double in a particular area at certain times.

Hawkins also noted that while there were sections of the hotel and surrounding resort facilities that seemed unfinished, there were definitely off-limit areas. Through his conversation with Yuri, trading stories about motorcycles and favorite shooting trips, Hawkins also managed to burn up the minutes that normally would have dragged on as he waited to see what would be on display. Also, as he talked, he made note of different men.

He even recognized several who were on most-wanted lists, both for Interpol and Homeland Security. This was truly a global assembly. Asians. Middle Easterners. Europeans. Africans.

All were clean and well dressed, and there was plenty of iron on display, both in terms of handguns in open and concealed holsters, as well as knives. This was a den of many wolves, and Hawkins could see that one mistake would serve him and the rest of Able Team up as appetizers to a bloody feast.

Hawkins wrapped his fingers tightly around the rubber grip of his pocket Magnum as the ballroom doors opened in three spots along the hallway. Curious criminals and terrorists lined up, invites checked, and filtered into the showroom.

Hawkins passed through the doors and stopped cold, his jaw dropping as he saw a ten-meter-long Dong-Feng missile sitting on a support scaffold. Huge, ominous, it was an unmistakable display of the vulgar firepower the auctioneer Jinan had assembled.

CHAPTER SEVEN

Hermann Schwarz gave T. J. Hawkins a prod in the back, urging him not to drop his jaw. "C'mon, Tex. We got a shopping list to fill."

Hawkins tore his attention away from the massive DF-21 antishipping ballistic missile. Though he'd been aware that Able Team might encounter such a mighty weapon, seeing it sitting in the showroom right in front of him was unmistakably a jaw-dropping sight. He'd idly wondered how the Chinese design was such a looming, powerful threat, but up close, he could tell the sheer power of it thanks to its girth and the large, bell-like nozzles of its rocket motors. Now he could see the kind of thrust that could push the Dong-Feng into low orbit at ten times the speed of sound, and then drop it on an American aircraft carrier and its support group. The nose cone was blunt and wide, big enough, he noted, for easily six or seven smaller warheads, or a full-blown nuclear missile or massive ordnance air burst bomb.

"Is that…?" Hawkins began.

"Obviously not," Schwarz answered. "It's a dummy, like the Soviets often used for their May Day parades. There's no smell of any form of fuel."

"It's a hell of a sight," Hawkins said. "And it's got MIRVs?"

"No. A Maneuverable Reentry Vehicle—a MaRV," Schwarz corrected him. "And even though it's capable of nearly 1700 miles of range, there're still a lot of questions about how it will track its target.

"We're not certain about their over-the-horizon radar systems or other sensors. Any long-range targeting might have to come from an outside third party."

Hawkins nodded. He didn't want to talk too much about what kind of guidance mechanisms would be on the DF-21 variant. While Thomas Jefferson Hawkins was someone who was interested in communications equipment and radars, Thomas Presley's interests were motorcycles, marijuana and machine guns. More than a little curiosity would cause suspicion, so he moved along.

Of course Jinan wouldn't put a real antiship ballistic missile in the middle of his hotel, even without fuel or active warhead, the effort to break it down and bring it into a ballroom and then reassemble it would be too difficult. Conversely, there were plenty of rifles and other firearms on display, as well as shoulder-mounted rocket launchers and even larger designs.

It was a hell of a display across 38,000 square feet of showroom. Hawkins even saw a number of "booth babes," though as he and Schwarz passed close by to them, he could make out the crumbly flecks of heavily caked makeup, which concealed whatever bruising they'd received the night before. Hawkins scanned the room to see if Lyons's "party favor" was around, but she was not in evidence.

This was still something that took Hawkins by surprise. Schwarz gave him a nudge in the ribs and led him over to a table with what appeared to be Heckler

& Koch assault rifles, but as Hawkins picked one up, he could feel that the balance was off. Checking for serial numbers or other marks, he noted that the writing on the gun was neither German nor English, looked vaguely Latin, but didn't resemble Spanish.

"Brazilian knockoffs," Hawkins said.

"Chinese Mausers," Schwarz responded. "What are you looking for?"

"Carl's girl," Hawkins replied.

Schwarz narrowed his eyes. "If he finds out that you're looking for her...or if our host does..."

"I'm just curious, man." Hawkins spoke up, falling into character. "Can't a guy be curious about the chick his bro's boning?"

Schwarz winked almost too quickly for Hawkins to catch. "Karl ain't the kind to share, and you aren't his 'bro.' You're Texas chapter, which means he can stand the smell of you, but you ain't Cali."

Hawkins showed Schwarz his open palm. There was a clearing of a man's throat across the table. The Texan glanced over.

"No fighting at the gun tables," the man said.

"These fake like that missile?" Hawkins asked.

"They have firing pins, but they are stored separately," the huckster said. "We're not stupid."

Hawkins nodded. "I don't see a lot of ammunition lying about."

"The only things ready to go in here are the bayonets and other blades," Schwarz mused.

The huckster touched his nose. "You still shouldn't make a fuss so close to the automatic weapons."

"Don't worry," Schwarz said. "We're moving this conversation elsewhere."

Schwarz took Hawkins by the arm and marched him away from the H&K look-alikes.

"You think they've got microphones and cameras in here watching us?" Hawkins asked.

Schwarz shook his head. "That doesn't mean we have to drop our guard."

"Nope," Hawkins added. "So, what do you think the Aryan Right Coalition would like in its stockings?"

"Grenades," Schwarz murmured.

Hawkins chuckled. "No, *you* want that for them."

Schwarz winked. "They sure ain't gonna like guns with Portuguese writing on them."

Hawkins shook his head. "We need to look for something more homegrown."

"In a manlier caliber than 5.56," Schwarz added.

Hawkins nodded his agreement, staying in character. "Let's take a look at the rifles. These chumps should have something in .308 Winchester."

Schwarz winked.

Even as the two men went to check out the rifles, a thought crossed Hawkins's mind. What was taking Lyons so long to get down here?

CARL LYONS HAD opted to take the morning away from the arms sales to take advantage of the half-completed gymnasium, which, when completed, would have been something absolutely joyful to be in. There were free weights and state-of-the-art resistance machines, as well as what looked like a 100-meter track for jogging, in addition to treadmills and stationary bikes. Lyons loaded up a bar, noting that he wasn't the only one devoted to physical fitness. There were blacks, Orientals and other whites.

He scanned the area, assessing who was present, looking for signs of being armed, indications of hostility. Space was kept between the individual members of various factions, but there was no sound of hostility, no trash talk or threats. There were only the subtle grunts of effort and the clanks of steel and rattles of weight plates.

Lyons went to a butterfly machine and got to work.

He ran out of steam after fifteen minutes and rose from the machine. Even though he was pushing his body to where it could benefit from the effort put into the exercise, he kept his mind on the situation around him. The workout bunch, Lyons noted, were in their own worlds, not looking for trouble, but instead dedicating themselves to their bodies, keeping them honed. This wasn't some kind of narcissist assembly. Lyons could see there were men working on keeping their agility up, while others were continuing the routines that kept them lean and hard during stays in prison.

And there were plenty of these former prisoners around. Lyons could easily make out the Yakuza by their multicolored, flamboyant shirts of ink, and could tell the Russian Bratva by their unmistakable and unique signs. He could see the rift between Slavs within the *mafiya* and those who had Nazi symbols scratched into their flesh, despite the fact that both groups used the selfsame prison methods and inks. Lyons tried not to think about what had been scrawled on his flesh, glad for the T-shirt that covered much of his, but his perspiration soaked the cloth to his skin and elements could be seen on his torso, not to mention the sleeves scrawled down his arms and on his neck.

Slowly, gingerly, one of the Russian neo-Nazis approached Lyons.

Lyons kept himself loose, eyeing the man as he stretched and warmed up his upper arms and shoulders from the reps.

"You are American, yes?"

Lyons grunted. He would have had to been blind not to see at least a bit of fellowship in regard to the tattoos that seemed to duplicate themselves, at least thematically, on what was visible of their skin. "What's it to you?"

The Russian looked around. "Nice to see someone with some of the same sympathies."

Lyons relaxed some. "Yeah. Just…you know…not sure."

"It's tense around here," the neo-Nazi thug said. "But as long as these guys don't try to move into my neighborhood, take my people's jobs, I don't mind them."

"They seem to mind Moscow 88," Lyons said.

The Russian's eyes lit up. "How did you know?"

"We've got some information about our allies in Europe," Lyons answered. "You're working security."

The Russian nodded.

"Your group has enough money for this auction?" Lyons asked.

"No, it doesn't," he said. "We're one of several groups working security for the auction. My name's Grigori."

"Karl," Lyons answered.

Grigori glanced back toward the Bratva gangsters who glowered across the gymnasium floor. Lyons noted that their number had dropped by two, but the motion of figures in the corner of his eye informed him the Russian mob members were on the running track.

Lyons frowned. "They don't like you very much," he said in a low rumble.

Grigori shook his head. "Some of them are too stuck in the Great Patriotic War. Others make money from the very scum we're trying to boot from Moscow."

"They've lain with the dogs. And they're looking at you like you got fleas," Lyons mused.

Grigori smirked. "Can I call my men over?"

Lyons nodded.

Three more of the racist Russians came over. Lyons should have felt comfortable, should have been glad to have these four slabs of beef between him and the Bratva goons whose memories stretched back to World War II. The goons acted as if they *liked* Lyons—or rather, Karl Long, American badass motorcyclist. That comradeship bristled under his fake tattoos, making him even more uncomfortable in his skin.

Then there were the two runners who slowed on their latest lap as they came closer to the Russian security thugs and himself.

"Do you think the gangsters will be stupid enough to go after Abalisah's staff?" Lyons asked out loud, sharply enough for not only the runners to hear, but also the Bratva goons across the gym floor.

Grigori looked over Lyons's shoulder, watching the joggers through slitted eyes. "No. Not even when we're not on duty."

"Shame," Lyons said. He cracked his knuckles and picked up a pair of fifty-pound kettle bells. "I'd love a chance to do some martial art."

"What's your style?" Grigori asked, picking up a similar set.

"Jailhouse rock," Lyons answered, not quite lying.

He was a devotee of Shotokan karate but life was never that simple. While he trained in that martial art, he had incorporated all manner of different maneuvers. His fighting style had boxing punches, wrestling moves and assorted dirty tricks like thumbs into eyeballs or bending elbows and knees backward, things that weren't in the conventional fighting style of Shotokan.

The two of them went to work on their cores, bent at the waist, legs spread, a kettle bell in each hand and moving that hand toward the opposite side's toe, arms rotating in an imitation of a windmill's propeller, hence the name "the low windmill." Lyons was glad for this particular exercise, as it could be done anywhere without exercise machines. Putting nylon web straps around 24-packs of bottled water, or just filling two duffel bags with the approximate same weight provided the same amount of resistance. It also kept Lyons's torso trim enough to share a waistband with a .357 Magnum revolver.

Grigori's buddies were loosening up, as well, working on free weights.

The Russian mobsters, however, took their cue not to mess around with the big blond bastard and his sudden pack of buddies in Abalisah's fighting force.

After an hour of working out, Lyons excused himself. No one seemed to have any wish to shower or clean up in the gymnasium's locker room, unless they happened to have the benefit of employment by Abalisah.

As Lyons made his way back to his room, he picked up a sensation at his back.

He didn't know who had taken the stairs behind him, but whoever it was, was lagging by thirty seconds. He heard him come out as he was nearing his hotel room door.

Trouble was on its way. Lyons slid the electronic key into the reader and stepped into his room. This wasn't going to be a stop off for a shower and a change from his workout clothes. He went straight to his Colt Python, checked it and then snatched some extra ammo.

Lyons hadn't put the latch across the door, instead waiting for his pursuer to make the first move. He knelt behind the bulk of his bed. A mattress wouldn't slow most bullets right away, but if someone fired through the door or the wall, the slugs would certainly lose significant penetration. If the enemy just kicked in the door, Lyons would shoot right away.

"Come on in," Lyons whispered softly, thumb safety clicked down. He looked over the sights toward the door, but made sure the front sight post was clear and crisp, letting him know exactly where his bullets would go. He might have been surrounded by criminals and killers, but if he accidentally took out one of Jinan's staff or mistakenly put a bullet into Schwarz or Hawkins, things would get very sticky.

The wait dragged on, but no matter how long it took for his follower to come up, he'd hold his position—a small target, barricaded behind the bed, his gun supported by the mattress as his shooting rest. He gently rested on one knee, one foot flat on the ground, ready to spring and retreat to the cover of the bathroom or to charge in an attack.

Even as his eyes made sure his aim was precisely aligned, his ears were peeled, waiting for the sound of who could be approaching. He heard two sets of footsteps just outside his door and held his breath to further filter out any extraneous sounds.

The door suddenly exploded, a hole bursting beneath the handle. From the looks of things, it was a big bullet that cut through. A second blast resounded and it was louder than a mere handgun.

Lyons heard a foot smash against the door. He saw the sole of a boot emerge through the opened doorway, meaning that the breacher knew what he was doing, using the wall as cover. Unfortunate for him, Lyons shifted his aim slightly and tapped off two rounds into that wall.

There was a gurgle and a screech of pain as a body toppled to the floor. A huge, almost cartoonish revolver poked through the open door on the other side of the entrance and a loud crash preceded the mattress in front of Lyons rippling with multiple projectile impacts. That was when Lyons knew what these guys were using against him—a Taurus Judge revolver.

Chambered for one of the smallest shotgun chamberings, it was big and formidable-looking. Able Team had looked into it, and the Farm's armorer, John "Cowboy" Kissinger, had attempted to brew up .410 shot shells for the big pistol. But it was just too little in terms of buckshot capacity to be any improvement of just .45 Colt revolver cartridges in the cylinder. The Judge was a good .45, holding five shots, but the cylinder was just too long for the capacity and power. They would have been better served with Taurus's old .45 Colt Tracker snub-nosed revolvers, which were lighter and shorter yet still maintained a full .45 punch. Even so, the .410 shot shell was nothing to ignore; it just didn't display a measurable improvement over regular old bullets.

Lyons shifted his aim and fired twice. Unfortunately, this gunman had the protection of the wall and his hotel room door. Another burst of .410 buckshot bellowed from the entrance, this time shattering the lamp to Lyons's immediate left.

The Able Team leader rose and took a few strides to the cover of the dresser, which also served as a cabinet for the television. Using that for cover, he was out of the sight of his attacker. The Judge bellowed another time and Lyons winced as a pellet punched its way through the particle board of the TV housing and sliced across his shoulder. The television, however, absorbed the other two buckshot pellets, sparing Lyons more serious injury.

Now bleeding, Lyons felt his patience dwindling. He stepped back from his cover and blazed out four rounds. Since the furniture was particle board, not solid wood, he didn't have to worry about returning fire through the same barrier. If one pellet could get to him enough to hurt him, then one of his hollowpoints would prove more than sufficient to bite his enemy back. There was a cry of pain, then the stumbling of feet. Another shotgun shell roared to cover the killer's retreat, but Lyons was in the mood to unleash some fury.

He paused long enough to look at the man on the floor outside his room. It was a Hispanic man, one with enough ink to inform Lyons that the Heathens' archenemies, the Horde, had their own representation here at the auction. The Able Team commander didn't pause to check if he was wounded or still in fighting trim. Acting the role of the ruthless ex-biker, he pumped a single round into the fallen attacker's skull, ending what suffering was still going on between his ears.

The other man at the end of the hallway paused and turned at the sound of the finishing shot. The guy had one more round in his big revolver, and he raised it toward Lyons. The Able Team leader wasn't risking the spread of buckshot somehow reaching him. He pumped three rounds into the Mexican outlaw biker, catching him in the upper chest.

The gunman's revolver blasted a storm of lead into the ceiling above him as he crashed backward, ribs broken, lungs torn apart by the fat mushrooms of lead and copper that smashed into him. Lyons ran closer to the fallen attacker, Colt leveled.

In instants, there were guards running up. Lyons lowered the pistol, muzzle aimed at the carpet beneath him. The men were in uniform, and he couldn't tell their nationality thanks to the shooting goggles covering their eyes. They regarded him cautiously, then looked at the body on the ground, pistol still in hand.

"Can I get an ear for my collection of Hordesmen?" Lyons asked.

The inscrutable guards looked him over. "No, but you can keep his gun."

Lyons bent and picked up the empty revolver. He patted the corpse, finding two speed loaders in the dead biker's pocket. One was full of .45 Long bullets, while the other had five .410 shot shells. "Thanks."

"Try not to get any more blood on the walls of this place," the guard grumbled. "We'll send up someone from maintenance to fix whatever they shot up."

Lyons took a deep breath, then nodded.

Their first morning at this auction and already someone had tried to kill him.

Lyons mentally shrugged as he walked back to his room. "You never did mind a target-rich environment," he muttered to himself.

CHAPTER EIGHT

Mei Anna's people in the bar were glad to see the man who had been trailing her, and who had killed one of their assets. While Calvin James was their usual chief of interrogation, thanks to his skill with administering scopolamine and following stress patterns through electrocardiograph readouts, they had left most of their equipment at a safe location outside the city of Hong Kong. In Aberdeen Harbour, there was as close to an entire floating city as one could get, and in one of those floating hulks, Phoenix Force had set up their safe house. It was in a neighborhood where the HKPD didn't go to, not without full military support and heavy machine guns.

As such, it was sacrosanct.

Getting there, however, after the battle in Statue Square and at the Cenotaph, would prove difficult. As such, Phoenix Force and Blancanales took their prisoner back to Mei's place. The assassin was dragged down into the basement and put into restraints.

"I don't like this," James muttered, looking around the bare, ugly little room where the prisoner was tied down and blindfolded. "This looks like a place where they stick bamboo shoots under your fingernails."

Mei snorted. "That went out with the Vietnam War era."

McCarter folded his armed, watching one of Mei's employees push a small cart into the room. It was a combination table and drawer, and there were syringes atop a small sterile square of cloth. Alcohol pads and bandages were present.

"You're not going to examine him to make sure he can take the pressure of the drugs you're using?" James, used to being the one getting information out prisoners, asked Mei.

She looked at him as if he had asked if they were going to give the prisoner a puppy. It wasn't the first time Phoenix Force had been in a situation where they had to work alongside others who didn't have the same impeccable ethics they personally possessed.

"We're not going to torture him, but this man killed one of my assets," Mei told him. "My folks can get the information out of him. And it's not going to be torture."

James's frown softened for a moment.

"We've got atropine and adrenaline if he starts having heart palpitations, because a prisoner who's dead can't answer questions," Mei added. "And we're not going to use torture because people will say anything to stop the pain."

"They're not rookies at this game," McCarter added, looking at James. "And they are good at getting information."

James nodded. He wasn't exactly happy, but he also wasn't the kind of person who liked to see a helpless prisoner executed. It was one thing to put down a foe in combat, but once left helpless and restrained, that brand of murder didn't sit well with him. He turned and left the room.

McCarter joined him, an arm resting around his tense shoulders.

"Your girlfriend is a scary lady," James murmured.

McCarter nodded. "How much of that discussion was your concern over the prisoner and how much was being sidelined?"

"Even," James admitted.

"Don't worry too much," McCarter said. "We'll see where the assassin came from and then we'll make a move. And don't forget…"

"Yeah, he was an assassin," James agreed "I saw what he did, but that doesn't mean I should like it when someone is set up just to die. Even when they're a cold-blooded killer."

McCarter looked at James and grinned. "I see your point. I really do. And this would be an amazing debate for some other day."

As McCarter and James entered the room, Gary Manning closed the communication program on the Stony Man laptop. The shell of the machine was a combination of aluminum and high-tech polymers that cushioned the electronics within, so it could be brought with them into the field. Manning had personally tested the durability of the prototypes as Schwarz kept making new ones for the commando teams' usage. This one was durable enough to survive a hit from an M-4 assault rifle. Anything heavier would be impractical. The compact, tough computer had more than sufficient radio transmission power to connect to satellite.

"What've you got off this mook?" McCarter asked about the prisoner. They'd taken his fingerprints and digital photographs and transmitted them to the Farm to check for facial recognition or his inclusion in FBI or Interpol files.

"They're checking his records, but what we have so far is that he's out of Moscow," Manning said. "He's listed in their police databases as a common gang member. He sells Krokodil and has committed more than a couple of hate crimes."

"Hate crimes, as opposed to…?" McCarter started.

James smirked. "Crimes of passion, duh."

"This one is a fighter not a lover," Manning added. "Greb Yulinstov."

"I'll get that to Mei and her people," James said. "The more they know of their interrogation subject, the better they'll be able to open him up."

"All right, relevant data is sent to your device," Manning explained.

With that, James jogged down the hall.

McCarter looked around. "Where are Rafe and Pol?"

"Rather than sit around like fifth wheels, they decided to look for the vehicle this guy used," Manning said. "Pol went through Yulinstov's pockets while we were bringing him back."

McCarter nodded, then turned on his phone, bringing up Yulinstov's file. He scrolled through, looking over the man's background.

Krokodil was a dangerous drug and it was usually sold by people just as deadly and nasty. McCarter could see several public disturbances, though in their inspection of the prisoner, they noted that Yulinstov didn't display any of the lesions indicative of gangrene, swelling of his legs or other tissue damage. Krokodil was a true narcotic, made from opium and delivering a high as powerful as heroin, though shorter in duration.

It was also incredibly easy to synthesize from codeine-based medicines, as long as you had sufficient other supplies. The name Krokodil came from the appearance of the damaged skin addicts invariably developed. No, Yulinstov was not a Krokodil addict. He had tattoos, but they were on skin drawn tautly over a well-muscled torso and arms.

McCarter turned to Manning. "You didn't let Pol and Rafe head out without a tracer, did you?"

Manning pretended to look shocked. "Oh, wait, I didn't join this team yesterday."

McCarter rolled his eyes. "They've got a direct link back to us. Did you at least send them armed?"

"Both stopped off at the bay to pick up sidearms," Manning replied.

Phoenix Force's safehouse in Aberdeen Harbour was in a low-profile area, the floating village that, officially, had a population of 6000 people on more than 600 junks. However, the area was such a mishmash of fishing families living on their boats and living off the water, and had so many tourists with ferries passing through the villages to and from some of the giant floating restaurants, that they had managed to bring in their own boat—*Dragonfin*—disguised as a sampans. Underneath was the hull of a fiery, stallionlike racing boat that had been first converted to a cocaine smuggler, but came into Stony Man Farm's possession and became Phoenix Force's open-seas, high-speed interceptor, capable of long-range sprints that could cross distances from Colombia to Florida in the space of a day. *Dragonfin* had proved quite capable in a recent mission, dealing with stolen missile-ship prototypes in both the chilling waters of the Antarctic and chasing down their final prey in the China Sea.

Up top, it was nothing more than a fishing boat coming into the harbor. However, underneath, there were supplies for Phoenix Force and Blancanales. Currently they had chosen Glock Model 26 autopistols, handguns that were less than an inch in width, six inches long and a shade under five inches tall, all while maintaining a ten round capacity of 9 mm Parabellum. As a backup weapon, it was as close to weightless as one could get thanks to its polymer frame, but it took the same ammunition as their chosen frontline submachine guns and service pistols.

Blancanales and Encizo were supposed to maintain a low profile, so being only barely armed, yet having spare magazines not much larger than cigarette lighters and pistols no bigger than two packs of 3 x 5 cards placed side by side was a huge improvement. To further keep the team clandestine, the Glocks were actually unlicensed copies from Brazil, but produced by very canny builders who knew a completely Glock-compatible pistol would be an easy sell, especially with so many millions and millions of magazines available for the knockoffs. Blancanales and Encizo, barring a head-to-head conflict with a fully equipped terror cell, would be able to handle scouting and tracking down things.

"All right. I'm going to sack out for a few. Wake me when business picks up," McCarter said.

Manning gave his friend a slight salute.

The Briton had been awake for the past thirty hours, so a short nap would do wonders to restore his thoughts and energy. If only he could get over his concerns for his friends out on their search for long enough to nod off.

RAFAEL ENCIZO WAS glad for key fobs with remote-access locks. Even though Yulinstov's car was a rental, it was fairly easy to locate within a radius around Mei Anna's bar headquarters. He was able to recognize rental plates and the brand of automobile from the key fob, as well, so all he and Blancanales had to do was to patrol, looking for an abandoned vehicle parked somewhere. The distance Yulinstov covered shouldn't have been far. There was another driver, the one who'd dropped off Blancanales's attackers, but he'd dropped them off *after* McCarter had first sensed the Russian Nazi thug.

Blancanales pointed to the rental car as its blinkers went off on Encizo's press of the button. The two men continued toward it, keeping their eyes peeled. There might have been others who were involved with Yulinstov and the extant driver, waiting to see who had captured their man.

As it was, the two men had their sidearms. Encizo also had his knives and Blancanales had come up with a replacement for his shattered cane. The two of them were up for anything short of a full-on HKPD SWAT attack.

That didn't mean that either Encizo or Blancanales underestimated their foes. Yulinstov's history tracked back to the Russian Federation of National Socialism. That group had gained notoriety in 2007 by murdering two Armenian immigrants on video and spreading the news across the internet. One man had been shot in the head. The other had been beheaded—and they hadn't used a long blade. Instead, they'd used a carpet knife and it had taken twenty minutes to sever the last threads of sinew and muscle connecting the skull to the rest of him.

These were brutal, sadistic butchers. Their presence in Hong Kong was something that was unmistakably insidious.

"You want to rummage the car or should I?" Blancanales asked.

Encizo shrugged. "Roshambo?"

Blancanales sighed, took the keys and slid behind the driver's seat. He hit the trunk release. "Check the trunk, Rafe."

Encizo chuckled, stepped away from the driver's side door, then stepped back. "I just thought of something…"

"Two Hispanics entering a car not their own?" Blancanales asked.

"Was that a coincidence?" Encizo countered.

"But we're the ones who wanted to get something done while the others waited on information from Yulinstov," Blancanales answered. "And we've got the keys."

Encizo nodded.

"If confluence were *really* making this a racist stereotype…Cal would be hot-wiring this buggy," Blancanales concluded.

Encizo rolled his eyes. "One of these days, we're going to hell."

"Not I, for mine heart be pure, and does give me the strength of… Hello," Blancanales said.

Encizo leaned in closer as Blancanales pulled out a crumpled piece of paper. Turning on a small LED light, they looked over the receipt. It was for cash, but it was from a nearby hotel.

Blancanales took a cell-phone picture of the receipt and transmitted it immediately to their teammates and uploaded it to the Farm. They also located the name of the rental-car company, which would give them a base from which to perform some forensic accounting to track down money trails and such.

They also uncovered more information. The hotel wasn't where Yulinstov stayed. There were other hotel gift shop receipts for coffee, for soft drinks and a couple of bar bills, as well.

Blancanales kept digging under the seats and through the glove compartment, finding and then photographing paperwork. Even as he did so, he made mental notes of addresses and slowly began building a ring of possible places where the Russian Nazi might have actually located himself and his allies.

There was a rap on the fender of the car. It was Encizo, giving the code that they had attracted attention. Blancanales peered over the dashboard and saw a familiar van, one that looked almost identical to the one that had dropped off his two sparring partners in Statue Square earlier that night. He gave a tap of his foot outside the open driver's-side door, acknowledging the receipt of the warning. As he did so, he slid the Brazilian-built Glock 26 from its pocket holster. Finger resting on the frame above the trigger guard, he was ready for trouble if their opposition decided to bring something loud and violent toward them.

Encizo, in the trunk, had his knife at the ready in case their attackers decided on something quiet but no less deadly. If it came to a melee, Blancanales had his replacement cane leaning against the side of the car, braced so it wouldn't be knocked off balance by either the movement of the vehicle or someone moving in close. The only way the stick could fall was if it fell toward his leg, where Blancanales could easily snatch it up.

One more rap, and that meant Encizo was on the move, getting away from the rental car. The trunk lid was still up, making it seem as if he were still present.

Headlights suddenly blazed through the windshield, making the interior of the car as bright as day. Blancanales cursed, then pulled both feet in through the driver's door, tucking his legs up against his chest. It was a last-moment reflexive action, but it saved him from losing everything below his knees.

The automobile shook violently, air bags deploying from the windshield and above the glove compartment, but thankfully Blancanales was prone so the rapidly expanding sacks didn't hammer him into unconsciousness. The main force of the carbon-dioxide bursts was straight out, toward the passenger or driver, and victims in accidents often looked as though they'd been hammered in the face afterward. Broken noses and shattered eyeglasses were common. Here, slipped beneath the bags, Blancanales was rocked by the impact of the collision, but the blossoming balloons provided cushioning without bludgeoning his prone form. Unfortunately the impact of the airbag struck Blancanales's gun hand, slamming it backward. His face and head were protected, but the gun had literally been punched from his grasp. His cane was lost. He was on his back in a tight space. And enemies were nearby.

Blancanales stretched and clawed at his fallen pistol.

CHAPTER NINE

Rafael Encizo had slithered down two car lengths and was out from behind Yulinstov's rented car after he had wordlessly communicated the presence of the strangers on the scene. He hadn't drawn either his knife or his gun, not wanting the blade to glint in the streetlight, or to commit himself to a shootout with the newcomers. They might not have noticed his presence, and the van might just have been innocently turning onto this street.

Either way, the Cuban wanted to be in position, ready to attack or retreat as necessary. That was when the van's lights came on brightly and he heard the engine roar. The sudden glare made him squint his eyes and recoil, and suddenly he heard the crash of metal. Still half-blinded, Encizo threw himself back onto the hood of one of the cars, raising his legs instantly out of the deadly chopping block formed by the fenders of the vehicles he was between.

Metal and plastic collapsed and Encizo rolled hard, pushing himself toward the sidewalk and landing in a low crouch. The enemy had gone full-lethal using their van as a weapon, and he tore the Brazilian-built Glock from its holster. A car crash was nothing short of murder, and this loud, Encizo knew that the only means of surviving this fight was to get loud and violent in response.

Thankfully, when the van crashed into Yulinstov's

car, its headlights had either been broken or were obscured by the frame of the rental. Encizo could see, so he didn't care about the exact details, bringing up the flat, powerful 9 mm pistol and looking for the shapes of men.

Sure enough, a tall man with a sawed-off shotgun stepped onto the sidewalk, moving around the crumpled front end of Yulinstov's rental and toward the driver's-side door where Blancanales had been. Encizo had last seen the Able Team veteran stretched across the front seats of the vehicle, but he wasn't sure how his partner had dealt with the van collision.

You don't get more intent on murder than shoving a shotgun through the window of a car and firing. Encizo didn't hesitate, bringing up the compact Glock and firing two shots, center of mass on the shotgunner. He hit with both shots, but the gunman turned instead of toppling over. He was wearing body armor, which accounted for the breadth of his chest and shoulders.

Encizo, a trained professional, brought the muzzle up higher, pinpointed his opponent's head, and fired one shot right into the middle of his face. Those bones were thinner and more fragile than the heavy shell of bone that protected the human brain. Encizo killed the shotgun ambusher with his third hit.

From the front seat of Yulinstov's car, the Cuban Phoenix warrior heard the crack of a 9 mm pistol, bullets barking in rapid succession in response to a figure just barely visible over the roof of the crumpled car. It was Blancanales doing the shooting, because the muzzle flash lit up the interior of the rented vehicle. Another shotgun blast roared, but the heavy weapon's flare was directed skyward, not into the car. Encizo lunged forward, racing to his fellow Stony Man commando's side.

"Approaching driver's side!" Encizo shouted in Spanish, hoping it would both spare the Cuban from being shot as he surprised Blancanales and still keep his intentions covered against being heard by their opposition.

"Gotcha!" Blancanales answered in response.

Encizo took a tug at the driver's-side door, saw Blancanales glance up toward him, but kept his pistol aimed out the passenger door. Through the tunnel of the car's interior, he could see the man Blancanales had shot. He was lying on his back, his face spattered with blood.

"They're wearing armor," Blancanales said.

Encizo nodded. "I know."

Blancanales lifted his hand and Encizo gave his friend a tug up to a seated position to squirm out of the car. The airbags had deflated, giving the spry Able Team member all the room he needed to get on his feet.

Encizo put the Glock back in its holster, then stooped to pick up his target's shotgun. It was a hand-cut sporting shotgun. A semiautomatic with its barrel sawed down to behind the end knob of the tube magazine, but it at least had a shoulder stock. Encizo couldn't tell what the capacity was, but there was a fresh round in the breech and at least one more shell in the magazine tube. He felt for more shotgun shells in the dead man's pockets, pulling three more out. He pushed one shell in and tried a second, but the gun was filled to the top.

Blancanales dumped the partially spent magazine from his pistol, feeding it a fresh box. There was no telling how many more people were in the van, or if they had other backup.

The windshield of the enemy van suddenly exploded, bullets smashing through the glass and popping into Yulinstov's wrecked car. Encizo and Blancanales both hit the ground, keeping out of the line of sight of the third gunman still inside the van. Blancanales popped up first and unleashed three fast shots toward where he'd seen the enemy's muzzle flash.

This was a distraction, and Encizo pushed off from where he'd ducked, racing around to the driver's-side door. Since steering wheels and lanes were reversed in Hong Kong, the Cuban Phoenix vet didn't have far to rush before he was at the window, scanning the inside of the vehicle. Anyone he saw was going to catch a burst of 12-gauge buckshot. Unfortunately, no one was visible from the driver's window.

Their quarry, the one who was still armed, had retreated deeper into the van. Encizo backed away from the window and dropped into a squat. It was lucky that he lowered his head as bullets perforated the side panel of the van. Already fairly short, he was lucky to have gotten out of the way of slugs sizzling over his head. Encizo knew that if you could shoot out, you could fire back in. He pumped two thundering blasts of 12-gauge, smashing fist-size holes into the side of the vehicle.

Blancanales, having gone out toward the street, also fired.

The gunfight had only been on for fifteen seconds, more or less, but neither of them could afford to dawdle. Encizo rushed around the back of the van, checking the rear door from a wide angle, staying out of a fatal funnel situation. More gunfire roared within the confines of the vehicle, and Encizo was glad for his standoff, as the bullets sliced through metal and punched through glass, but didn't come close to him. However, in the flare of the gun's firing, he could see the silhouette of the shooter.

Encizo hit the man once with a shotgun blast. The shadow of the figure staggered backward. The Phoenix veteran fired the shotgun again, then threw it aside, reaching for his holstered pistol in lieu of reloading. The second swarm of buck pellets anchored the gunman fatally in the back of the van, ending his threat.

"Pol! ID these guys, quickly!" Encizo said, tearing open the rear doors of the van.

"On it," came the reply from Blancanales, even as the Cuban took a digital flash photo of the gunman in the van. He also dipped the man's fingers into the man's own blood and then pressed them against a paper bag left on the floor. He took photos of the prints. It wasn't the neatest, or the most precise means of getting prints, but at least it was something.

"Need paper?" Encizo asked through the broken windshield.

Blancanales shook his head. "Using the fender for these two bodies."

Encizo nodded. He quickly uploaded the photographs he'd taken, sending them back to the Farm via Manning's laptop.

That's when he heard the first distant warbles of police sirens. Blancanales stiffened at the same sound.

"Let's go," Blancanales ordered.

Encizo jumped out of the back of the van and the two Stony Man warriors took to the nearest exit. The last thing they needed was to be detained by the Hong

Kong Police Department. If they were even detained.
They'd just engaged in a raging gun battle in the street.
The HKPD were not going to show up unarmed to this
set of arrests.

They cut through the nearest causeway between
buildings, making their way to an alley as fast as their
feet could carry them. While they'd left the appropriated shotgun behind, as well as some scattered 9 mm
Luger shell casings, they kept the spent magazines for
their weapons in their pockets. Because they'd been
going through paperwork after breaking into Yulinstov's car, they'd both been wearing latex gloves to
keep their fingerprints off any objects. They had also
taken care to not get fingerprints on the ammunition
they'd put into their guns.

Any evidence of their presence in Hong Kong would
simply be circumstantial. Phoenix Force had made
enough enemies with the Ministry of State Security's
more corrupt elements that they didn't require the ani-
mosity of those who were actually fighting crime and
terrorism on the HKPD.

They listened for the sound of sirens approaching
the battlefield behind them and were glad they had
made the trek to the car on foot. There had been no
traffic cameras on the street where the battle had taken
place, but there were some on main street intersec-
tions, so driving to or from anyplace would have left a
trail that could lead back to Phoenix Force's safehouse
or Mei Anna's headquarters. Nothing was quicker at
alienating an ally like blowing their cover on an ama-
teur mistake.

So Blancanales and Encizo kept to alleys and side
streets after having rushed hard to get a few blocks of

distance from the conflict. Now they strolled at a leisurely pace, having doffed their gloves down a distant sewer grate and making sure any blood or gunpowder had been wiped from exposed skin. Each of the two men wore dark clothing. Blancanales was in a burgundy pullover sweater and navy blue slacks. Encizo was in a Lincoln-green turtleneck, with a near matching hue for his denim jeans. It was "urban camouflage."

The color of the clothing wasn't complete black, which would have actually drawn eyes to it in the neon splash of downtown Hong Kong. The subdued, muted colors, however, were what people naturally wore, and wouldn't seem out of place. The two Hispanic men looked like tourists dressed for a little nip in the night air. Untucked hems over hips allowed for easy concealment of their handguns and knives.

Blancanales looked nonplussed to Encizo. "What's wrong, Pol?"

"Lost my second cane tonight," Blancanales answered. "Sure, I have spares, but in our rush to get away, someone might link the broken cane at Statue Square to the one at the car. I don't want it tracking back to us."

"I doubt it," Encizo returned. "If it was knocked away in the van crash, you didn't use it in combat. If you didn't lose it in combat, then there wouldn't really be a reason for them to think you're the same one who killed that goon at the park. Also, there are a lot of stick-fighting styles in the world, four or five of them from China itself."

Blancanales nodded, but he was still tense.

"We're covered," Encizo stated. "Don't let it occupy your mind."

"I'm distracting myself with more pressing matters," Blancanales replied. He frowned. "Police at that intersection ahead."

Encizo squinted, seeing several HKPD Toyota Prius wagons, their lights flickering. He also noted a tow truck on the scene. "Automobile accident. Those are from the traffic division."

Blancanales nodded. "If the tow truck's there and not doing anything, that means that someone's taking photos of the accident. Steering clear of that is our best bet."

Encizo hummed in agreement. "Just because we're paranoid doesn't mean we're not in enemy territory."

Blancanales clapped his friend on the shoulder. "We'll just take our time."

"Tourists out on the town," Encizo agreed.

With eyes and ears peeled, the two men cautiously wound their way through Hong Kong, wending their route back in a circuitous path to Mei Anna's hideout.

HERMANN SCHWARZ LOOKED at the wrecked door to Carl Lyons's room, then leaned in, looking to see if his attackers were the only ones who had left behind bloodstains. He found Lyons sitting on the bed, looking over two unusually large revolvers with their cylinders swung out for ejection, balanced against black markers.

"Already buying firearms for the cause, Carl?" Schwarz asked his boss.

Lyons looked up from the small bedside table and the .410 shot shell he had in his hands. "Hey. How did the display room look?"

"They've got a mock-up of a Dong-Feng that made our little friend almost shit himself," Schwarz answered. He moved closer to the table. "Those .410 shot-shell revolvers?"

Lyons nodded. "A couple of bastards made a try at me with them. Security said I could keep them for souvenirs."

Schwarz picked one up. "Did you get hit?"

"Only after the buckshot passed through furniture and the TV," Lyons said. "Not like I ever find anything good to watch on the idiot box…"

Schwarz laughed and then asked, "Are you staying in this room? Or do you want to come over to my room?"

Lyons tilted his head. "I don't like sleeping with tweakers. And they're bringing a new door."

"Didn't ask for a replacement TV?" Schwarz teased.

Lyons shook his head. "Like I said before…nothin' worth watching."

There was a rap on the doorjamb. Schwarz glanced over his shoulder and saw a mountainous figure in the empty space. It was the big brute who'd also come by last night, bringing Herman Shore his nightcap of methamphetamine.

Schwarz nodded in acknowledgment of the man. "I didn't order room service."

"No, but your friend there did," Lump said. He stepped aside and a tiny little creature appeared from the shadow of his enormous bulk. It took a moment for Schwarz to figure out that this was the girl Lyons had been with the night before. She had concealer makeup on her bruises and a brown adhesive bandage barely lowered the profile of a fresh laceration she'd received.

Schwarz looked back to the sullen Able Team leader. He could feel the waves of guilt emanating from his friend. Lyons hadn't done anything violent to her intentionally, only reacting against what he'd perceived as a threat to him. Even so, she'd gotten banged up enough to firmly establish Lyons's identity of Karl Long as a woman-beater and a rapist. Guilt gelled in Schwarz's friend; he could see it coagulating into grim anger.

"What took you so long?" Lyons barked.

"You did a good number on her," Lump answered. The big freak in the hall looked at the bare hinges on the doorjamb and then observed spills of blood on the carpet in the corridor. "You didn't take anything out on one of our maids…"

Lyons scowled. "This joint has lousy security. A couple of Bratva thugs tried to kill me."

"The security is to protect the product and the staff on hand," Lump told him. "We don't give a shit if some of you meatheads try to kill each other."

"Right," Lyons said, annoyance dripping from his words. "Get in here, Sanay."

The hard edge in Lyons's voice wasn't completely an act, but Schwarz knew his friend. He could be ruthless, brutal to his enemies, to men who had profited and celebrated their own violence. Hurting an innocent woman, especially a prostitute who was more pathetic victim than society-crushing criminal, sat in the ex-cop's gut as if it were cold lead.

The girl padded in, her step a light spring as she rushed to his side. Lyons held up his hand, keeping her at arm's length.

"When's the door going to get here?" Lyons asked the Lump.

The big Samoan shrugged. "I'll check on it. Why?"

Lyons rolled his eyes. "Why do you think?" he said sarcastically, looking pointedly at Sanay.

"There's always the shower, Nazi," the Lump growled. "And I can tell from here that you need some goddamn soap."

With that, the big Samoan spun with nearly impossible ease on one foot and stormed off down the corridor.

Lyons took a whiff of his own armpit, then wrinkled his nose in silent agreement of the Lump's assessment. He took Sanay by the wrist and then looked over at Schwarz.

"What about you?" he growled.

"You're really going to get naked and helpless while you only have a bathroom door between you and strangers?" Schwarz asked.

"Never helpless, Shore," Lyons returned. "But if you want to stand guard while I work off some more tension…"

Schwarz waved his hand. "Just get down to business."

"I intend to," Lyons muttered. He shot his friend a wink, gently put his arm around Sanay's shoulders and guided her toward the bathroom.

CHAPTER TEN

Carl Lyons tugged on Sanay's tank top, pulling it up over her head, her pearlike breasts jostling freely before settling on her. She looked up at him with big brown eyes, lips pursed as she seemed uncertain at the way he'd spoken of her only moments before. He lifted her gently and carried her to the shower. He reached out with one brawny arm and turned on the water, which poured from the tap.

With the slap of droplets splattering against porcelain, a situation of white noise was created where Lyons could lean in close and speak softly into the woman's ear.

"I hope you know that I don't…"

"Yes," Sanay answered, her full lips softly brushing against his cheek as she stood on tiptoes to answer him. Even as they spoke, he tugged down on her shorts, flinging them out of the shower stall to the floor where they wouldn't get soaked when he pulled the stopper to make the water come through the shower head "This is a role you're playing. You were nice to me. Kind. Soft. And that wasn't the man I was told I'd be given to."

"Thank you for covering for me," Lyons whispered, holding her tight. His hands brushed up and down her body, exploring her with tenderness, but he was being thorough. He couldn't make a mistake and speak any more loudly than necessary, not until he was certain there was nothing on her person that could betray him.

He even brushed his hand over the bandage covering the cut on her cheek. Nothing untoward could be felt under the adhesive strip or the gauze placed over the cut. The swelling had gone down, but Lyons couldn't be too careful. Tiny microphones were nothing new to him. Putting them on in place of the gauze was something that Schwarz had done on more than one instance.

This was an auction of stolen and otherwise illicitly gained technologies. Guns and missiles weren't going to be the only gadgets the auctioneers would have on hand. Able Team had no clue as to who was arranging the sales, or even where they kept the majority of their stash, but to assume they were not being spied upon meant that Lyons had to go over Sanay's bronzed curves closely and carefully.

"The things I do for my country," Lyons murmured under his breath as his frisk turned to gentle caresses. Her lips were hot and hungry against his as she wrapped both arms around his neck. Lifting her up easily, he rested her against the shower wall, getting down to a far more pleasurable business between the two of them. The running water would go a long way toward maintaining the reality of the tattoos put on his skin. They would not rinse or run, but after a few weeks, they would disappear, metabolized by the dermal tissues. For now, he was in good shape, if by good shape meant being covered in indelible hate graffiti.

In their tight embrace, she was able to talk and,

thankfully, Lyons was only pretending to be making love right now. He wanted to hear what she had to say, his discipline fighting with his manhood for control and winning out. There was far more than one reason why they called him "Ironman."

"Jinan wanted me to get very close to you. Who are you?"

"I'm someone who is Jinan's worst nightmare," Lyons returned. "The less you know about me off the bat, the better."

She kissed the side of his head, nibbled on his ear, suckled at his neck. It was getting difficult to keep up a charade of making love and just getting to the meat of the matter.

"I don't want to know right now, but I need something…"

"I'll feed you. But he can't expect anything off the bat. We'll make sure you—"

There was a hard knock at the door.

Lyons turned off the shower. "Stay here."

He toweled himself off, then wrapped a second around his waist, knotting it so that it was tight enough to support the Colt revolver he tucked into it. Opening the door, he stepped out and saw his two partners entertaining a group of Russian men with tattoos that looked similar to theirs.

"Sorry," Hawkins said. "They wanted to talk to you."

Lyons nodded. He kept his expression grouchy. He hated being torn away from Sanay, so it wasn't so much of an act. It was the group that both he and Hawkins had been making inroads with among the auction's staff.

"What's up?" Lyons asked.

"Just giving you a heads up," Grigori told him. "The punks you dropped…"

"Yeah. They're part of the Horde," Lyons said. "They've been knocking heads with my brothers and me for decades. Leave it to a bunch of beaner bastards to bring these Brazilian things to a gunfight with real .45s."

"Still took one into the shower with you," Grigori noted.

"I didn't want my Colt to rust. This won't," Lyons said. "'Sides, it's nice, it's big, it's growing on me."

"So does fungus," Schwarz interjected. "Grigori, tell him who ordered the Hordesmen to tackle us."

"The Bratva," Grigori answered.

Lyons frowned, nodding. "They didn't like the two of us getting chummy."

Grigori shrugged. "They never liked us at all."

"That's because they're mostly Commie holdouts. They made their big killing when the government was a dictatorship. Now they've spread out, and some of these bastards are thinking back to Grandpa, killed in their Great Patriotic War by the men who wear our lightning bolts," Lyons offered. "Of course they're not going to have good memories of the group who nearly put them out of business."

Grigori nodded. "We were fools to have broken that accord. We would not have had to worry about the mud washing upon our shores."

Lyons nodded. "You still have a chance." He grimaced, hating his words of support for a neo-Nazi pig, but it was the role he had taken. He swallowed the bitter pill of his acting, saving it for later.

"A Hordesman tried to slip a knife into my ribs," Grigori said.

"I thought Jinan didn't want anyone stepping out of line and attacking his staff," Lyons said.

Grigori lifted his shirt, showing the fresh, bloody bandage. "That news only gets to our boss if they want us to. Can you take the heat for a broken neck?"

Lyons narrowed his eyes, the corner of his mouth twitching. "Certainly."

Grigori nodded. "I'll let you get back to your shower. Just to make certain you do not end up looking like a prune."

Lyons glanced back at the bathroom door, and Sanay, who waited beyond. "Don't worry. Sometimes a man needs to do things in private."

Grigori looked around the room, then shook his head.

And just at that moment Lyons realized the hotel room was definitely not bugged. Otherwise why would he have said anything about the Hordesman trying to kill him and then ask Lyons to take the heat of the beef?

"I'm just wondering how much we're being watched," Lyons murmured softly.

Grigori waved him over conspiratorially. "Jinan has us watching, but not electronically. He trusts us, our senses of smell."

Grigori tapped his nose for emphasis. "That goes for all the groups watching things."

Lyons nodded. "Human intelligence…always better than mere bugs."

He glanced over at Schwarz. If there was one thing the electronics wizard of Able Team always believed in, it was that human judgment was only enhanced by technology. Gimmicks were no substitute for the investigative instincts or intuition of a person in the field. Even so, Schwarz, in his role of tweaker, wrinkled his nose.

"Of course, if we're doing this, you guys better be on your game," Yuri spoke up. Lyons recognized him from Hawkins's description of the man with whom he'd had a long conversation.

"Of course. The Bratva will try a little harder. And the friends of the Horde will want a piece of us," Schwarz noted.

"That's going to be a list," Hawkins said. "And a lot of them are here."

Lyons sneered. "Let them take their shot. Jinan doesn't mind if we take the pricks out, right?"

"Go right ahead," Grigori told him. "Just try not to destroy the hotel or take down other bidders who aren't trying to kill you."

"Don't worry about that," Lyons said. "We are not those miserable Crips or Bloods who shoot with their guns tilted sideways and hit everyone but their target. When we kill, we aim to kill. And God help you if we wing you."

Both Hawkins's and Schwarz's eyes widened at the darkness that loomed over the hotel room. "That just means we're going to take our time letting you die."

THINGS WERE GOING a little better, Barbara Price observed. Phoenix Force, in Hong Kong, had found plenty of information about the Russian thug they had taken prisoner. Receipts and other tickets in the Russian's wallet and automobile had been photographed and relayed back to Stony Man Farm, where Huntington Wethers went to work. He was able to narrow the potential headquarters of the operation in Hong Kong.

Even as Wethers was accomplishing that bit of detective work, Carmen Delahunt was delving into the traffic cameras of the Hong Kong Police Department.

One thing the Farm's cybernetics crew had as their most important secret weapon was not that they could hack into the web security of dozens of different agencies. It was that they *had* hacked into those agencies and kept backdoor entrances into those systems.

Price was presented with the layout of the location in Hong Kong where all their forensic accounting and traffic camera hacking had determined the Russians belonged. Akira Tokaido had also come up with identification of the dead men photographed by Encizo and Blancanales in their latest conflict.

These men were members of the Russia Patriot Union, a skinhead organization that had drawn a lot of heat and attention since the mid-2000s. They started out "defending" their home city of Moscow from non-Slavic immigrants, but as was the case of all such gangs as these, the military structure, the aggressiveness and violence of the group, bubbled up into something that proved to be useful and good for organized crime.

At first they had been courted by the Bratva, but after a while the Russian mob's friendship and compliance with those "foreign intruders" had driven a wedge between them. The RPU and its action arm—Moscow 88—went into their own business, and after a wave of brutal conflict between the neo-Nazis and the ex-spooks turned mobsters, things quieted down. Even so, skirmishes broke out at the drop of a hat and the RPU sought out allies abroad who would provide them with succor and support.

Unfortunately for the world, there was no lack of

white supremacist groups who sympathized with the Russians. That growth led to conflict with not only "immigrant-based" biker gangs across Europe, but also strengthened their own status and economic standing.

Now it seemed the RPU was getting some spread, especially if they had a presence in Hong Kong. They didn't have contact with Able Team on the island, but Price would have been interested in knowing if the Moscow 88 were on the island in an official capacity.

That would not take long to discover. Hermann Schwarz would be sending a rapid info-dump on schedule, their skills and equipment willing. Stony Man had been waiting for forty-eight hours for the first contact, trusting Able Team to check for privacy and security. If anyone could find a bug or transmitter, it would be "Gadgets" Schwarz. The brilliant electronics expert would be able to sweep and jam any system, given that much time.

If it weren't to come, then things would serve to be too perilous for Able Team to talk, or they would have been discovered. It was a tenuous balance between trusting in the remarkable abilities of the three operatives and writing them off as discovered, captured and murdered. So Price kept her ears open, waiting for the call. Waiting for that squirt of high-speed data, the reassurance that she hadn't sent three men off to their deaths, was more stressful than the worst firefight.

At least in a battle, you could *do* something more than wait, impotently, on the sidelines for news.

Price's tablet blinked. The upload had arrived. Her heart thumped loudly at once at the sight, a burst of relief rushing through her chest. The alert allowed her to relax her tensed shoulders and she set the tablet down.

It would take the Stony Man software a minute to unpack the compressed data stream sent by Schwarz; she took a few moments to go to the fridge for an ice-cold bottle of water. She didn't realize how parched she'd made herself by waiting, and opening her mouth produced a sudden pop, her teeth aching without the continuous pressure of her clenched jaw. The swig was good pouring down her throat.

She picked up the tablet and opened the formerly compacted folder with its dozens of photographs, including one of the Dong-Feng 21 mock-up. She spotted a heavily tatted security guard for the auction and she tapped on the photograph to open it up.

She recognized the ink as a similar set of patterns and themes belonging to most Moscow 88 soldiers, the Russian neo-Nazis who had also showed up in Hong Kong opposite Phoenix Force.

"Barb, David and the team have the confirmation data for going up against the Russian operation in Hong Kong." Aaron Kurtzman spoke up. "Giving you the heads up."

Price nodded. "Throw in that the RPU and Moscow 88 are at the auction acting as part of the armed security force, so we're not positive that the Gobi incident and the Able Team mission are linked, as well. Let them know about the missing scientists from our base's attack—Robert Baxter and Beatrice Chandler."

"Why would you think the scientists are there?" Kurtzman asked.

Price shook her head. "Just a gut instinct, and the fact that there's no way that the auction would want to keep the brains behind those toys so close to that client list."

"Pay now, receive later, and not get ripped off immediately," Kurtzman agreed.

Price nodded. "There might be missing Chinese scientists stationed there, as well. If they can't find them themselves, there might be links or clues as to where the kidnapped techs were taken."

"Adding it to their heads up," Kurtzman replied. "Given the dimensions of the Russian base, I can see there might be some room for more than just stock."

"Get them rolling, Aaron," Price ordered.

PHOENIX FORCE AND Rosario Blancanales were back together at Mei Anna's headquarters. Encizo and Blancanales had arrived just as David McCarter returned with suitcases full of long arms for their upcoming raid on the headquarters of the group Yulinstov belonged to. So far, the enemy group in action in Hong Kong had suffered some serious losses, but that didn't mean that the five men of Stony Man Farm were going to take any chances.

So far, the small, mobile team had been sending out its forces in even tinier fractions of their main force. The Russians showed all the hallmarks of being professionals at this; McCarter knew they would have operatives in reserve back "home."

Thanks to the paperwork Encizo and Blancanales had discovered, the crew at the Farm had managed to focus in on where the Russian group might have been hiding out in Hong Kong. Right now, they were awaiting a collection of street-surveillance data and the positioning of a satellite infrared camera to make certain they had the right target.

"I could have someone in my contacts look in on the place," Mei Anna said.

McCarter shook his head. "It's a tempting offer, but we don't need you to jeopardize your operation just on our account. Let us use some of the resources we've got."

Mei smirked. "Technically, those aren't your resources. They belong to the Hong Kong Police Department and SAD."

McCarter smiled back. "Not everything we have is related to hard work."

Mei winked.

McCarter looked at the rest of the team. They were going over their main weapons for the upcoming assault. While each had their personal sidearms—a Glock Model 34 and a Glock Model 26 for backup—their main weapons would be VBR-B Compact PDWs. As the VBR also took a Glock magazine, it was very useful, being a long gun with a completely telescoping stock and a foregrip akin to an FN-P90 under the barrel. The PDW was a stable, full-auto and burst-fire platform with excellent sights. Chambered for 9 mm Parabellum, and capable of handling high-intensity armor-piercing ammunition, the VBRs could be collapsed to the size of a large Magnum-caliber handgun and yet still be extended to a quick handling, accurate machine pistol. The VBR was so compact, McCarter was able to fit all six into one suitcase, while another was packed with 19-round and 32-round extended Glock magazines to feed the little buzz guns. The shorter magazines would be put into the chatterbox pistols for concealed carry, but once their load was spent, it would be time for the extra-capacity magazines.

"According to the estimates by the crew back at the Farm, we could expect three-to-one odds," McCarter told the team. "Even after all of the losses we've inflicted on their group."

Mei Anna shot a glance laden with worry toward McCarter. "Three-to-one odds. That sounds tough."

David McCarter gave her his most confident smirk. "Anna, sweet, we call that Tuesday."

The Stony Man warriors bid their allies a temporary goodbye and went off to war.

CHAPTER ELEVEN

Robert Baxter sat in the cell, on the naked stone floor, his back pressed to the wall, hands over his face, alone and in the dark. There was no clock, no sense of time or pace with which he could measure his imprisonment. Even his sense of hunger and thirst was imperfect. The kind of sedative he had, he was not certain if his memories of eating and drinking were dream or reality. Baxter knew about sleeping-pill addiction and "sleep shopping" or "sleep driving." Being hungry or dry-mouthed wasn't apparent, so he could not be certain of that.

All he could do was attempt to count his heartbeats, count his breaths, and even that was uncertain. With no visual reference, he could not tell if his eyes closed and he nodded off to sleep or not. The aftereffects of the drugs in his system also left him groggy, so he was not sure if he was staying awake or sloughing back into unconsciousness.

And as usual, in his dream state, he was caught up in a fugue state of nightmares, and was not certain if Beatrice Chandler was shouting invectives of hate and rage at him, or he was merely projecting his guilt on to her, giving his own emotions her voice in an effort to make himself feel worse. He groaned, gave himself a pinch with fingertips that felt more like solid rubber—

numb and useless—than anything that had once been a part of his hand. Baxter wished for even a spark of an image, a hint of light stimulus on his retinas.

This was madness, and the silence and darkness were beginning to close in on him like a crushing weight, a bathysphere sent to the bottom of the ocean into pressures that began to crumple the steel ball as if it were an aluminum soda can. Desperate for physical input, he ground his knuckles against the cold stone floor. He pressed the back of his head hard against the unyielding wall until it felt as if his skull was ready to explode.

No one had spoken to him, and he did not know if it was a matter of hours, days, weeks…eternities. Every possibility was exposing itself to him. All he knew was that there were Chinese-appearing men, and even that was no certainty of guilt or who'd actually taken him captive.

This way laid madness and horrors that he could not survive. He bit his tongue, giving him a single point of focus. He pulled up mathematical formulas and began working problems, deconstructing and rebuilding the solutions step by step. Science was his refuge, his anchor. Science and math would not change.

Math would not twist itself to fit hallucinations. One thing Baxter prided himself on was the fact that when he dove into it in dreams, it actually worked in the waking world.

Now he was feeling calmer, better. The horror and chaos that had gripped him was at bay, behind barriers of logic.

Through his thoughts, his focused calculations, he began structuring the world, staving off the semi-drunken stupor of his current state. The darkness would no longer haunt him, no longer smother him. He found his light.

After a time he pleasantly lost himself in, he heard the door open, the silence having been so complete that it sounded as if the walls around him shattered with the clack of the turning door handle. He looked up into a blaze of brightness burning across his eyes.

"Come. Now."

Baxter weighed the option of a smart-ass remark, but knew that as a prisoner, he would suffer for it. And the cruel men would make sure to use every inch of that pain to loosen his tongue and be far too disciplined to give him sweet release.

So Baxter rose, still barefoot, bare-chested, skin itching where thousands of tiny cuts and scrapes healed. He walked, aching from sitting still for too long, and as his vision cleared he realized that the blaze he had envisioned came from a weak 40-watt bulb hanging naked in the hallway.

As it was, the globes of burn still filtered everything he saw; he could barely make out his surroundings. A hand slapped against his chest, slowing him. His vision began to focus better and saw that he was at a doorway. One of a twin set of metal, green-painted fire doors swung on silent, well-oiled hinges.

"Move!" came the gruff order.

Baxter continued along, jolting to a halt as the door slammed shut behind him. He glanced back and saw that he was alone in the room. The rack and heavy clunk of metal informed him the door was now barred behind him.

The room was dim, the only light source coming

from small cracks through which he could tell there were windows on the opposite wall from him, covered with thick curtains. The thin slits of light gave him more than enough illumination now, and he could make out a small form sitting in the corner by the windows, to the left of them. Baxter took a few steps closer, hearing a breath escape lips, the soft exhalation sounding feminine.

"Don't worry, I'm not here to hurt you," Baxter said.

"Another prisoner." It was a girl's voice. A voice heavy with dread and disappointment. All she could do was look past her bare knees, folded up all the way to her chin. Her bare arms were wrapped around the folded legs, and her dark eyes locked on a segment of floor.

Baxter frowned. "I'm sorry."

"You can sit beside me if you want," she said. "I suppose we're in the same boat."

Baxter took a seat. "This doesn't feel like a boat."

"It was a figure of speech," the girl said. Her English was too good, without accent. Baxter wondered if she was a plant, a means of putting him off balance, a means of getting inside his head. This disturbed Baxter, however. They already had Bea Chandler, a woman who was known to have an emotional relationship with him. Where was she? Or would they both be forced to observe what horrors were inflicted upon her?

"So what did they bring you here for?" Baxter asked. "What's your area of scientific expertise?"

"Chaos mathematics," she answered.

Baxter tilted his head. It took him a few moments to see how such a thing would be useful to missiles. "You're not working on antiship missiles."

She looked at him. "What are you talking about? I was taken by a group of men from San Francisco."

Before she could go any further, the curtains were pulled aside. Baxter's eyes felt as if they'd been set on fire, harsh fluorescent light streaming through the windows on the side of the cell. He heard the girl give a squeak.

Both blinded, they sat against the wall, waiting for something else to happen, to give them some clue as to why they were here. Even as his curiosity was piqued, the back of his mind brought up a fact. Chaos mathematics was the source behind predictions of air currents and their effects upon weather.

Things began turning in Baxter's mind. Surely a nuclear weapon utilized against a fleet would be tantamount to a declaration of nuclear war. But with the proper seeding of a cloud and an injection of intense heat, a hurricane or other massive sea storm could be thrown against an opposing naval force without fear of reprisal. This woman from San Francisco had the mathematical acumen to predict such a thing, and with a proper warhead, something fast on target with GPS precision, such as the weapon he'd been working upon…

"No fair talking to each other when you will not give us what we want," a voice said. There was a vocal distortion over the speaker, low and vibrato, rumbling to the point of recognizability.

"You have not requested anything yet," the girl said. "I want to go back to Berkeley, so I will give you whatever you wish."

"Dr. Ling Fu, you are in no position to make demands."

Baxter wanted to look at the girl, but now he knew who she was. Professor May Ling Fu. The Chinese government did not like her very much because she utilized her position to criticize the Communists in Beijing.

She most definitely would *not* have been part of the Chinese group that had raided the testing facility.

But she *had* been part of the kidnapping.

"Dr. Baxter?" the distorted voice asked through the speaker. "Are you listening?"

"Not particularly," Baxter answered. "Where is Bea?"

"As I told Dr. Ling Fu…"

"Are you going to use her against me?" Baxter asked. "I just want to make this interaction as simple as possible."

"You want this simple as possible," the speaker repeated. There was a chuckle, but it was different. Odd. Inhuman and grating against Baxter's spine.

Ling Fu looked at him, her otherwise smooth forehead wrinkled as she scrutinized him, anger seething in her dark eyes.

"I'm attempting to be practical," Baxter said to her. "These people attacked a desert weapons-test facility. They are deadly serious, and no doubt, they will torture and kill us."

"So you'll betray your home?" Ling Fu asked.

Baxter did not say anything in answer. The less he said, the more he could hedge bets. He knew these men would execute him once his worth was used up. The best that he could hope for was to make his demise provide as much of an opportunity to spite these madmen before they made their move. Already, he was recalculating his propulsion designs for the sake of making any missiles useless to them. It would be off by only millimeters, by thousandths of a calculation point, but it would be just enough for the kidnappers to blow themselves up with their first efforts.

Sure, it would have been more glamorous to refashion the missile parts into a weapon with which to smite his captors, but he did not have that kind of wild imagination as to actually design a powered suit of armor.

That kind of mechanization was not within Baxter's purview. He was a propulsion specialist. A rocket scientist, not an amazing inventor.

Sabotage by mathematics and materials was his only weapon.

He had no delusion that there were any top-secret commando teams out there searching for him. It would have been nice, but pure logic told him the government would rather obliterate any chance of his knowledge being used against them. If they could find these men, they would send guided missiles, equipment he'd likely improved the efficiency of, and turn this prison into a crater.

With that knowledge, that he was dead one way or another, a calm settled onto his heart.

"I will go to my death as I see fit," Baxter said to Ling Fu. He looked away from her angry glare.

"You seem to be appropriately agreeable," the voice from the wall speaker said. The glare from the windows was too bright, too intense for his eyes to adjust, to see more than a pair of shadows. He did not doubt that they could see much better from their side of the window.

The rocket scientist did not make any assumptions of the reality of this tableau. They were in a room.

There was light streaming through two windows. There was a large speaker on the wall through which someone spoke, and there was certainly some means by which they were being watched and heard, but this could have been all an illusion. After all, why firmly lock the doors when there was a pane of glass that could be broken through? Not that there were any objects with which he could smash the glass.

Baxter looked around. His sense of distrust, the few factors in his imprisonment, all of this was altering his thoughts and he could not find a place to lock his mind down, to anchor himself. The strange woman, even if he was aware of her identity, the presence of the voice, the figures behind the mirrors, all served to unsettle him. Mentally, he was losing his grip, the slope of sanity he'd clung to disintegrating under his grasp.

He grit his teeth, praying for this madness to end.

But when he opened his eyes, he was still a prisoner in a strange room, alone with May Ling Fu. A scared little whimper choked out of his throat.

DAVID MCCARTER TOOK the point for Phoenix Force and Rosario Blancanales as the five men stalked toward the headquarters of the Russian skinheads doing cleanup in Hong Kong. Ideally, the group would have made their assault from two vectors, and Gary Manning would have been on sniper-rifle duty, putting down guards and sentries with deadly, quiet bullets to even the odds and cut down on the chance of their opponents realizing they were under attack.

But this was the world of Phoenix Force, and Barbara Price had already informed them that a van had left the HQ of the Russians, taking a group of bodies with them. Phoenix Force was tracking not only stolen technology, but kidnapped people.

"Put the finishing touches on the Hong Kong operation. We'll track the van," Price informed McCarter through his radio headset. "The last thing we need is a moving gun battle on the streets of that city, and maybe you can pick up intel on what's present."

"Just don't lose those bodies," McCarter returned.

"Drs. Baxter and Chandler are too valuable to lose," Price said. "I just hope they are part of that group."

"Doubt it," McCarter said. "Smuggling Americans into China is stupid, especially since the Chinese would *love* what's between their ears. These guys are getting their Chinese geniuses out of Hong Kong."

"All roads will lead to them, in that case," Price noted.

"We can hope," McCarter said. "Going radio silent, guns loud."

The Moscow 88 goons had assembled in an old, rancid former apartment building that had been turned into a brothel a layer of filth ago, but the building eventually had run down completely, too rotted and unusable for anything but opium addicts and drunkards who wouldn't feel the necessity to move to relieve their bowels and bladders. McCarter could see the demarcation line where the Russians had claimed their territory.

There were lost souls—skeletal, ghostly figures—huddled, wearing an assortment of rags that armored them against the cool, wet nights of Hong Kong. Phoenix Force was no stranger to the undersides of cities and nations. Yet as much as McCarter empathized with the homeless, frightened figures who tucked themselves into nooks along the side of their alley, he knew that any effort to assist them before they cleared out the neo-Nazis would only endanger themselves.

These were men who were used to hiding, used to staying out of the path of authorities and all manner of trouble. McCarter put his finger to his lips in a universal sign for silence, then unhooked his VBR machine pistol. He gently eased the stock to its full extension and made certain that the suppressor was firmly locked at the end of its threaded barrel.

There was a brief flash of amazement in the eyes of a couple of the homeless men, but they put their fingers to their own lips in a sign of acknowledgment of McCarter's request for silence. McCarter and his men were here to clean the infestation of Russian racists out of their former home. They did not look as if they were going to stay.

The smell of cigarettes and alcohol was an overwhelming wave emanating from their former home.

McCarter silently motioned for his team to split up. McCarter and James advanced slowly, carefully under the watchful gaze of Manning, Phoenix's primary marksman. Covering Manning were Encizo and Blancanales.

McCarter and James were going to get in through the roof, scaling the iffy-looking fire-escape scaffolding. With them working from the top down, they would flush out the enemy to where all three other members would form a solid perimeter.

First, however, Manning locked his holographic optic on the head of a lone, heavily tattooed man standing guard at the back door of the building. He'd put the selector switch of the handgun-turned-carbine to single shot and brought the red laser dot at the center of the sight to a point at the bridge of the man's nose. Through that part of the face, a single bullet could penetrate deep into an enemy's brain and shut his body off with scarcely a sound or reflexive action.

Manning stroked the trigger evenly and cleanly. With a soft chug, the Russian thug slumped bonelessly to the ground. His face was splattered with blood, though not even a sound escaped his throat as he'd fallen. One down and well over a dozen to go.

McCarter and James moved with a slick, silent grace, and spread out so that McCarter took a five-yard lead so as not to overstress the ancient metal grating clinging tenaciously to the side of the old apartment building. As soon as McCarter cleared one flight, James followed. These two were the most slender and relatively lightest members of Phoenix Force, as well as the pair most trained at scaling buildings should something go wrong with the metal steps.

Even as they advanced upward, McCarter could feel the give and creak of the metal. He was glad for the suppressed PDW in his hand, because he was worried and certain that someone would hear the racket of their ascent.

Luckily, they only had four stories to climb before they reached a top-floor window. It was dark, but McCarter didn't risk anything by moving across it. He perched on a ledge and helped James onto the stony lip as they avoided the darkened window. They moved along, McCarter pausing outside another opening along the top. To call it a window would have been generous, as the glass was gone and the reek of long-dried human waste wafted out the black hole in the wall. Just to make certain, he angled a small pocket mirror so that he could look within. It was to an unoccupied room, the only light within being a small sliver of spilled glow underneath the room's door.

The fact that the room stunk, even though it was a dry stink, meant that the room was used very little.

McCarter slipped through the hole, followed by James.

The two men gave a single-tap signal on their communicators, the transmission buttons giving a crackle to their allies in the alley, but that was all that was released. Without speaking, they would not attract attention and no sound would be heard on any radio scanners. Anyone listening would merely assume it was a burst of static.

A response click came back from the trio on the ground.

James swept the floor with a red-filtered flashlight, then tapped McCarter on the shoulder. In the corner, there were several fresh cigarette butts. This room was being used as a bathroom, at least a place for the Russians to empty their bladder while staying on alert. McCarter nodded with acknowledgment when the slim strip of light from the hall was obscured by two shadows.

The door handle moved and the two Phoenix Force warriors turned just in time to see the door swing open, a couple of smokers talking to each other as they came through the door. An inked hand brushed the wall and flipped the light switch, exposing McCarter and James to the attention of the two guards.

CHAPTER TWELVE

Though the Phoenix Force warriors had suppressors on their machine pistols, the weapons were not completely silent. Gary Manning's sentry-removal shot was only kept to the sound of a polite cough because he'd chambered a single round, one that was loaded to produce a minimum of muzzle blast, yet maintained enough weight and energy to destroy a man's brain at the range of forty feet. He also had the bolt on the weapon locked so as not to produce any mechanical sound, either.

It was a risky prospect, one that could have left Manning with an inoperable weapon.

So when they heard the muffled rattles from the empty fourth-floor window, Manning, Encizo and Blancanales knew that the battle had begun in earnest.

And as much as every instinct told them to make their move on the lower floors, David McCarter ordered them to hold their ground and keep the thugs inside the building from escaping. Once more, Phoenix Force was operating on the very edge of the law, but the concern for innocent bystanders was one of their most important considerations. The last thing they wanted was for a group of armed, racist savages to burst onto the streets of Hong Kong. Even the most downtrodden and hopeless opium addict was worth twenty of the bigoted Russian goons. This was going to be the end of Moscow 88's Chinese operation, and it would send a brutal message to whoever was further up the chain of command for this pack of maniacs.

Suddenly the run-down apartment windows blazed with fresh light, curses issued in ugly Slavic grunts. The rack and chatter of weapons being loaded accompanied those curses. The trio of Stony Man warriors had encountered enough hardcore Russians to understand the foul words they grunted and barked, as well as the orders to move up and take out the intruders.

Just because the three of them were ordered not to enter the structure did not mean they were going to sit idly on the sidelines. Two of the Moscow 88 thugs pushed out of a window and climbed onto the fire escape, obviously intending to climb the scaffolding to the top floor and outflank McCarter and James.

Manning and Encizo raised their weapons and fired, triggering bursts into the two neo-Nazis, 9 mm slugs ripping into their torsos and churning up internal organs. One of the gunmen on the fire escape struck the railing and the rusted metal gave way, allowing his body to sail to the alley floor, landing in a brutal crunch of bones and spurt of flesh and blood. Blancanales kept his eyes on other windows and the doors to the alley in case someone else decided to come out to escape.

Sure enough, a ground-level door kicked open. A man whose upper body was clad only in a white tank top and sleeves of black or blue ink burst into the alley, the red-gold single eye of a cigarette tip visible amid a wisp of smoke. Blancanales had his VBR shouldered and ready. As soon as he saw the shotgun in the Russian's hand, he tapped a short burst right at the glowing cigarette's end. Bullets crashed into the man's face, snapping his head backward in a murky cloud of spattered gore.

"Business is picking up down here," Manning said over the shared radio network. By now, with all the gunfire, McCarter and James might have known the whole building was on alert, but caught in the middle of their own conflict, they might not have heard otherwise, especially as the Russians who had left the building hadn't gotten a shot off first.

That could change soon enough, Manning realized. While their allies were upstairs, exchanging gunfire with the Russians, others on lower floors would know about the activity outside the building, especially with the deaths of three of their own.

Sure enough, windows that still had glass in them shattered, panes and splinters knocked out by roughly swept gun barrels. Manning was prepared for this, pulling a small, hard disc from a pouch on his assault harness. He depressed the primer in the center of the circlet of plastic explosives and hurled it with a deft flip of his wrist toward one of the windows.

The Russians were unable to see Manning, Blancanales and Encizo, thanks to the suppressors on the ends of their weapons. Without a visible muzzle flash, their foes were literally in the dark, but it wouldn't take more than an instant for them to switch on flashlights, especially if they were mounted on rifles and submachine guns. The disk, however, would give them something new to think about. The mini-Frisbee was actually made out of carefully shaped and stiffened plastic explosives.

The disk sailed through one of the windows and

detonated after a few moments of flight. There was no shrapnel in the ring, but the edges of the death Frisbee were molded to maximize the ring of shock force created by the detonation. Overpressure would at least stun and deafen their opposition. The crack of the blast vented out the window, along with the upper torso of one of the Russian gunmen. He hung on the sill like a dirty shirt, weapon torn from numbed fingers.

Another of the Moscow 88 gun thugs turned on his rifle-mounted light and received a stream of high-velocity 9 mm lead through his head. Encizo tapped off that fatal flurry of bullets, dissuading their opposition from turning on more lights to illuminate the alley. Even so, the Russians' weapons roared, lines of fire coming close to where the trio of Stony Man commandos had dug in. Fortunately the three super-pros knew better than to not take a secure shooting position with something solid between themselves and their opposition.

Above, Manning could see the flash of Russian small arms flaring through the windows on the fourth story. If those guns were active, that meant McCarter and James were in the thick of it, and the warriors left behind in the alley would not hear those weapons. Their only consolation was the racket of guns on the top floor, slowly dying out as their fellow Phoenix warriors whittled down the enemy numbers.

Manning flicked another of his deadly disks through another window, making certain not to throw anything close to his partners. A subsequent blast blew out the remaining glass in the windows on that level of the building. Another ragged form slumped over a sill, flesh blackened to a crisp by a close range burst of explosives.

"Enough." McCarter's voice came over the hands-free radio setup. "We're moving down."

"Confirmed," Manning answered. He checked and noted that both Encizo and Blancanales had received the call. Though neither had grenades, they would make certain they would not blast any figures near the windows on the third floor. Their Phoenix allies would call out as they descended story by story. Manning had already outfitted McCarter and James for their dangerous task.

Things were getting loud and bloody, but that would be no excuse for sloppiness on any of their parts. Either they finished this pack of armed thugs in Hong Kong or they would lose several kidnap victims.

DAVID MCCARTER AND Calvin James opened fire within milliseconds of each other as the Moscow 88 men entered the door to the darkened bathroom. It was a swift, fatal response to the Russian gun thugs, and neither man fired more than a 3-round burst into his target. McCarter's target took the trio of slugs to the heart and the next man jerked violently backward as his face exploded with a salvo of 9 mm launched by James.

With the two Russians dropped, so, too, was any hope of a quiet infiltration and sentry removal. Though suppressed, their machine pistols still produced sounds over 90 decibels, which raised cries of confusion and alarm on the top floor of the building. McCarter took the lead, charging ahead not only as his role of Phoenix Force's field commander, but also by the very nature of his training and personality. James was no shrinking violet when it came to armed commando assaults, but McCarter had developed a reputation for short temper and knee-jerk reactions. Though the role of leadership had mellowed him, calmed him, turned him into a seemingly more reasonable man.

But when things came to close quarters, battle at a range where you could smell the dying breaths of your opponent, where gunfights blazed at ranges in inches, David McCarter was still balls to the wall, a controlled explosion of mania and aggression. He was like a shaped charge, otherwise unfocused destruction funneled to a precision point.

A Chinese sentry stepped into the hallway, confusion crossing his features, but the sight of a shotgun in the man's fist immediately informed the Phoenix Force commander that this was an armed hostile. The VBR SMG sputtered out its quick 1000-round-per-minute song, and the local muscle smashed violently back into the doorjamb. His figure slumped to the floor, gun clattering beside him. Another figure from a nearby doorway, just a little behind McCarter's shoulder, popped into view. There was a bark of some manner of Slavic epithet and the Briton made out the motion of a weapon in the corner of his eye, but a sickening crack resounded.

Calvin James was a little too close on McCarter's heels to bring up his subgun, but when the tattooed goon shoved his pistol toward his friend's head, the Chicago badass didn't have to think twice about his response. With a violent snap of his leg, James crashed the sole of his foot into the Russian's knee, producing the ugly, wet bursting noise. Femur, patella and shin bones all separated with the elastic pop of shredding tendons and dislodged cartilage.

The Moscow 88 goon fell, the gun dropping from his fingers as agony seized control of him. He was now far more concerned about his wrecked leg than putting a bullet into the back of McCarter's skull. Unfortunately, James was not about to let the neo-Nazi thug make up for his mistake. As soon as he fired off his knee-breaking kick, the black Phoenix Force pro stepped back far enough to accommodate the length of the VBR's suppressor. A snarl of 9 mm slugs shredded through the injured goon's face and upper chest.

McCarter surged on, glad for James as backup. The Chicago warrior checked the room the Moscow 88 soldier had burst from, hearing the rumble of suppressed gunfire preceding the rise in unmuffled gunfire. McCarter kicked a door to one side, the panel smashing into a figure on the other side of it, arresting its opening. The Briton sidestepped, drawing his weapon to shoulder level. Holes burst through the wooden door, bullets spearing toward the Phoenix Force commando in the hallway. McCarter fired through the wall, ripping 9 mm figure eights through the interceding drywall. A scream of agony rewarded McCarter's probing sweep of fire, ending the blaze of fire tearing through the door.

James hadn't come from the door he'd entered, but then, he heard the unmistakable roar of a Kalashnikov rifle. It began in that corner unit, then moved. McCarter assumed that his partner either had blown open a connecting door or simply weakened the drywall between two rooms with a relentless spray of someone else's ammunition. Either way, McCarter caught

James in motion through the doorway, throwing his commander a thumbs-up.

More gunfire resounded, but none of it seemed to occur on this level of the building.

"Business is picking up out here," Manning confirmed through his headset. McCarter smirked and ducked into the room he'd slashed through. A wounded Hong Kong gangster lay splattered on the floor, his once-white shirt soaked red from a half dozen injuries. Another Chinese gunman struggled to fit a new magazine into his spent rifle.

McCarter transitioned to his Glock 26, the stubby little compact pistol clearing leather with impossible speed. Giving up sight radius quickened the draw, and the stiffness of the 3-inch barrel still managed to maintain razor-edge accuracy. The subcompact pistol barked out three quick shots into the reloading thug, two bullets cutting just left of center of the man's chest, the third snapping through the bridge of his nose. The entire exchange took less than two seconds, and the local gunman was lifeless, sprawled in a bloody heap.

McCarter glanced to his right and saw that there was a doorway there. This one had nothing in the empty arch between rooms.

Something shook the building, a cracking boom that McCarter knew by ear. It was one of Gary Manning's personally designed plastic explosive disks. Rather than a conventionally hurled fragmentation grenade, it was a flying shaped charge that threw out a ringlike guillotine of high-pressure, neck-snapping force. In an enclosed area, it was brutal and invariably lethal. In the open, it was able to hurtle much farther than even a standard grenade, riding on currents of air.

The hallway erupted with sheets of gunfire as the defending guards on this floor swung into the open, blazing away at where they assumed the Phoenix Force intruders came from. McCarter stepped through the empty archway, seeing a pair of men, both firing their guns into the corridor. One was a small Asian man, the other was a thug with blue-black prison ink sleeving his bare arms. Both were armed and both were enemies trying to kill him and James.

McCarter reloaded his PDW with a few swift hand movements, then opened fire, drilling both murderers through the back, hurling their riddled bodies into the hallway where they caught more gunfire from their friends. The gunfire increased even more as the two dying men showed themselves as targets. That was the thing with these paramilitary Moscow 88 thugs: they had little sense of discipline, seldom identifying what they were shooting at before opening fire. It was a simple bit of safety to know what you were pointing a gun at.

The scorn he felt for these maniacs only continued to rise as more subguns stopped shooting on the other side. James was clearing out the enemy. McCarter double-checked for anyone playing possum, then kicked on through into the next room.

This was the last one on the floor. And even as McCarter entered, an Asian turned and crashed into him. The two men snarled against each other. The Chinese gangster likely had realized their attackers weren't using the hallway and had turned to the connecting doors. The Chinese man let out a clamor, and McCarter knew enough Chinese from his many stays in Hong Kong to know that this guy was a local.

McCarter also understood the man who'd barreled into him, batting aside his submachine gun, was warning his allies about the intruder's presence. McCarter didn't bother fighting for control of the PDW, but jammed his thumbs into his opponent's open mouth and dug his fingertips behind the guy's jaw. With a turn and a quick duck, suddenly he was concealed behind the clever Hong Kong outlaw, but a grunt in Russian preceded the blast of a shotgun. The Asian criminal slammed against McCarter, and he let the toppling form push him beyond the line of sight of the other figures in that last room. On his back, he pulled the Glock 34 from its hip holster and lined up the enemy's position around the doorway on the other side of the wall.

This time, he didn't wait for the enemy to start pumping bullets through a wooden door. He began firing, spreading out all eighteen rounds in the long-slide Glock, eliciting cries of surprise and pain. One man stumbled into view of the doorway, firing his shotgun once again.

Again, the Chinese criminal's body shielded McCarter. He pulled his backup baby Glock and drilled that man: two to the pelvis, two to the chest and two to the face.

With a surge, he got out from beneath the dead Asian and crouched, scanning for targets. He performed a quick reload, putting a 17 rounder into the baby Glock, then fed the Glock 34 another 17-shot box. He holstered both, and saw James wave his hand in the doorway. McCarter motioned. The floor was cleared.

Below, a second detonation shook the structure. Plaster dust rained from the ceiling.

"Enough," McCarter ordered through his headset. "We're moving down."

"Confirmed," Manning answered.

Their opposition would be watching the stairway, knowing that it was the only way down, though they would also likely keep away from the fire escape, watching those windows in case McCarter and James decided to flank. However, no one would expect what the two Phoenix Force commandos really intended.

James unfolded a web of high-velocity explosive in cord form and placed it in on the floor. McCarter could hear orders coming up through the floorboards, and knew that this particular part of the building was where the Moscow 88 gunmen and their Hong Kong allies had set up to protect their territory.

The breaching web was locked into place, and both McCarter and James moved out into the hallway to reduce their odds at injury. James pressed the detonator and a powerful crack made the whole building heave, even though the web was designed to focus its force in one direction. Screams filled the air.

McCarter and James stepped to the edge of the hole the detonation carved in the floor. Splinters of wood rode on sheets of air compressed by the explosion, turning into shrapnel and raining down upon the heavily armed gangsters. Men were scattered around, some dead, some jerking in pain from their injuries and some merely staggering, stunned by the overpressure of the blast.

The standing gunmen received the initial bursts of subgun fire, bullets ripping into them with ruthless efficiency. Once the able-bodied gunmen were downed, McCarter and James switched to single-shot, putting the wounded out of their misery. Outside, more gunfire blazed, as the breaching charge and rain of deadly lead had likely informed the men on the first and second floors that they were in truly deep shit. And, once more, the crack of Manning's unmistakable explosive resounded, the high-explosive disks serving as flying guillotines, pressure waves snapping necks and crushing ribs.

James braced himself, took McCarter's arm and lowered the Briton to the floor. McCarter covered his partner as he climbed down through the hole.

Sure enough, the third floor had been cleared of gunmen. The brain trust of Moscow 88 goons had thought that by making one room a fortress they would be secured from the hallway and the windows. McCarter and Phoenix Force, however, worked in three dimensions.

"Let's look for intel. Quick sweep. Even in this rotten neighborhood, all this shooting will draw an army of cops," McCarter ordered.

CHAPTER THIRTEEN

Grigori was glad for Karl Long's allegiance. The big, brawny American was a true believer in the power of pure blood, as well as a canny warrior. Already, he'd proved his capability in combat, and thus was to be a revered brother. He was not Russian, but not everyone could be perfect.

On the other hand, he wished that he'd never thrown in his lot with Abalisah.

Walking back to his room now that his shift was over, he paused, looking at the gymnasium.

It was empty. Quiet.

Maybe he'd take some time to work out the kinks in his shoulders. He could settle into the rhythm of exercise and clear his mind, meditate, recharge himself.

Even as he entered, peeling out of his uniform shirt, something felt wrong about the empty gymnasium.

"I am with security," he announced, resting his hand on the butt of his pistol. He glanced around the semidarkened room. There was a strange vibration in the silence, something that set his nerves on end. He thumbed the strap on his holstered pistol. He had a Grach pistol, one of the new handguns of the Russian Federation, and he knew that he had eighteen shots to deal with any problem that could burst from the shadows. He let the shirt drop to the floor and looked around, moving toward the locker room and shower.

As soon as he got to within a few feet of the locker room, he stopped, smelling the stink of fresh coppery blood and voided bowels and bladders. Grigori pulled the gun, then yanked his radio from his belt. "We have a situation in the gym. Send men now!"

He spotted a hand as soon as he moved closer to the open door. The confirmation of his command resounded in the distance, his mind not filtering it, keeping it distant as he recognized the face at the end of the arm. It was Yuri, his eyes wide open. The poor kid's arm was bent backward, elbow broken and twisted to an unnatural angle. The kid's handgun was in his other fist. He must have tried to fire the gun, but something had stopped it. Perhaps it had snarled and jammed with a live round stuck in the breech.

The handle of a knife jutted between Yuri's ribs. Some distance away, another figure was folded and huddled on the ground. A spent shell casing showed that Yuri had fired his shot, and the puddle of blood pooled around the second fallen figure informed Grigori that at least the kid had done what he could.

So why hadn't a gunshot roused the whole building? Surely Yuri hadn't been alone in here.

Then he thought about the snarled, jammed slide of the handgun.

The muzzle must have been jammed into the soft belly of his attacker, human flesh enveloping the muzzle blast and effectively silencing the gunshot.

Grigori approached the fallen man and noticed a knife still in his hand. The Moscow 88 fighter stepped closer and kicked the man onto his back. There was a sticky slurp as his body broke free from coagulating blood, a bullet hole through his sternum having gushed almost half the blood from the corpse.

The man was another of the Horde bikers who had been brought in as extra muscle. Grigori knelt and looked closer, just as more of his allies came in. "Don't shoot, it's us."

Grigori stood. "They killed Yuri."

"That guy is with the Horde?" one man asked. "He doesn't look American or Hispanic."

"That's because he's a Muslim. Those half-blooded Hordesmen opened up a branch in Germany and allowed Muslims to form the core membership. They could be working with French, German or Italian organized crime, and by extension, with the Bratva," Grigori explained.

"Why Yuri? They should know goddamn well that making a move against one of us is an attack on the whole Abalisah organization," Greb, one of the Moscow 88 brethren, said.

Grigori locked the man with a hard stare. "Because we're making inroads with the Reich Low Riders. And they feel threatened by our chance to grow."

"Fucking Horde," the other guard said. "There's more blood, a trail leading away."

Grigori snapped to attention. "Take me to it."

He replaced his radio with a flashlight. Together, the Russian neo-Nazi and his two men followed the trickle of blood until it reached a broken window. "Call someone to start checking the perimeter…"

With a sudden burst of violence and noise, a greasy-haired figure slammed against the pane of the window. In the glow of his flashlight, Grigori was able to see Karl Long, scowling and punching at the figure. Ugly, wet crunches filled the air as bones broke under each punishing blow.

Long's large hands were wrapped around the other man's head. Grigori could see the blood spattered on Long's fingers just as there was a savage push, the crack and crunch of neck bones giving as the head was pivoted on the sill of the window.

With that, the Horde biker died, foam issuing from rubbery, lifeless lips, dark eyes wide and bloodshot with horror.

"Karl?" Grigori asked. "Was he the only one out there?"

"Yeah. He came through the window," Lyons returned. "He was sprayed with blood…then tried to attack me. Who is this goon? It's too dark to see."

"He's with the Horde. He killed Yuri," Grigori said.

Lyons spit on the dead man.

"Thank you," Grigori said. He held his hand out for Lyons, who took the offered hand up, then crawled through the window and into the locker room.

"They screwed their chance at me, so…what? They attacked one of yours?" Lyons asked. He watched as Grigori's two Moscow 88 brethren hauled the dead Arab through the window. Sure enough, the man's arm was drenched with Yuri's blood, likely from the deep arterial puncture by the knife currently sticking out of Yuri's ribs.

Grigori gave the corpse on the floor a kick. "These animals. The Bratva sends the least of their mud people to kill a pure-born warrior for the cause."

Lyons could see the tears begin to well in the Moscow 88 commander's eyes. The other two men were busy talking on their radios, preparing to set up a sweep.

He knew just enough Russian, and saw the expressions on their faces, that he was able to add together the assembly of the brothers on the island to unleash hell against the Horde and find out who had ordered the hit.

"You're going to make things bad for Jinan," Lyons spoke up.

All three Russians turned, stopped what they were doing and looked at him.

"You're going after Jinan's moneymakers," Lyons added. "Suddenly he might think you guys are expendable. And when you are expendable…"

"There's a reason why he picked from four groups as security," Grigori rasped.

"Jinan brought us here, all of us. Sure, he means to make money, but he doesn't seem to give a damn if his customers kill each other, or burn out on the drugs he's providing," Lyons told him. "Why is that?"

Grigori raised an eyebrow. "We've been working with them on operations in China, as well."

"The operation to get that Dong-Feng? The one Abalisah is selling, not the cardboard mock-up in the huckster room?" Lyons asked.

Grigori nodded.

"Because you and whomever you were working with are deniable resources," Lyons said. "This happened to us, too. Me and my brothers barely escaped when the Aryan Right Coalition was hit last time. Those ARC bastards used the Heathens as human shields. I'm finally at the end of my patience for this bullshit."

"We've heard of that," Grigori stated. He looked back toward the corpse of Yuri. "We're nothing but cannon fodder for those who think themselves so clever."

Lyons nodded solemnly. The Able Team commander made certain his frown and sadness matched Grigori's.

"Damn…"

Lyons put his hand on Grigori's shoulder. "Listen. We can deal with the Horde. We can figure out who hired them, too. We can work our way up the food chain. We just need cover. Help."

Grigori's eyes narrowed. "What do you need?"

"I need a body or two. We're gonna fake Shore burning up in a meth-cooking accident. That way…"

"That way no one will look for him," Grigori added conspiratorially. He looked at the Horde he'd stomped into a bloody pulp. "Can't use him…we'll use the other Horde prick."

Lyons nodded. "Good."

"We'll make sure things are right in his room. We've got some time, so we'll get it all done in the next thirty minutes," Grigori said. "Get Shore out of his room."

Lyons smiled. "Thank you, brother."

The two tattooed men clasped hands, a symbol of the strength of their burgeoning bond. The auction was a hellhole, a trap. The two groups present were surrounded by hated enemies, and their only reliance could be on themselves.

With that, Grigori motioned for Lyons to leave, to head back to his two brothers.

With the deaths of three men, Carl Lyons was well on his way to driving this auction to his advantage. The Able Team leader knew that for him to ingratiate Able Team to Grigori and his crew, there had to be a sense of deep brotherhood. That involved giving them something to bond over.

Lyons took revenge on the Horde biker out in the woods.

Similarly, the two Horde members from Germany were innocent of the murder of Yuri. That had been the work of Hawkins. In the meanwhile, Lyons and Schwarz had grabbed the two Muslim bikers, picking them up from a bodyguard detail with the Corsican Union. The two Able Team warriors had gone over enough information to know that the Bratva had informal ties with the Corsicans. That would give Grigori more than enough fuel for his paranoia.

Under the guise of a friendly kindred spirit, the leader of Able Team would do his best to pit allies against each other. Getting in good with Moscow 88's contingent of hired guns would allow them to further threaten the unity of this auction. That three thugs were dead was only icing on the cake, three fewer killers Able Team would have to annihilate on the way out of this island.

THE MAN WHOM the assembled auctioneers had come to call Jinan sat on his couch in his office. He was busy listening to snippets of conversations going on throughout the hotel. Sleep would be saved for after he finished this round of evidence gathering. One would have thought that the gangsters, the terrorists, the petty warlords would have all taken the time to enjoy a night's sleep in a comfortable bed, but the thugs who assembled at this grand bazaar of high-tech and untraceable weaponry weren't on vacation.

They were networking, spying on their rivals and

enemies, making plots and wondering how they could outbid for certain items.

The former Heathen bikers seemed especially suspect. They'd arrived with an invitation, intended for Kevin Reising, who was attached to yet another incarnation of the Aryan Right Coalition. The three men were graduating from road fiends to high-level traffickers, and this was their debut trip.

Herman Shore showed potential; he had a lot of intelligence. Even with the debilitating effects of a methamphetamine addiction, the tweaker had accomplished some remarkable electronics work. The radio had been dismantled and turned into an impressive electroshock weapon, something Jinan would love to get his hands on.

Hiring him on would be good. Right now, he was busy converting the components of a television into a directed laser, taking hits off his meth pipe every so often. It was fascinating watching the man's hands work, his eyes light up, and his genius enabling him to create a beam of coherent energy that lit a small dot of wall on fire, literally.

Abalisah's representative, who'd chosen the name Jinan to represent his place in the birthing of a great army, saw this man as someone as worthy of taking to their Sri Lanka hideout as the scientists from China and America.

Jinan would not let any of the lower tiers of the security in on the truth of his designs upon Herman Shore. Instead he called in his takers, Manjun and Junun. Soon, Shore would be on his way across the ocean. He would have to see what Karl Long and Thomas Presley would do when their friend disappeared without a trace.

HERMANN SCHWARZ HATED the stink of the meth in the pipe. He'd done his best not to inhale too much, but already his body was starting to rebel against this part of his charade. He desperately needed fresh air.

On the other hand, the laser he was building from components of the television was coming along so nicely. It might have been the meth, the obsessive focus the drug gave him, that kept him from moving until he'd perfected the television parts into a powerful directed-energy device.

He gave the trigger another press and the next beam, this time directed at the porcelain wall of the tub, flared for a few instants, then burrowed through. Wisps of smoke showed on the other wall of the bathtub, and Schwarz grinned with satisfaction, killing the beam instantly. Sure, he was using the power supply from the hotel, something that couldn't be put into a backpack, but he'd achieved good penetration on the beam. It was only visible where it landed, and it took only instants to burn through materials.

The only problem would be a small enough pack to generate the energy for the beams, and that technology was years away, even for Schwarz's genius. The man called Gadgets would have to make do with conventional firearms, grenades and missiles for the time being. He set the device aside and opened the window, leaning out and sucking in fresh Hawaiian air, the scents of the forest and the saltiness of the Pacific Ocean going a long way toward recharging his mind.

Schwarz closed his mind and fell, almost immediately, into a Zen state of being. For him, his relaxation was not the kind of the brawny Lyons. Certainly, Schwarz possessed considerable physical ability; one simply did not become one of the world's greatest fighting men without muscle and limberness. However, for Schwarz, it was metaphysics and internal exercises that honed his body.

The door clicked open behind him and Schwarz ended his meditation. The sound was soft, nonthreatening, but he was aware that none of his friends had a key card that would allow them access to this room. They would have to knock or utilize a master key.

Schwarz turned to his intellect and keen senses as two figures entered the hotel room on quiet feet. He could already detect the early wisps of chloroform.

So they're going to kidnap me, he thought. This relaxed him, and he continued his seeming meditation, all the while maintaining his deep breathing, flushing his bloodstream with as much oxygen as possible. Whoever these two men were, they were good and skilled, capable of getting close to him.

A tweaking biker wouldn't have noticed a single thing about them, but Schwarz had already estimated their weight by their tread on the carpet.

He was glad that his boots were full of electronics that he could assemble into a secure transmitter, but were inert and unnoticeable otherwise. To even a trained eye, they were simply battered, well-used footwear, not the kind of thing that would be packed with equipment from a James Bond movie.

A hand with a chloroform cloth appeared out of the corner of his eye and Schwarz stirred, showing a sign of recognition of something wrong. By then, his captors had already determined his reflexive actions were too late, too little. The soaked rag was pressed over his mouth and the Able Team electronics genius, already holding his breath, made as if he were trying to suck in fresh air. He twisted, writhed, and then began to quickly subside. During the struggles, he kicked at the wall, leaving a message for Lyons; otherwise, there would be trouble. Without panic seizing him, Schwarz was able to leave his boot-black message quickly and efficiently.

In a few moments an average of the amount of time it would take for a person to normally succumb to chloroform—Lyons wasn't the only member of the team that did lots of research—he was limp, feigning unconsciousness in the arms of the two kidnappers. He mentally retreated, body gone raggedy and insensate. They pulled him into the hallway.

We'll see where you guys are taking me. And once I find out, it will be your funeral, Schwarz mentally promised.

Inside, the genius smiled.

CHAPTER FOURTEEN

Carl Lyons entered Hermann Schwarz's room a good five minutes after he had been taken from it, finding the door already unlocked and the area empty. There was a smoldering meth pipe sitting on the table, next to a small laser projector. Already, he could tell the after scent of something aside from the meth. There was no sign of a struggle. Nothing at all.

He was busily at work, going through the room with every ounce of awareness and investigative know-how he possessed. His sharp eyes picked up several clues.

The meth pipe still smoked, only dying out within a few moments of his double-checking it. He looked at the window, which was open, and noted a few scuff marks on the wall, just at floorboard height. There were dots and dashes made by the scuffs.

Three dashes atop two dashes around a dent.

Even being kidnapped, you remember your Morse code, Lyons thought. Schwarz had coded "OK."

That meant he'd known he was being taken. That was why there were no signs of a struggle and why the room was empty. Lyons looked around and saw that Schwarz's laser was still warm from the powerful beam it had generated. Schwarz had gotten pretty good with the design, even cutting through porcelain and leaving scorch marks on the wall.

The radio-Taser that Schwarz had bragged about making that first night here in the resort was gone, as well. Lyons knew he hadn't taken it apart for materials to run the new laser, but he was also aware that it was rechargeable and could hold a couple of shots in the batteries already within the clock-radio mechanism.

They'd come for Schwarz and they'd taken the example of the man's incredible inventive skills. The laser was larger and too bulky to take within the brief instants the attackers had come for him. Lyons leaned up and looked to see that there were scratch marks on the sill, made by Schwarz as he seemingly studiously ignored whatever threat was creeping up behind him.

Here, in the window, Lyons could smell the too familiar reek of chloroform. If Schwarz had smelled it, as well, then he could have maintained consciousness and the clarity of thought to have deliberately kicked and clawed the "OK" on the wall just above the floorboard. Given Schwarz's wits, and his ease of multitasking, he'd likely faked a fight for consciousness while leaving behind that message. What was more, as he'd waited for them to make their first strike, Schwarz had made two tally marks on the sill with his thumbnail. Two attackers.

Hawkins was at the door, eyes wide and concerned at Lyons's presence, scanning for clues. Lyons waved him in, then looked around.

"All right, I made plans with Grigori," Lyons said conspiratorially. "Shore is going to have an accident so he can disappear. Grigori and his pals are bringing along a fresh corpse to make it look like he burned himself up."

Hawkins looked a bit bewildered, but nodded, following Lyons's lead. "Lasers and meth don't mix."

Lyons tapped his nose and then motioned toward the wall below the window. Hawkins, with his Ranger and Delta Force training, would have known Morse code like a second language. The Texan nodded with realization that Schwarz was in good condition.

"Listen, I know that Jinan isn't supposed to have microphones in these rooms…" Hawkins began.

Lyons shrugged. One thing Schwarz had located first thing when they'd arrived was a whole electronics suite of miniature, passive bugs hidden all over their rooms. Though Grigori and his Moscow 88 comrades seemed unaware of the surveillance in the rooms, they had not had Able Team's resident technology guru on their side. Right now, they were acting for the sake of whoever was listening.

"Shore left behind the laser to make the fire seem a little more plausible, I guess," Lyons said.

Grigori and his allies were at the door now.

Lyons waved them in, a dead Horde thug carried between them.

"Where'd you get him?" Hawkins asked.

"Yuri shot him before he died," Grigori answered with solemn dread.

"Yuri's dead?" Hawkins asked with such shock, Lyons forgot for a moment that it was the Texan himself who had slid the knife between Yuri's ribs. Hawkins glared with hostility at the corpse. "What happened?"

Grigori gave Hawkins the timeline he had determined from the evidence. With a little bit of grim smugness, Lyons was pleased to have manipulated the Moscow 88 goon so readily and completely. Just one more victory.

"Yeah… We'll find out who ordered the hit. Shore will give us the leads we need once he disappears," Hawkins confirmed. His voice was grim, his eyes hard.

"Get out of here," Grigori said. "We'll set up the burn."

With that, Lyons and Hawkins disappeared from Schwarz's room. They found one of the blind spots Schwarz had located and, after a quick double-check using their Combat PDAs, they were satisfied no one was looking in.

"Grigori is making like he doesn't even realize that someone took Gadgets," Hawkins mused, speaking softly.

"Which means, whoever took him was someone with a lot of connections, or Abalisah themselves," Lyons said.

"Abalisah is the name of the group. It's the plural of Iblis," Hawkins stated. "Iblis was the first of God's angels, except instead of clay, he was sculpted from fire. Blue fire, likely lightning."

Lyons nodded. "I occasionally read books without a lot of pictures in them."

Hawkins smirked and chuckled. "So, Abalisah took Gadgets. According to what we got from the Farm, these auctioneers have been taking American and Chinese weapons designers."

"So, Hermann, doing his tweaker thing, inadvertently made himself a valuable target," Lyons said.

"We play it like we originally planned?" Hawkins asked.

"What else can we do? We'll let the Farm know that

Gadgets is in motion," Lyons noted. "No doubt, he'll be putting together a tracker for himself, and they'll pick him up on satellite no matter where he is now."

"No doubt," Hawkins repeated. "In the meantime, we play stupid and tear through Moscow 88's competition."

Lyons shrugged. "And the Heathens' too. Jinan wants that from us, apparently. So let's give the man what he asked for."

Hawkins nodded. "In spades."

The two Stony Man operatives didn't mention to each other that they were now down a man, and that someone had showed more than enough interest in their group to take one of them. While they were confident of Schwarz's skills, there was no guarantee he would be able to put his wizardry to work while a captive. There was only so much a person could do. Even if he was a member of Able Team.

Things looked dark and dangerous in the coming hours.

Their best bet was simply to follow through with their original plan. Fire and maneuver. Ambush and kill.

And when the smoke cleared, they could only hope that they made it through the battle alive.

BARBARA PRICE GRIMACED with frustration as she looked up at the gigantic computerized projection of the Hong Kong traffic cameras on a wall screen. The HKPD traffic computers were out, knocked down for thirty seconds, likely through some manner of hacking or sabotage.

"We're still scanning traffic cameras now," Kurtzman said. "Thing is, this might have been a deliberate bit of evasion."

"You think?" Price asked. "Sorry, didn't mean to snap at you."

"No, I get your frustration," Kurtzman answered. "Don't worry. Phoenix is tearing up their old head-quarters now. It's a rat hole of filth, but they brought their latex gloves and are digging wherever they can find a nook."

Price nodded. "How's the search from our end— any idea where Baxter and Chandler might have left the country?"

"Nope," Kurtzman said. "There were glitches in standard surveillance, much like the ones we just experienced in Hong Kong, except this was spread across several ports."

"They cast out all manner of phantom false leads," Price grumbled. She took a sip of coffee, grimacing at the thought there might not be a means of trailing the missing scientists and technicians. So far, Phoenix Force and Rosario Blancanales had been at the site Moscow 88 was using in Hong Kong, and they had been looking for several minutes.

The one saving grace was that their tap on the HKPD communications network told the Farm the team had another fifteen minutes of grace to tear through the files and any leftovers from the Hong Kong operations. Police units were talking, and a perimeter had been set up for several blocks around the site of the firefight.

Knowing HKPD SWAT tactics and procedures, the fifteen minutes of search time would still allow her people more than fifteen minutes to find their hole in that perimeter and escape. Phoenix Force had been surrounded by cops before, and if there was one thing they could do, it was disappear without engaging in an unnecessary conflict with local law enforcement.

Nothing good would come from causing harm to policemen simply trying to protect their city.

And right now, Phoenix Force's eyes on the ground were exactly what was needed to fill in the holes of their computer and satellite hacking.

Her tablet blipped, alerting her to an incoming message from Able Team in Hawaii.

She pulled it onto the screen.

Gadgets in wind. Taken by Abalisah. Track him.

Barbara Price felt a wave of semirelief come over her. Yes, Hermann Schwarz was in enemy hands, but the bad guys might as well have taken a time bomb to their chests.

Ears are open. Need him now.

As of this moment Schwarz was the only thing that Price and the rest of the home crew had to locate Abalisah's captives and presumably their store of major weaponry. Schwarz had sent them pictures of what the auctioneers had currently on hand in Hawaii, an impressive array of communications equipment, some nearly as sophisticated as what the Farm itself had, thanks to Schwarz. There was also all manner of small arms, ammunition samples and video displays of high explosives.

The major stuff—armored vehicles, long-range missiles, even short-range antiaircraft and antiarmor rockets—was not going to be kept on site. Not with all those crooks in such close quarters.

Price also could see that the Abalisah group had assembled far more than simply Moscow 88 thugs. There were Chinese-appearing men on the staff, but after some facial recognition work, Akira Tokaido had been able to determine that they were actually Kyrgyz separatists, picked for their resemblance to regular Chinese, despite having Turkic roots.

That meant that this group was East Turkestan separatists. Price remembered that members of one of those groups were responsible for a mass stabbing back in early 2014. Dozens died and hundreds had been murdered by an organized, focused mob of knife-wielding maniacs in China. It was news worldwide. This group's tattoos identified them as East Turkestan Freedom— ETF.

Besides the Moscow 88 and the ETF, there were also Syrian rebels, Colombians and Vietnamese. Most of this information received courtesy of Lyons's buddying up with Grigori, and confirmed by facial recognition through Schwarz's photography of the guard staff.

Another message came through.

Striker special served.

Price may not have been around since the very beginnings of Stony Man Farm, but she knew exactly what Lyons was talking about. Even before Able Team had been sent in undercover, there would be no doubt that anyone sent to the resort would be terribly outnumbered and outgunned And yet, whenever a summit of

criminals occurred in this manner, it was a specialty
of Mack Bolan, the aforementioned Striker. He would
slip in among them, appearing as a fellow criminal or
terrorist, and by playing on old prejudices and fears,
pit his enemies against each other, ramping up the tension and distrust until a violent paroxysm shook down
everything.

Price texted a reply.

Watch your back.

It wasn't something she needed to break communications silence for, but it still made her feel better.

She wasn't certain how long it would take until
things turned hot and bloody for Lyons and Hawkins,
but as of now, it was a mere matter of details. On the
other hand, there were still missing scientists, and
Schwarz was on his way. She contacted McCarter's
device.

Gadgets en route to join hostages. Any news for intercept?

There were a few moments.

En route out. Discovered laptop. Plugging into link
now.

Price smiled, then turned to see Kurtzman lift a
thumb, indicating there was now a direct link to the
laptop they discovered. Within moments Stony Man
would have access to every bit of communications received through the device. Another file popped up, this

time a cell phone's memory. In all, the men of Phoenix Force had recovered four possible communication platforms and sifting through all the porn and cat videos would be quick and easy for the cybernetics team.

It was better than nothing, and it would also help them home in on any location Schwarz would be broadcasting from now.

Leaving early to avoid rush. Don't wait up, luv.

Price smirked.

Things might actually turn out not to be a disaster, after all.

Barbara Price caught that thought and broke into a deep frown. That kind of thinking was exactly the hubris that would bring down tribulation to the teams.

Price returned to watching the HKPD, to make certain they weren't tightening their noose on Phoenix Force too soon.

DAVID MCCARTER WAS in the back of the Phoenix Force van as Rosario Blancanales and Gary Manning continued to pore over the stash of electronics they'd recovered from the Moscow 88 headquarters. Calvin James drove and Rafael Encizo was riding shotgun, dividing his attention between the actual streets and the police scanner on his Combat PDA. One of the things that Blancanales noted was that a couple of the phones that had not yet been connected to the Farm came off a Chinese man supposedly in the employ of Moscow 88. Rather, he'd turned out to be a Kyrgyz, a blend of Chinese and Turkic, who could, at times, facially pass for true Chinese.

Knowing Phoenix Force's luck, the East Turkestan man was part of a minority of Kyrgyz Muslims who were adamantly separatist, willing to commit all manner of violence to further their cause. Since kidnapping weapons designers from the People's Republic of China military would be a big blow against the government, the East Turkestan separatists would jump at the chance to aid in the operation.

The donation of manpower would also give the Moscow 88 plenty of Chinese-appearing scapegoats for the attack on the Naval Testing Ground where Baxter and Chandler had disappeared from. McCarter checked through the listings on the man's phone and confirmed his suspicions about the group. Just to be certain, he gave Mei Anna a quick call.

"Kyrgyz? We've got a few sympathizers who are keeping their eyes on the People's Republic for us. And then, there are those who are a little too crazy for espionage. They call themselves K-SET," Mei told him.

"Kyrgyz for the Separation of Eastern Turkestan?" McCarter asked.

Mei chuckled. "It sounds kind of cool."

"It sounds like they should be selling spray-on hair and pocket fishing reels on the late-night telly," McCarter returned. "Thanks for the heads-up."

"Never a problem," Mei said. "Moscow 88 and K-SET are two groups of psychopaths who do no one a lick of good. They are hateful, bitter maniacs."

"And yet they were close bedfellows when we hit them," McCarter returned.

"Money is a good salve for some discomforts," Mei offered.

"And the opportunity to hurt mutual enemies is all

the more golden delicious," McCarter concluded. "Just like my lads and your operation."

He could feel Mei's wink over the phone line.

"Except our amity isn't from money."

"I could say something about golden skin..." McCarter purred.

"But you're among your teammates." Mei's laugh was a delight, even through the tiny speaker on the phone. "And you already did say it."

"Don't worry. I've got thick skin and a hard head. I can take their kidding. You stay safe, pretty lady."

"I will," Mei responded.

McCarter ended the call.

"So aside from some nooky talk, you found out about a group called the Kyrgyz for the Separation of Eastern Turkestan," Manning said. "We've located similar stuff in the laptop we haven't hooked back to the Farm."

"I'll send a message to Barb to confirm we've sighted these blighters on hand here. Chances are, though, Carl and the gang already know about K-SET," McCarter said. He fired off the message to base.

"K-SET? Didn't they used to make Mister Microphone? 'Hey, I'm on the radio!'" James spoke up. "'I'll be back to pick you up later!'"

"I always thought they had the boring music collections," Blancanales returned.

"All right. All right," McCarter chuckled. He looked at his screen.

Independent confirmation of Kyrgyz presence on your end. K-SET and M88 are on the payroll in multiple locations. Thanks.

McCarter smirked. Of course, his counterparts in Able Team would have picked up on that information, but that would have been only shared if it were relevant. And now, it was relevant for Phoenix Force's mission.

In fact, McCarter got on the horn to Mei Anna once more. And this time he wasn't cooing sweet nothings into her ear.

CHAPTER FIFTEEN

After having lost the convoy via satellite and traffic cameras, it was Mei Anna's organization with their Kyrgyz contacts that managed to drop a line to Phoenix Force as to the Hong Kong "transportation hub" of K-SET. Like most smuggling operations, it was at home on the seedier sides of Victoria Harbour's docks, and sure enough, as the van passed by the building, there were the two vans they had all seen leaving Moscow 88's erstwhile headquarters.

Phoenix and Rosario Blancanales refreshed the ammunition they had spent in their magazines, making sure that they had full loads.

This time, however, the Stony Man commandos were not interested in a quiet hit. They had their personal hearing protection—electronic earbuds that filtered sounds capable of causing permanent hearing damage down to manageable levels. Stealth was replaced by swiftness and violence of action. Encizo, Blancanales and James supplemented their PDW machine pistols with portable grenade launchers. James and Blancanales were both the M-203 men on their teams, often utilizing M-16s or M-4 carbines with the detachable grenade launchers mounted beneath. This time, however, both were using the stand-alone version with a collapsing stock and pistol grip.

Encizo's personal favorite 40 mm launcher had been the old HK-69 A-1, but the newer HK-320 was something he'd learned to utilize well, being a big fan of Heckler & Koch. Unfortunately, finding a HK-320 would have been difficult. At this moment, he was making do with an M-203, which he'd fortunately become quite familiar with thanks to its use by his teammates and fellow Stony Man warriors.

"Knock on the door for us while we check out the back," McCarter said. The VBR-PDW was full to the top with a 33-round extended Glock magazine.

Gary Manning had his close-quarters gear, forsaking the machine pistol and the Glock sidearms for his more favored tools: a short-barreled 12-gauge shotgun and a pair of .357 Magnum revolvers, both Philippine knockoffs of the legendary Colt Python, one with a six-inch barrel and the other with a two inch. Manning also had breeching rounds for the shotgun, as well as a full supply of other portable munitions. The 12-gauge was a pump gun, the M-5 based off the old High Standard Flite King. This weapon came in nickel, and had polymer- and fiberglass-filled furniture for greater durability and waterproofing. It was a good, solid weapon, and one that was deniable, as were their Glocks and the VBR.

The grenade launchers popped as McCarter and Manning closed in on the warehouse, 40 mm shells detonating with loud cracks. Currently the Phoenix Force grenadier team was launching smoke and distraction devices that shattered windows and began filling the building with clouds of obfuscating chemical fog.

The noisemakers weren't lethal, just like the smoke grenades, but they allowed the Stony Man artillery barrage to draw attention entirely away from McCarter and Manning. Once at the rear entrance, Manning fired his breeching round at the fire-door lock, blasting the dead bolt into useless garbage. Two more pumps followed by trigger pulls resulted in the hinges on the door disintegrating and allowing McCarter to rip the door from its frame and hurl in a flash bang.

McCarter had earned the "bones" for his Stony Man service as a member of Britain's elite Special Air Service, and the SAS were among the very first forces to utilize the flash bang. The noisy, brain-numbing device was as much a part of McCarter's repertoire as his right arm and personal Browning Hi-Power—a Philippine copy residing in his hip holster—so he knew exactly how long the fuses would go. He entered the room immediately upon the bang, right at the moment when whoever was on the other side of the door was left insensate.

On the other side of the door was a K-SET guard, staggering uneasily, but the Chinese AK in his hand was all the evidence McCarter required to judge him a threat. The Briton brought up his machine pistol and tapped off a short burst that shredded the Kyrgyz separatist's heart. Blind and deaf, the sentry was dumped unceremoniously in a boneless heap on the ground. McCarter leaped over the body and continued on into the ever-more cloudy and obscured warehouse.

The Phoenix Force commander was thankful for his hearing protection, and even more pleased that he and the team were wearing night-vision goggles, the projected infrared beams of the goggles' built-in illuminators reflecting through the thickening mists. Off to one side, Manning's M-5 boomed and a K-SET fanatic's attempt to ambush McCarter was ended in a swarm of .36-caliber pellets that chopped through flesh and bone, shattering ribs and tearing internal organs to mush.

Two down, but the odds were not going to be that light or easy.

"Go to burn," McCarter ordered.

In a moment the trio of portable artillery launchers were reloaded and new shells sailed through emptied windowpanes. This time when the shells struck, hitting the walls of the warehouse, the 40 mm Ferret shells burst through Sheetrock and disgorged payloads of oleoresin capsicum. As soon as the airborne pepper spray met the K-SET staff on hand, cries of pain and dismay filled the warehouse, making it all that much easier to locate and target the gunmen.

OC spray was one of the most powerful means of disabling an opponent's senses short of actually cutting out their eyes and sinuses. In many instances, the victims of airborne capsicum actually wished that someone would take a sharp knife and remove their eyeballs and tear ducts, the pain was so intense.

Behind their goggles and face masks, McCarter and Manning only had minor whiffs of the intense fog, and even then, tears came unbidden from their eyes. To experience the clouds of OC, however, was akin to feeling like your face turned into lava and was trying to eat through your skull. Both the Briton and the Canadian had experienced blasts of the natural chemical agent. Any person who engaged in paramilitary operations had to subject themselves to working while in tear-gas filled environments. There was rarely ever a case where someone truly "got used to" the crowd-control sprays. It was endurable, but it was never an environment one wanted to stay in long.

There was no ignoring the sudden surges of mucus flooding from nostrils, nor tears produced by burning eyes. The body tried everything to flush the vile, powerful pepper resin from its sensitive tissues, rendering people blind, incapable of speech or suffering difficulties while speaking.

Garbled voices rose, trying to communicate with each other. The renegade Kyrgyz gunmen tried to scramble as swiftly as they could, some searching for means of protecting their agonized faces, others trying to look through the smoke and their own blurring tears for the intruders who were firing SMGs and shotguns into their midst.

McCarter dove for cover, barely avoiding being cut down by a spray of Kalashnikov fire from one hardy opponent. Through the night vision, he could see it was one of the larger Moscow 88 gunmen, his tattoos glowing brightly in the illumination beams of his goggles. The Russians had dispatched some of their number with the captured Chinese techs. Additional muscle.

In their normal environments, neither side would have tolerated each others' existence, let alone worked together. However, now they were fighting shoulder to shoulder, showing loyalty and tolerance for each other. McCarter almost felt bad when Manning smashed a whole the size of a grapefruit in the Russian's chest.

Here, two groups of bigots were learning to put aside their hatreds, and here was Phoenix Force, killing off everyone making that spiritual growth.

Fortunately, it was likely that these bastards were only showing teamwork because they were facing a common foe—the warriors of Stony Man Farm. The desperate thugs found themselves even more hammered with new waves of Ferret shells and noisemakers.

One of the guards stood too close to one of those bangers and he dropped his rifle, clamping his hands over his ears. Blood spilled over the poor bastard's fingers like oily ink, his ruptured eardrums gushing. McCarter triggered a burst of 9 mm into the deafened gunman, cutting his suffering off with a trio of bullets through his brainpan.

"Cool it with the noisemakers. You blew the ears out of one of these goons, and we don't want the hostages hurt," McCarter ordered.

"Roger that," James said from outside. "Should we bring it in close?"

"Do it," McCarter replied. "We've got them off balance and confused. Time for the knockout."

"On our way," Blancanales spoke up.

McCarter motioned to Manning. "Keep laying down fire on these mooks. I'm going to look for the kidnapped techs."

Manning nodded. The Canadian knew it was only logical. The shotgun he had was not a precision weapon, though he could easily keep it topped off and possessed unequal stopping power in the close quarters of the warehouse. Making a hostage-rescue shot with his shotgun would mean a transition to his superbly accurate .357 Magnum revolver. As fast and capable as the men of Phoenix Force were, that was still milliseconds longer than simply bearing down and flicking the selector switch to single shot.

McCarter would have to make the rounds of getting

to the captive techs. He swept through the darkness, the IR illuminator casting the world ahead of him in ghostly greens. There was a figure in the distance, but the Phoenix commander held his fire, not seeing anything in the person's profile that indicated that he was armed or a hostile. He jogged forward, keeping low and glad for the crepe soles of his boots lowering his profile, even among the flash-bang-deafened opposition.

"David, we've got an arrival out here!" Encizo called out.

"HKPD?" McCarter murmured, getting closer to the mysterious shape in the darkness.

"Worse," Encizo said.

That was when the glare of a spotlight blazed through the warehouse window.

And if it wasn't the Hong Kong authorities, or the Chinese military, then it was the Abalisah organization come to pick up their prize.

McCarter returned his attention to the warehouse floor and grunted as a powerful blow knocked him off his feet.

The mysterious figure was big, brawny and had just laid out David McCarter with a single hit.

OUTSIDE THE WAREHOUSE, Blancanales lowered the machine pistol on its sling and brought up the stand-alone M-203 grenade launcher. The helicopter was a big, fast beast. It was a Harbin Z-9, China's knockoff of the Aérospatiale Dauphin. To Blancanales, the aircraft looked more like a shark in profile than an actual bottle-nosed dolphin.

Then again, he was trying to make sense of French nomenclature, and this was right in the middle of their raid on the K-SET transportation hub. He had a noise-maker loaded into the breech of the 40 mm grenade launcher, a Def Tec Aerial Warning and Signaling munition. It was supposed to be a noncombat round, but the thing put out 170 dB of sound pressure and over 5 million candelas of light. This was what he and the others had been hammering the warehouse with, and one of these devices had blown the eardrums, literally, out of a Kyrgyz separatist. The only reason McCarter and Manning had been able to operate at all was due to their protective goggles and the earbuds, which had built-in audio filters. The rest of the K-SET group, he knew, had staggered around drunkenly.

Blancanales swung the muzzle of his M-203 toward the Z-9 and tried to peer through the blaze of a spotlight on the nose of the hovering beast. It was a smart maneuver on the part of the pilot, making it difficult to see the body of the craft after the initial pass-by.

The Abalisah aircraft kept its hover orbit far enough away for the spotlight to hamper the vision of him and his Phoenix Force allies, but not to make itself an easy target.

"This is getting annoying," Encizo said.

"Just keep laying down cover fire against the warehouse," Blancanales said. "Cal, you got an angle on the son of a bitch?"

James shook his head. "Using the noisemakers?"

Blancanales nodded.

A sputter of gunfire suddenly came from the side door of the Harbin Z-9. From the impact divots they made on the dock, Blancanales knew that someone was using a .22 center-fire rifle, be it an American-style M-4 carbine or the QBZ-85 that was Chinese issue. There was no way to be absolutely certain the bird was not part of the government, but the fact that only one gunner was shooting, and it wasn't the usual heavier, standard door guns from the military-grade bird went a long way toward convincing Blancanales these weren't cops or soldiers doing their job and bringing down the hammer on the Kyrgyz separatists in the warehouse.

The fact that the knockoff Dauphin had room for nine passengers, as well as the pilot, meant that this was going to be the transport for the hostages brought here via the convoy of vans. With the extended range and quick speed of the helicopter, it could easily pick up three or four hostages, their guard, and bring them all to a ship waiting in international waters.

Blancanales grew tired of being a sitting target for all of the two seconds it took him to determine the helicopter was part of the conspiracy that attacked China and America. A conspiracy that hoped to gather a group of scientists to press into slave labor service, making missiles and other weapon systems as cutting edge as possible. He aimed at the spotlight and fired his Aerial Warning Device.

The shell was designed to detonate at 100 meters, as it was meant as a stand-off device. However, the fuse was time measured, thanks to its initial velocity. James fired his M-203, as well, but this one had a different grunt than his. He was using the Ferret rounds, which were meant to strike barriers and penetrate windows and thin metal, disgorging tear gas on the other side.

Either way, the thunderclap above was unmistakable. The flash bang was so bright, it eclipsed the spotlight's glare, and Blancanales could feel his teeth vibrate with the detonation of the charge. The Harbin swerved violently, the pilot either dazzled by 5 million candelas—as bright as the sun—or he was now currently trying to operate the helicopter while having his mucus membranes inflamed.

It was also likely both the Able Team and Phoenix Force grenadiers had managed that one sweet spot where both of their attacks were more than enough to turn the enemy's helicopter advantage into a flying deathtrap. Losing control, a figure screamed as he was hurled from the side door, falling to Victoria Harbour's night-blackened waters.

Blancanales swiftly reloaded, deciding to stay with the Aerial Warning, just in case he found an opening in the craft to sail the shell through. The Harbin swung wide and away from the docks, however, its tail wobbling as the pilot struggled to keep her under control.

He quickly traded the M-203 for his Combat PDA, getting on a direct line back to the Farm.

Barb, pickup aircraft by docks. Hit it, it's flying off. Track it.

Almost on the heels of the transmission, Price answered him back.

Got it. On radar.

James and Encizo looked over at Blancanales. He gave them the thumbs-up. They could now turn their attention to getting into the warehouse and helping out their allies, Manning and McCarter. Just to further soften up the enemy awaiting them inside, all three cut loose with another volley of Ferret rounds.

THE MAN WAS huge as McCarter looked up from the floor. The combatant was over six feet, easily, and his shoulders were wide and broad. He wore athletic tape wound his large fists, darkened by soot and everyday life, straps around his lowest knuckles and over the tops of his fists, the soiling on them making it as low profile as his black shirt. His skin was dark and dusky, and the Briton could see elements of the subcontinent in his fleshy features. Tears rolled down his cheeks, the wafting effects of tear gas that had penetrated this far into the warehouse.

"These men are to be delivered to Abalisah," he said softly in English, his voice containing the rolling timbre of a sleepy lion.

"Not on my watch," McCarter grumbled. He was back to his feet in one swift movement, snatching for the PDW as it dangled on its sling, knocked away by the savage ambush that floored him. Even as the gun rose, the stranger's long leg lashed out, striking McCarter in the forearm and jarring the weapon from numbed fingers. Luckily, while he saw the kick coming in time to allow himself to flex with the attack, saving his arm from being snapped like a twig, the impact still knocked the gun from his fingers.

The Briton realized he was just in too close to hope to draw a firearm fast enough to deal with the stranger. Rather than retreat, he lunged forward, ramming his shoulder into the Abalisah henchman. Just for the sake of brevity, he labeled the giant "Iblis" so he could keep his focus on the man. The impact was like hitting a tree trunk, but even while slamming into that tower of rock-solid muscle, he was able to take his foe off of his feet.

Iblis clawed his fingers at the shoulders, trying to maintain his balance, but McCarter hammered off a brutal left hook into the other man's kidney. The giant let out a grunt and croak of pain as the punch was one of the cornerstones of dirty infighting. All the muscle, all the martial arts skill in the world, could not minimize the nearly paralyzing pain of such a blow. It was a cruel, unfair bit of fist work, but McCarter was here to rescue kidnapped people and prevent the Abalisah organization from getting hold of their technical knowledge to build their own fantastic weaponry.

Iblis stumbled; legs gone to rubber from McCarter's skillfully placed cheap shot. With a savage chop, striking the man in the side of his knee, the British warrior used the bruiser's own weight and the traction of his footwear to turn an otherwise uncomfortable impact to a tendon-and-muscle-tearing, close-quarters blowout. The tall Indian's leg folded sideways and his lungs produced an insane screech.

Collapsing to the ground, McCarter snatched his foe's wrist with his good hand, then pulled his opponent's arm straight and his elbow to meet his own knee. The elbow bent backward, bone snapping, cartilage popping off the joints. He'd seen the power and effectiveness of his foe, but rather than go to a more elaborate form of martial arts, the Phoenix Force commander went to his strengths. Most fighters like this one seemed to be more in tune with the ritualized, honorable face-to-face battles.

The world that Phoenix Force battled in, however,

was one where McCarter was facing this towering freak with an injured forearm—his dominant hand actually—and with his head wrapped in more than enough equipment to cause him considerable head trauma if he took a punch to any of it. The goal was winning, not proving his skill or manhood.

All right, so hauling back and kicking the downed, agonized man right in the jaw was an act of malice. The sound of bone bursting like a beer bottle against a concrete curb told McCarter that he'd scored a telling blow on his foe. Unconsciousness claimed the man instantly. Stepping back from the fallen giant, he turned to see Gary Manning, watching. With him were three wide-eyed, distressed Chinese men, each rubbing raw wrists from where they'd been untied.

"Thanks for the help," McCarter grunted.

"I was accomplishing the task we came here for. Besides, you handled it," Manning returned.

McCarter addressed the trio in Cantonese, a language he had some familiarity with from the time he'd spent in Hong Kong both officially and unofficially. He was not fluent in the language, but he could communicate simple thoughts easily and quickly.

"Are you all right?" he asked.

The men nodded.

McCarter looked like hell, but they seemed to warm up to him since he'd destroyed the man who'd held them captive.

"We can take you somewhere that you can contact your employers," McCarter added.

One of them began to speak in English. "Thank you. But I do not believe the Chinese government would like to know of your involvement with our recovery. It is

better you leave, but my friends and I do wish to give
you some information before we part ways."

McCarter smiled and bowed his head to the man.

Stony Man Farm was due to get another update soon
enough.

CHAPTER SIXTEEN

It was midday, and Lyons and Hawkins had managed to sleep, in shifts, to keep their energy up. Both men knew the importance of sleep, and covered for one another while the other got his rest. Dreaming was a vital part of maintaining sanity. They took the time to sleep in until noon, thanks to the mayhem of the faked fire in Schwarz's hotel room.

Sanay curled up with Lyons while he slept, and the Able Team leader felt good with a warm, soft body beside him in the bed. The sound of her breathing helped him to focus and enter a deep, restive state. Having gone through the mourning, the act of anger, the quizzing by Grigori's allies, the two men hadn't gotten in until six in the morning.

Before settling in to sleep, and while Hawkins got his rest, Sanay informed Lyons of the questioning she had received. Naturally, Abalisah was interested in Karl Long, his preferences, his behaviors, his habits.

"Let him know I'm unconcerned about the disappearance of Shore," Lyons told her. "I mean, the death of Shore."

Sanay nodded. "You want me to make it seem as if you're covering up for his disappearance."

"Exactly," Lyons returned.

"But what really happened?" Sanay asked.

"He's sneaking around the grounds," Lyons told her. He hated to lie, but he didn't want to jeopardize Schwarz. He hated not being able to trust the woman completely, but right now, things were on a razor's edge. Besides, it wasn't as if they weren't being listened to. He'd done everything he could to conceal information from electronic eavesdropping. Here, lying in bed with the dusky beauty at his side, there was no guarantee that they were not spied upon now.

Especially with Schwarz/Shore in Abalisah hands.

He waited to see what would come of Jinan and his fellow devils learning of "Long's delusion."

As soon as the two men were up and about, Sanay disappeared, doing exactly as she had been given leave to. She was to tell everything to the Abalisah representative. As Lyons went to the drawer where he stored the Taurus Judge, he saw a package next to the big revolver. He picked it up, noting there were ten .410-gauge shells inside.

There was a small slip of paper with the package of shells.

"Remember the old gyro-jet rocket bullets? Same theory here. You'll like the execution."

Schwarz, always thinking ahead. He'd made something from the less than optimal mini shotgun shells. Lyons didn't have to test it out. Not from the description.

Lyons did not know how Schwarz had managed to get actual 12-gauge destruction out of a mere .410, nor did he really care.

There was a sudden boom coming from the direction of Hawkins's room, and Lyons knew the Texan had not learned to entirely trust the genius of Hermann

Schwarz. He loaded up the Taurus and used it to balance his Colt Python before jogging to the doorway where Hawkins looked at a door with a hole punched through it the size of a basketball.

Grigori's Moscow 88 brothers rushed to the scene, as well, the Phoenix Force veteran scratching the back of his head as he looked at the devastation wrought on the door. The wall opposite the door was also scorched and dented as if a massive fist had struck it.

Hawkins looked with a bit of lost abandon at the massive punch. "I…"

"You did that with a baby .410?" one of the Russians asked.

Hawkins nodded.

"So much for the element of surprise," Lyons groaned.

There was a bleep from the Moscow 88 guard's radio and he picked it up. Hasty words were traded in Russian, Lyons only understanding enough of the language to pick up every fourth word. What he did pick up, though, was that Jinan wanted to see him and Hawkins as soon as possible. Hearing their cover names helped, too.

"You'll have to leave your weapons with us when you go in to see him," the guard said, walking them toward Jinan's office.

Lyons and Hawkins didn't say anything. They were aware they would eventually attract attention. They had been speaking with Grigori rather openly about taking on Moscow 88's enemies in exchange for some looking the other way and other considerations. All that talk would undoubtedly have attracted the attention of the Abalisah organization. With this summons, Lyons began to feel a little more vindicated in his choice of battle tactics.

As they walked through the lobby, they saw a corpse being wheeled along on a cart. It was a lifeless mound under a sheet, but Lyons had seen more than enough homicide victims to know the shape and smell of the recently murdered. This one had the stink of burned flesh, which meant either another case of arson, or perhaps an electrocution.

"Someone else is playing rough, too," Hawkins noted.

Lyons nodded.

"It makes me wonder what's really going on here," Lyons murmured under his breath.

"Not an auction," Hawkins mused. "More like... an audition."

Lyons's answer was a grim frown. He was a man who was more for straightforward action. It didn't mean he was not familiar with deception and duplicity. He'd spent plenty of time as an undercover agent.

However this situation was one where things were becoming less and less under control. His team was split, thanks to Schwarz's kidnapping. The Abalisah organization also had planted a spy into Lyons's bed, Sanay, even though he was more in control of that situation, knowing that she was to listen in on him. He controlled what she told them.

But now, they were going to be face-to-face with the main man.

Lyons and Hawkins handed their sidearms over to the Abalisah guards, then were escorted through a set of heavy doors, obviously internally armored.

Jinan sat at a large desk. He was bracketed by a pair

of men, large and brawny, but both were sharp-eyed and attentive to the two men who entered their boss's presence. Lyons couldn't quite make out their nationality behind their sunglasses. Their hair was black, slicked down with product, and their skins were dark, but that could have easily been a tan as well as a native complexion. They were in BDU shirts and pants, and the arms that extended from their short sleeves were straight and wound with coils of powerful muscle.

"Mr. Long. Mr. Presley," Jinan said.

Jinan himself was a man with flowing brown hair. He was white, at least in terms of how his nose, brow and lips appeared to Lyons. Jinan appeared that he hadn't used a razor for a few days, but that was more of an affectation because the whiskers along his jaw were uniformly trimmed and well shaped.

Lyons and Hawkins remained silent, only acknowledging his greeting with a nod. There was an uneasy tension in the room as Jinan examined them. His eyes were sharp, bright and observant, taking in the two men's builds, their mannerisms, their stances. This was someone who knew what he was looking at, and looking for.

"You were talking to Grigori about the scheduled disappearance of your friend, Mr. Shore," Jinan stated. "It was an attempt to get him outside of the resort, so he could operate more freely to eliminate some of his competition."

Lyons and Hawkins both jolted with the surprise they remembered when Schwarz first went missing. Remembering that oddity, that discomfort, was a way to root their acting in something truthful.

"What have you done with him?" Lyons growled,

taking a step forward. Even as he made the menacing motion, the two guards glared at him. Lyons could see their shoulders shift, but they could see that the Able Team commander wasn't committed to attacking their boss. However they kept their attention on him and Hawkins. The bodyguards weren't stupid sacks of cement; they knew what they were doing.

These two were much more professional than the guys hired to wear uniforms and carry guns outside of doors. This made Lyons feel a little better. Professionals often were more predictable in their responses, and Lyons could get inside that mind-set. That knowledge didn't mean it would be easy to counter them, however.

Jinan didn't react to Lyons's aggression, meaning that things were even more under his control than it appeared. Even without firearms, both Lyons and Hawkins were dangerous men, but there was some other advantage the Abalisah representative had.

"He's been hired on," Jinan stated in answer to Lyons's question.

Lyons looked around the office. "Hired?"

"When he wakes up, he'll be more properly debriefed," Jinan said.

"And we're disposable?" Hawkins grumbled, not quite as menacingly as Lyons, but still nothing to ignore.

Jinan shook his head. "If you were disposable, you would not have crawled out of your beds this morning. No, you three show some creativity together, and the two of you seem to have properly snowed Grigori and his goon squad, which is no small feat with those paranoid apes."

Lyons stood a little straighter, tilting his head to

indicate he was more interested than threatened. "Snowed them?"

"You obviously have no more concern with a group of Russian also-rans than you would with the Russian organization," Jinan stated. "If you truly were out for blood, then you would have planted two actual mobsters instead of a couple of disposable mooks."

Lyons smirked.

Hawkins glanced at Lyons. "He's on to us?"

"Of course he is," Lyons returned. "This guy has been getting weapons out of China. He's managed to have all of these gangs and groups assemble without a major agency landing on the auction. Maybe not Jinan himself, but his people, they have some brains."

"Astute," Jinan told him. "We like men with initiative."

"And you also like to stroke us off until we like you," Lyons said.

Jinan smiled.

"What do you need us to do?"

Jinan's smile disappeared. "What do I want you to do for your audition?"

Lyons nodded.

"Simple," Jinan said. He snapped his fingers. A door at the side of the office opened and another brute came out; it was the Samoan from before. He came with Sanay, in handcuffs, her eyes red-rimmed from tears.

Jinan took out a handgun, laid it flat on its side, then swiveled the handle toward Lyons. "Kill this bitch. I'll give you a replacement."

Metal rumbled on the wood of Jinan's desk as he slid the pistol toward Lyons.

The Able Team leader looked down at the ugly hunk

of metal, then to the girl he promised to help out of this mess. His fingers closed around the handle, feeling the soft rubber tacky against his palm.

He only had moments to figure out how to get out of this without killing a woman he had placed under his personal protection. Lyons was now caught in a trap, a trip-wire decision.

Kill Sanay or die.

HERMANN SCHWARZ FELT the plane begin to alter its speed and altitude. He allowed his eyes to flutter open from the meditation he had placed himself in, looking around in a state of confusion that his captors would have expected but that he didn't feel. He wished he could have kept the boots he had packed with electronic components sandwiched in padding and between leather plies.

Unfortunately the Abalisah kidnappers were simply too on the ball. They had made note of his inventive abilities and gone over him with a fine-tooth comb. He was dressed in a set of sweats, which had replaced his normal clothing, cut off and unraveled at the seams.

Schwarz knew these men were going to find something on him, and they would go further than trying to see if he had a hollow boot heel with components stashed within. And yet, even as he "woke," he could see the contents of his boots in a clear plastic storage bag on the seat next to his.

He was not bound by his wrists, nor was he otherwise restrained, except for a seat belt over his hips.

"Good morning, Mr. Shore. Or should I say afternoon?"

Schwarz yawned. "What'd you do to my boots?"

"That is all you're going to ask?" the speaker returned.

"Well, I don't want to walk around barefoot," Schwarz answered. He reached over and picked up the electronics bits and pieces in the bag. A quick glance informed him that everything from the boots was in it. These kidnappers had been thorough. That also meant that he could not expect to build something under their noses and expect to use it to contact the Farm.

He was alone, and over a barrel. Abalisah had separated and isolated him from his Able Team and Phoenix Force brethren. As if to answer Schwarz's need for footwear, a pair of plastic, disposable shoes was set on the seat where his components had been placed.

"They're in your size," the speaker said.

Schwarz looked himself over, then grudgingly tugged the plastic slippers over his feet. "Well, you guys sure ain't the kings of fashion. Who are you?"

"I am," Schwarz thought he heard the man say.

"That's exactly what I asked."

"No. Iyam," the man told him. He spelled it out.

"Well, imagine that," Schwarz said. "We could have done an old comedy skit back and forth."

Iyam smirked. He was ruddy-skinned and the nose was unmistakably either Pakistani or Indian. Schwarz couldn't quite get the exact nationality, as Iyam's clipped, slightly British accent smothered what base language lay beneath that western veneer. Not that Schwarz could do much more in discerning the difference between the two subcontinental nations' dialects.

"You Abalisah guys could have simply given me an invitation to visit you instead of taking me down with chloroform," Schwarz told him. He flexed his feet in the hard-shelled shoes. They were a bright lime-green, which only made him feel more self-conscious about wearing them.

Iyam rested his hand on Schwarz's shoulder. "We did not intend to give you a choice."

"So that's how it's going for me?" Schwarz asked. "What about my partners?"

"They're back where Jinan can utilize their particular form of muscle and skill," Iyam told him.

Schwarz nodded.

Great, they want to hire me on as their weapons inventor, and they're going to make Carl and T.J. clean house, Schwarz thought to himself. "Who do they have to kill?"

Iyam chuckled. "You have your own situation to deal with."

The Indian sat in a seat, buckling in.

Schwarz knew the inside of a Learjet, having ridden on various incarnations as both Federal agent or undercover with a corrupt politician. This flight was only about four or five hours long, giving him an approximation of range and speed for the aircraft. By his reckoning and estimates of the comparative speed of the jet plane, they had come a significant distance. This would have put them around the Indian Ocean, as farther north would have taken them to the Arctic Circle and Alaska or Russia, and there were no significant land masses to the south.

"And my situation is to be pressed into work for Abalisah," Schwarz mused. "If I say no?"

"Why would you refuse?" Iyam asked. "After all, we will give you all the resources and money you could ever ask for."

"And a bullet in the base of my skull if I refuse," Schwarz added.

Iyam shrugged. "Get paid. Die. Is it that hard of a choice?"

Schwarz looked at his components in the bag. One thing that had not been found, fortunately, was the small transceiver implanted in the sole of his boot. Even if someone had torn every seam apart on the pair, it had been injected into the molded rubber of his soles. It was a passive transmitter, and hopefully, Lyons and Hawkins had already given word about his abduction earlier.

If not, then Schwarz was out of luck.

This is Carl we're talking about. The man thinks belt and suspenders aren't preparation enough, Schwarz told himself.

"What kind of money are we talking? And is there good pussy and prime drugs to spend it on?" Schwarz asked, beaming a wide smile.

"Just enough that you don't become useless to the Abalisah organization," Iyam answered.

Schwarz nodded. That kind of evasive answer was more telling than Iyam suspected. Herman Shore was intended to succumb to indentured servitude in a Third World weapons sweatshop. If he fried his brains, or ended up with some manner of disease, then he could be discarded for the next hot brain in line.

Schwarz looked out the portal to see an ocean view extending into the distance. Judging by the velocity of the aircraft, as well as their earlier stop around the Philippines to refuel, they were over the Indian Ocean. Twelve hours of flight, with a good tail wind, and he'd managed to ascertain that they were not on a Learjet but on a Cessna Citation X, one of the fastest midsize jets in the world at 700 miles per hour. As they reached the Philippines to refuel about half the journey back, and the familiar aircraft had only about 3200 miles of range, then their position now was bringing them farther than the Malaysian archipelago, but short of India, depending on if the airplane had extra fuel in the tanks.

The island they were coming to had its own airstrip. It wasn't long, and as they touched down, Schwarz could see another aircraft parked in one of the hangars. There were guards out in the open, wearing the same crisp, dark BDU uniforms that the Kyrgyz separatists, Moscow 88 thugs and Colombian gunmen had worn in the abandoned resort in Hawaii. These guards, however, were not marked with tattoos.

Iyam escorted Schwarz off the plane. On closer examination, he could see that these men were more along the lines of true believers, dressed crisply, their faces focused on their tasks.

This was not a hodgepodge group of guns for hire, assembled to collect paychecks. Or if they were for hire, they were professional mercenaries, not members of a glorified urban militia or rebel group. Schwarz also could see a large dish array that looked as though it easily could contact any place in the world and pick up satellite communications from around the globe.

This private army was more impressive to Schwarz than the one back at the auction.

There were also a couple of helicopters kept under camouflage netting. From their silhouettes, they were French Dauphin or some knockoff design. The netting also didn't quite obscure the winglets on the sides of the aircraft, showing missile and gun pods.

Two heavily armed gunships meant that this had to be ground zero for the Abalisah organization. It also began to make more sense to Schwarz, especially with Iyam's appearance.

Schwarz could only hope that he could figure some way to send out a message.

A guard in the Abalisah uniform came off the private jet carrying a bag of garbage. This bag was swiftly thrown into a fifty-five-gallon drum. The drum's contents were then immediately lit on fire.

Anything left in that trash, including the transmitter that Schwarz had injected into the rubber of a boot sole, would be destroyed with sufficient heat.

Schwarz could only hope the transmitter had been active long enough for the Farm to pick up his location.

If not, then he would just have to invent his own way out of this gilded cage.

CHAPTER SEVENTEEN

Carl Lyons looked at the handgun offered by Jinan, rep for the Abalisah organization, to shoot Sanay. He and fellow Stony Man warrior T. J. Hawkins were undercover to arrange enough violence to scourge these arms dealers from the face of the earth.

Schwarz had been appropriated by Abalisah and taken off the tiny Hawaiian island to an undisclosed location. Without Schwarz, Lyons was without the one man he could rely upon to turn fertilizer and a cement mixer into a blockbuster bomb, among other works of dangerous and mad brilliance.

Lyons looked at the gun. It was a big, burly Glock .45 automatic. He wrinkled his upper lip, then looked around the desk. With a surge, he grabbed the lamp and unplugged it. Ripping the cord from the base of the lamp, he then turned and walked toward Sanay.

"What are you doing?" Jinan asked.

"Are you messing with me?" Lyons asked. "A .45 on this brown little bitch's skull? Your office will be stinking for years. Brains don't come out of carpet and wood. And they reek."

He wound the ends of the electrical cord around both of his hands, pulling the wire taut. Sanay's eyes were wide, but she kept her mouth shut. The terror was real.

"Still going to make a mess," Lyons rumbled. "Should

have put down plastic if you wanted me to off this bitch…"

"Wait!" Jinan shouted.

Lyons turned back and glared at the Abalisah representative.

"What now?" Lyons snarled. "You want me to kill her…"

"I was expecting to see you aim at her…"

"And what? Pull the trigger? These things aren't worth a goddamn bullet."

Jinan grimaced. "But they're worth my lamp?"

Lyons rolled his eyes. "Oh, you're pissed about that…"

"No," Jinan said. He rose and picked up the pistol. He racked the slide, but nothing ejected from the breech. "This is empty."

"This was a test," Lyons growled.

"Yes," Jinan said. He looked at the cord in Lyons's hands. The two guards were watching Lyons, who had just put on one of the best bluffs of his life. He was ninety percent committed to strangling Sanay, at least into unconsciousness. Anything less and Jinan's two guards would have known whether Lyons was out for the kill or not.

Shooting her would have been a no-win situation. The strangling, however, could be aborted. Or it could be faked that she was rendered lifeless. Or he could have had at least a few more moments to think of some way out of this macabre trap.

"She's a fine piece anyway," Lyons said, unwinding the cord. He threw it to Jinan.

Sanay's eyes were still wide. Lyons didn't know what was going through her mind, and to tell the truth, he wouldn't have blamed her if she wanted him dead, and then gave away his whole charade.

Jinan and his twin monsters and the Samoan blob of fat and muscle would have only been the first, but if he and Hawkins somehow got past them…

"Please…please, I'm sorry," Sanay sobbed, lowering her gaze to the floor. "I won't displease you again."

Do not take this route with me, Lyons prayed inside. He still held his gaze as hard as stone and as cold as steel. But he was beginning to weaken, to feel worse for the simple knowledge that what she was saying was her in on the deception. She was still helping, still letting him know that he was dictating the rules for this deadly charade. If Jinan were to decide to execute them, she would go down as a coconspirator.

She was loyal to Lyons.

"Keep your damn mouth shut," Lyons snapped, maintaining the charade.

She glanced up at him, then looked swiftly away.

Lyons swallowed hard and turned back to Jinan. "Are we done with you screwing with me? Because if not…"

"No, you don't have to prove anything else to me," Jinan said.

"So you're done with us?" Lyons asked.

"Yes," Jinan said. "Get something to eat or rest or something. Then I'll discuss what I need for you to do later. At dinner."

"Dinner," Lyons repeated.

"Yes," Jinan confirmed. "Go with them, girl."

Sanay nodded, following Lyons and Hawkins.

The trio immediately went outside. A quick glance at their Combat PDAs ensured there were no surveillance devices in the immediate vicinity. They continued on until they were clearly out of sight and earshot of the resort.

Lyons touched Sanay's chin gingerly. "Are you okay?"

Sanay looked up, hair falling across her face. Her cheeks were wet with tears and just the small bit of contact with her conveyed the tremors of terror she suffered from. "I know it was an act... I know now..."

Lyons rested a hand gently on each of her shoulders, meeting her frightened, bloodshot gaze with his own. "I didn't know if the gun really was loaded... I couldn't risk shooting at you."

Sanay nodded. "Would you...have ended it?"

Lyons wrapped his arms around her, letting her rest her cheek against his chest. "I'd have tried to figure something out. I'd have maybe put you to sleep... proven something, faked strangling you all the way..."

"We need to wrap this up." Hawkins spoke up. Lyons could hear the reluctance in his partner's voice. "They're going to wonder where we went, what we're doing."

"Ease up. I'm getting the stuff we set up for Shore," Lyons growled, slipping back into character.

BARBARA PRICE FROWNED. They had been tracking the private plane from Hawaii. It was moving quickly, about 700 miles per hour, and it had taken off just a little before midnight in Hawaii. Unfortunately, twelve hours later, the airplane had activated a counter tracking device, or it had found a pocket in satellite and radar coverage. Whatever the means of disappearance, they had at least a range of disappearance.

The aircraft had landed in the Philippines, a scheduled stopover for refueling that had gone quickly at Luzon. Kurtzman had hacked into the airport's records and found out that the airplane had listed itself as a Cessna Citation, but its fuel intake was 2500 gallons, not the standard 1900 or so, which extended the range of the aircraft.

"About 8300 miles, more or less," Price murmured. "Do you have anything on the map at those ranges?"

Kurtzman pulled up a map. "I'm doing calculations, especially based upon the tail wind the plane received over the Pacific and their course when they disappeared."

"And you've got fuel range and calculations off that sudden turn?" Price asked.

Kurtzman nodded. "The range of the upgraded plane will let them land anywhere around Sri Lanka, as they've been taking care to avoid Chinese airspace."

Price nodded. "Phoenix's new captive is from that area. He was in control of the transfer, and he told the captives that he would be bringing them to his home."

"That also ties in with the ship that was moored out to sea, which would have picked up the helicopter that Blancanales and company shot at," Kurtzman added. "Still, we're looking at a huge area."

"Twenty-five thousand square miles, and that's not counting offshore properties," Price said. She frowned. "If Gadgets could have gotten us a better signal…"

"Give him some time," Kurtzman said. "Given what we know about the distance traveled, he's only been on the ground for about an hour. They're likely still processing him. I know the files we have made for Herman Shore's background were just accessed forty-five minutes ago."

Price nodded. "They did go looking through his record, and lined up his fingerprints. Hopefully the ink he's wearing matches well with the sets we put in."

"We omitted some of the fresher-appearing tattoos," Kurtzman said. "If things lined up too perfectly, the enemy would think something was up."

Price hated waiting for one of her men while they were out of contact. However, one of the reasons the eight warriors of the Stony Man Farm action teams had been chosen was their ability to adapt and survive. Hermann Schwarz was an especially resourceful and adaptive operative.

If anyone could get a message out of deep within enemy territory, it would be him.

And if he couldn't…

Barbara Price fought the urge to think more along those lines.

DR. ROBERT BAXTER squinted as the door opened and a heavily tattooed man entered. The flare of light into the formerly darkened room was a blast of pain, and the sight of the newcomer, complete with the Nazi symbolism scrawled on his skin, made things only more uncomfortable for Baxter.

May Ling Fu, his fellow captive, sitting in for the long-missing Bea Chandler, cleared her throat as their vision once again had to adapt as the door closed behind him. This new guy was clad in a set of sweatpants, a short-sleeved shirt and lime-green plastic shoes, an assembled fashion that was a train wreck no matter how you looked at it. The guy—a biker? Baxter asked himself—didn't look comfortable and glanced at the door closed behind him.

"Who are yo—?" Baxter asked.

"You think this freak speaks English?" Ling Fu cut him off.

The biker looked at her, then folded his arms.

"That is a hell of a way to greet someone," the man said. "I'm another prisoner here."

Ling Fu narrowed her eyes, looking him over. "With all of that ink, you should be used to it. Where were you? Lompoc?"

"I don't need to answer you."

"Wait!" Baxter said. He stepped between the two, holding his hands up to put the brakes on in case one or the other charged. Baxter looked at the arms sticking out of the sleeves of the T-shirt on the biker. They were powerful-looking, though not toned and cut. The ink, however, was indicative of how much bad news this newcomer could be. "We're all stuck in this together. We don't need to be at each others' throats."

"I'm just in here for a little bit," the new man stated. "They have to do a little more checking on my background. Then I can leave you two to whatever you want."

"I'm Robert Baxter," the rocket scientist offered. He held out his hand to the biker.

"Herman Shore," Schwarz answered. He took the captive's hand. Even if they had not been briefed over the disappearance of Robert Baxter and Beatrice Chandler from the Naval Weapons Testing Center, Schwarz would have recognized this man. He was one of the premier propulsion specialists in the Department of Defense, and an inventive genius who managed to produce a compact engine capable of Mach 10 velocity without having to rely upon a ballistic-missile-size launch vehicle.

Ling Fu said, "He's a Reich Low Rider."

Schwarz turned, faking an angry glare for the Chinese American woman.

May Ling Fu was not a stranger to Schwarz. She was a coworker with another brilliant computer expert who had long ago been on Stony Man Farm's elite roster, Lao Ti. In his many visits to Lao Ti, Schwarz had gotten to know Ling Fu, and the woman recognized him.

As Ling Fu was part of the high-security company Lao Ti founded, and was a trusted subcontractor of the Sensitive Operations Group, the missing woman was aware that Schwarz was likely here in an undercover status. Her hostility was just a means of keeping Schwarz's cover. This was a small favor, especially since it would continue to give Schwarz the time necessary to devise a means of escape.

"Reich," Baxter repeated. He looked over at Schwarz.

"Considering we're wearing the same crappy clothes as each other, I think I can tolerate your presence," Schwarz said. "But keep that little yappy dog on her leash."

"I'll show you yappy dog," Ling Fu snarled as Baxter crossed to her.

Schwarz didn't think the scientist could put up much of a fight. He was too light of build, and his stance was all wrong, but his courage was admirable and unmistakable. Even if he wasn't of great value to the defense of the United States, Schwarz would not hesitate to keep the young man safe from harm.

All of that would count upon Schwarz's getting a

weapon and communicating with the Farm. Any hopes of being traced right now were up in smoke in a barrel fire. Schwarz didn't know how to fly a helicopter and he was aware that May Ling Fu was not a pilot, either. He wasn't certain about Robert Baxter's aviation skills, but he didn't care to risk the man's life behind the stick of a Dauphin or even one of the jets.

Schwarz took a seat on the far side of the cell from Baxter and Ling Fu. He was aware that Chandler was not present, which left him in a lurch. How would he even know about her existence, let alone ask about her? One mistake—and this cell was undoubtedly bugged—and Schwarz could kiss his cover identity goodbye. They wouldn't trust him for an instant, if they even did at this moment.

"Did you see another woman out there?" Baxter asked. "While you were being brought to this detention…possibly another captive?"

Schwarz turned to the scientist. "I can't say that I have. She your girlfriend?"

Baxter looked as if he'd just been put on the spot, made uncomfortable.

"They were taken from the same facility," Ling Fu said. She still had a strong note of hostility in her voice, but she was helping him get his bearings here. "Goes by the name Bea. She's got long brown hair, got a desert tan…"

Schwarz shook his head. "And Baxter's girl."

"Listen, I'm just worried about her," Baxter answered.

"I'm not giving you any shit," Schwarz countered. "The way you froze up when I asked you if there was something between the two of you…"

"If you do find her, I'll be so grateful," Baxter said. Schwarz nodded. "No problem."

"And what do you get out of this?" Ling Fu asked.

Schwarz locked eyes with her. "I get this guy grateful to me, he might work for my new bosses a little easier. A little more leeway and benefits for my ass. I wouldn't mind getting you less pissed off, either…"

Ling Fu narrowed her eyes. "Really?"

"You ain't hard on the eyes. Just sayin'," Schwarz told her. That wasn't a lie, and the truth was, in his visits to Lao Ti's firm, he and May had dated quite a bit, developing an off-and-on relationship that was along the lines of friends with benefits. There was an attraction, but it could only be part-time, simply because of the nature of Ling Fu's anti-PRC activism and her scientific career and Schwarz's own responsibilities to Able Team and Stony Man Farm.

The door opened. "Shore!"

Schwarz stood, regarding the newcomer. It was one of the professional gunmen, and he didn't seem particularly hostile. He waved Schwarz to the door and the Able Team pro looked back into the room.

"Smell you assholes later." Schwarz tossed the words back in way of seeming dismissive. The guard chuckled as he closed the door firmly, locking it.

"So there're some more willing lady folk on this base?" Schwarz asked the gunman.

The guard took a belt off a nearby hook and handed it to the undercover Stony Man. "We got some chicks… but you got one in mind?"

"Nerd in there asked about the chick he came in with," Schwarz said. "Knowing those geeks, she might have six chins…"

"Nah. The Chandler girl's pretty good-looking," the guard said.

Schwarz noticed that his Beretta was in the gun belt, complete with a pair of spare magazines, as well as a few of his tools. He put it around his hips, feeling a little better.

"I thought you bikers didn't like foreign-made guns," the guard said.

Schwarz tipped the Beretta slightly out of its sheath and tapped the slide. "Made in the U.S.A."

The guard nodded. "Makes sense."

"Damn straight," Schwarz answered, tucking the pistol back into its holster and keeping it secure. "Where are we headed?"

"To get you some decent clothes that don't make you look like a New Jersey landlord," the Abalisah trooper said. "I'm Beck."

"You know I'm Shore...but you can call me Gizmo," Schwarz answered.

"Yeah," Beck stated. "We got a look at your Taser. That's some nasty shit."

Schwarz smirked. "Thanks."

Beck had his blond hair trimmed to peach fuzz, the mark of a professional who didn't want an enemy to get a good grip on his head. Of course, Schwarz knew that yanking on an asshole's ear was a better handle in hand-to-hand combat. Either you ripped the ear right off the side of the guy's skull or you got him in a pretty good come-along. Of course, reaching for that ear would extend you and allow your target to trap your hand and wrist, giving him the leverage to snap your arm.

Hand-to-hand combat was a game of mental chess,

and there was always some part of Schwarz's brain
going over the options. Even now, Schwarz assessed
the pros and cons of his situation. He was glad to have
his sidearm back, as well as the multitool in its scab-
bard. He also had a plastic storage bag full of electronic components. However, there also seemed to be
plenty of surveillance on hand, and there were dozens
of men like Beck, savvy and professional gunmen who,
with their superior numbers, could overwhelm even a
combat monster like Carl Lyons or David McCarter.
Abalisah either figured it could trust Schwarz, or it
could keep him contained. Schwarz intended to bide
his time, make more observations of the area. There
was one motto by which the Able Team genius lived by.

Knowledge Is Power.

It was time to charge up.

CHAPTER EIGHTEEN

Phoenix Force and Rosario Blancanales were in the air, following the last hints from the Chinese technicians they'd rescued in Hong Kong, and their captive, the tall bruiser whom they'd discovered was named Kotte.

Blancanales had led the way in figuring out who the Abalisah henchman was, getting fingerprints, as well as photographs and the beginnings of information simply from observations of the unconscious man, his appearance, his clothing labels and the contents of his pockets. It turned out that Kotte was on the payroll of yet another separatist group, this time for the Tamil in Sri Lanka. Blancanales remembered his mission to that island. There was no small irony noted by Blancanales over the fact that the Tech War he'd battled then had involved stolen weapons, also up for bid.

This time, however, Blancanales knew that he wouldn't have Carl "Ironman" Lyons at his back, and that if they were going to pinpoint the enemy, they would have to do it by clinging to the same shadows as they'd had in Hong Kong.

Whereas the Stony Man commandos had been on Chinese territory without authorization, but ultimately working for the best interests of the People's Republic as well as the United States, going into Sri Lanka was entering a realm where civil war left fresh, raw scars.

Separatist groups were savage, but the government was no less brutal in cracking down on its opposition forces.

Then again, the last time Able Team hit Sri Lanka, crooked government officials released Tamil separatists en masse, armed with machetes and photographs of Blancanales and his brethren in arms. When Able Team was found in a public bazaar, it was everything they could do to contain the army of blade-swinging maniacs and prevent countless bystanders from being injured.

Nowadays Sri Lanka's government was still under the scrutiny and criticism of multiple Western governments, including the United States, as well as Amnesty International and other global human rights agencies. Stony Man's arrival on Sri Lankan territory could be met with official hostility or more subtle betrayal. When Phoenix Force arrived, it would have to be low profile.

One thing Blancanales was glad for was the presence of four-fifths of Phoenix Force. He would have preferred Lyons at his side. If anyone was at home surrounded by hostiles, it was the big, brawny ex-LAPD cop. It wasn't so much that Lyons liked a target-rich environment, it was more that he felt better cutting loose with Able Team's phenomenal firepower without fear of gunning down innocents or cops or soldiers who were simply doing their jobs.

Abalisah, however, in its dealings from the southwestern United States to China, showed that they had a considerable reach, especially hiring on gunmen and other thugs from as far away as Moscow and Central Asia.

Kotte was not a government operative, Stony Man's

cybernetics team determined, but that didn't mean Abalisah didn't have law enforcement in their pocket. Again, the high-tech thieves once looking to knock Able Team off their trail had gotten police flunkies to release dozens of Tamil mass murderers. In that instance, it had been Lyons's fully automatic custom assault shotgun that had broken the back of the horde of blade-armed killers.

Blancanales pulled down his Pelican case with his M-4/M-203 assault rifle and grenade launcher combination to double-check it.

"You all right to go?" David McCarter, Phoenix Force's field commander, asked him.

"Yes," Blancanales answered, smooth and calm, despite the fact that he was double-checking the springs on his rifle's magazines.

"The Farm is putting every satellite resource they have into locating Gadgets," McCarter added.

"I know," Blancanales replied. "And I know the four of you can punch your way out of a paper bag."

"So, you still look a little tense," McCarter said, resting his hand on Blancanales's shoulder. "Uptight."

Blancanales nodded, taking a deep breath. "Sri Lanka can be a pure shit hole. Sure, there are clean spots for the tourists to come by, but we've been deep inside the bowels of the country."

"That was a while back," McCarter countered. "Not that we're going to be taking this lightly."

Blancanales shook his head. "I'm not implying you guys are. But you have your way of doing things…and we have ours."

"And by 'ours,' you mean 'yours,'" McCarter returned.

Blancanales let out a long exhalation. "I'm feeling by myself, when I don't have a right to. I've got one brother surrounded by bastards in Hawaii. I've got another, likely on the island of Sri Lanka who's surrounded by other bastards. I want to tear myself in half and help 'em both."

"And I'm worried about T.J.," McCarter said. "But you've got a stubborn Texan and that LAPD Viking working shoulder to shoulder. So far, things are going all right for them. They haven't been discovered, even if they have been separated from Gadgets."

Blancanales managed a smile for his compatriot.

"We're bringing him back. No one is going to make a mistake when we go after Abalisah on their home ground," McCarter promised. "This isn't the first time we've grabbed one of you out of a tight spot. And you've done the same for us."

Blancanales clasped hands with McCarter, a show of solidarity. He turned back to checking the ammo in his magazines.

McCarter returned to the work he had been doing on the flight in. He had numbers to call for contacts in the region himself, and he had terrain issues to put together. Manning was double-checking his pack of explosive devices. James ensured that his medical supplies were in order.

The Stony Man warriors had their mission ahead of them, and luck willing, they would find Schwarz and the missing scientists.

And if not, then the unspoken promise would be a swath of bloody vengeance against the many devils.

Either way, they intended to increase the population of hell by a considerable amount.

Carl Lyons, T. J. Hawkins and Sanay returned to Hermann Schwarz's abandoned hotel room. It was the only one with a solid door, and one where they were certain Schwarz had set up a kill switch for whatever surveillance was on hand. Lyons bore a bag full of gear that Schwarz had assembled for his flank, maneuver and kill operation while on the premises of the resort among the other bidders at the auction. He also did not want to trust anything was in the hands of Jinan's men.

At least until he had the opportunity to field strip and examine his surrendered sidearms. As Schwarz's gear bag had not been disturbed, Lyons took the firearms from within, including a spare Taurus Judge complete with Schwarz's tricked-out .410 shells, five in the cylinder and ten more to spare.

"You want this?" Lyons asked.

Hawkins shook his head. "I'll take his Beretta."

Lyons handed the spare handgun over. He looked around and was surprised to note that Schwarz had his other M-9 with him, meaning that when he'd been abducted, they'd taken the genius's personal gear along with him. Schwarz's pistol had not been left in the room when they'd scoured through, looking for clues and details of the disappearance.

Lyons took a quick moment to send a text to the Farm. It wasn't much, but if Schwarz still had his sidearm with him, then there was a means of locating him outside of the components in his boots.

Activate base plate transponders.

Schwarz had devised a series of miniature transponders to be implanted in the rubber base plates of his

Beretta's magazines. Utilizing the length of the magazine springs as an improvised antenna, each transponder could transmit for miles and miles. Of course, they needed to be activated by a pulse signal, but it was a general transmission on the part of the Farm. Once activated, however, the cyber team could home in on Schwarz thanks to the presence of his favorite sidearm.

That is, Lyons figured, if Abalisah had stopped stripping down and examining Schwarz's belongings when they'd discovered the hidden gear in his clothing. They might not have looked at Schwarz's personal weapons. Even then, it was unlikely his pistol's magazines would have been stripped down.

However, there was always that bit of luck. Someone might have thought to look into the removable grips of a Beretta service pistol, check the ammunition, but not take apart magazines. If Schwarz was lucky...

"Carl," Hawkins spoke up, breaking Lyons from his reverie.

Hawkins had his Beretta up and ready. Lyons picked up his shot-shell pistol, rising as he saw the shadows of feet through the crack beneath the door. No one had knocked yet, but there was a definite presence out there.

Lyons shot a glance toward Sanay, motioning for her to seek cover behind the bed.

"Mr. Long? Would you come out for a moment?"

It was a Russian-accented voice and Lyons half rose, his muscles taut, his finger off the revolver's trigger. Hawkins barricaded himself behind the bed with Sanay, but he was up with his handgun held in both hands and at arms at full extension.

Lyons opened the door, keeping himself clear of

both Hawkins's line of fire and out of the door frame so he wouldn't catch a bullet from either direction. "What do you want?"

He had his Colt Python tucked behind him, out of sight, but ready to go in a mere shrug.

"Jinan has a demonstration of the big showcase item," the Russian said. Lyons didn't see any tattoos that showed that he might have been with Moscow 88, nor did he have the hand ink of a Russian mobster. He was big, grizzled and professional. Lyons could place him as a military professional, as he stood with the same precautions Lyons had in regard to the fatal funnel of a doorway. "It will be ready in fifteen minutes."

"All right," Lyons said. "He wants us to watch this with him?"

The soldier at the door nodded. "Get your gear together. I'm leaving a case in the hall for your presents. Make certain to wear the shirts."

Lyons glanced down, seeing both a standard duffel and a hard case meant for long arms.

"Welcome to Abalisah," the Russian told him.

He then walked off.

Lyons bent, scooped up both bags and tossed them onto the bed after closing the door.

Hawkins immediately undertook an inspection of the sidearms.

"Anything?" Lyons asked, pulling out two dark uniform shirts. They were each sized for Lyons and Hawkins. The Able Team leader took one of Schwarz's detector wands and ran it over the clothing, and the rifle case. They were clean.

"Think we might be too paranoid?" Hawkins asked, putting his lightweight Magnums back together. He took one last glance at the lock work and slide of his disassembled SW-1911 and returned it to working order.

Lyons ran the wand over the offered BDU cargo pants and found them clean. "Change into your new uniform."

Sanay looked down at the five-shot revolver Hawkins offered her.

"You know how to use one?" Hawkins asked.

She nodded. "Will it hurt? It feels so light."

"I loaded regular .38s into that one. With the grips, you'll be fine and cushioned," Hawkins said. He also offered her a couple of rubber strips with handgun cartridges poking out of them. "This will keep you from dropping ammunition everywhere when you reload. Stick the bullet in the charging hole and pop the strip off its bottom."

Sanay indicated she understood the procedure. She took a deep breath. Being armed, she seemed a little more relaxed. Hawkins and Lyons continued dressing as she watched. Lyons put Hawkins's rifle on the bed in front of him.

"AK-12 for me. I take it you want the Benelli shotgun," Hawkins said.

Lyons's response was a smirk. "Actually, there's one of each, but you never struck me as the shotgun guy on your team."

"I never knew it was an option. And Gary usually takes one for himself," Hawkins mused. "Nah, I'll go with something with range."

He shrugged into his load-bearing vest with its pouches holding six spare magazines for the AK-12 rifle. It was in 5.45 mm Russian, just like the one Yuri had.

"What do you make of the delivery man? Spetsnaz?" Hawkins asked.

"Yes," Lyons answered. "And he's someone who has been with this group long before Moscow 88 was hired on for security."

"Grigori and his boys don't handle doors like that," Hawkins said to Sanay as an aside. "He was behind cover, putting a solid wall between himself and any violence Carl would have opened up with."

Lyons did a check on the rifle and shotgun that he had not checked. A quick disassemble and he was relieved to see the firing pins were in place on both weapons and neither appeared damaged. He nodded for Hawkins to take the one he'd inspected while he transferred ammunition to the second shotgun.

"Check out a Caracal for Sanay, too," Lyons ordered. "She can use something that doesn't need reloading every five shots."

"How many does this have?" the island woman asked.

"Eighteen in the magazine, one in the spout," Lyons returned. "There's no safety catch and the trigger is light, crisp and easy. No finger inside the trigger guard until it's time to put a bullet in someone."

Sanay nodded.

Hawkins proclaimed the Caracal pistol ready for business.

"Where should I be?" Sanay asked.

Lyons took a knife to a set of uniform pants that had been given to them, turning them into shorts, but giving her pockets.

"Out of sight," Lyons said. "Go to where we got Herman's bag. Don't shoot us, but if anyone else comes by, you hammer them."

Sanay looked a little frightened, even as she slipped into the cutoffs. She cinched the waistband tight with a small belt. Another web belt, slightly larger, hung at a jaunty cant, but held a holster, spare magazines and a small device with which Lyons and Hawkins could communicate with her. She was loaded and ready for anything that might come her way, but also kept in touch so that she wouldn't accidentally shoot someone who wasn't an enemy.

Lyons made certain the earbud and microphone were secured over her ear. There was a moment to test the com, and then it was time for them to get to Jinan's side.

And even as he left her, watching her head to the safety of Schwarz's old cache, he hoped that she was still on his side.

THE RESORT HEARD the sudden, thunderous roar even as Lyons and Hawkins left their hotel room. A scar formed from pillowy clouds of rocket exhaust stretched across the crystal-blue skies over the island, and the direction was unmistakable. It was flying west, and it was moving at an impossible speed.

Lyons and Hawkins paused, looking at each other.

"There's no way they should have a missile moving that fast. Not with just having taken Baxter or hitting the testing ground," Lyons said.

"Yeah, that's a hard thing to grasp, but that's flying west. Toward Asia," Hawkins said. He had his Combat PDA out and was rapidly texting and hitting Send. The Texan's thumbs flew and he had the device pocketed again. Around the resort, all eyes were locked on the spear that carved its path through the air.

"Part of the specs on the missiles these guys promised was a top speed of Mach 10. Which means, depending on its course, it'll get there in forty, fifty minutes," Lyons said.

"Victoria Harbour, forty-four minutes," Hawkins said.

"Fast math," Lyons said.

"Gary and Gadgets ain't the only ones quick with numbers," Hawkins returned.

"Are we sure that it'd be sent toward Hong Kong?" Lyons asked, picking up the pace to get to their summons by Jinan.

"The guys reported that they ran into a helicopter sent to pick up the scientists," Hawkins returned. "Not quite certain where the helicopter was going, but it must have been to a ship."

Lyons nodded. "That better be the case, because if it's a Chinese naval craft and they somehow track the missile from here in Hawaii, that's an act of war."

Hawkins paused. "The helicopter retreated to their ship. What if that's also where they intend to film the test?"

"So it could be something else struck," Lyons said.

"We've got five minutes to join Jinan for the show," Hawkins said. "And another thirty-eight to see if it hits Victoria Harbour."

Lyons and Hawkins jogged along faster.

Sure enough, when the two Stony Man commandos got to the ballroom, things were in the last stages of setup on stage.

Then, it was a case of hurry up and wait. The screen

behind Jinan had a small display of Victoria Harbour on live video. Lyons and Hawkins were informed to simply stand guard, along with several others who both undercover men recognized as former bidders now hired on to join this ever-growing group.

Jinan spoke, at length, about rocket propulsion and weapons systems, talking about antishipping missiles. All the time that Jinan went on, at length, he made the auction seem more like a motivational-seminar speech.

Lyons counted down the time to the missile reaching its target. He kept his hands crossed in front of him, the Benelli M-4 shotgun slung over one shoulder, cruiser loaded with a full 7 + 1. There was an extra shell "ghost loaded" into the gun, giving him nine rounds of on-hand 12-gauge mayhem. And, considering that these were 00 buckshot, each pull of the trigger would put out nine .32-caliber projectiles in a tight fist of flying death, essentially a third of a magazine from an Uzi or a MP-5.

With nine pulls of the trigger, he could unleash three full magazines worth of auto-fire, eighty-one projectiles in all. It wasn't his old beloved Konzak combat shotgun, the original Atchisson AA-12, which had been retooled by original Stony Man armorer Andrzej Konzaki, but the Benelli would still cut a swath of gore and devastation when called upon.

All thoughts of gore and devastation vanished from Lyons's mind, however, when Jinan's tone perked up.

"And now, gentlemen, I present the star of this auction—the vulgar display of power known as the Mach Ten Feng!"

The graphics faded away, the small inset of the live video growing in size and focusing on an ever-growing dot of white in the sky. Lyons gritted his teeth, watching as the dot stretched, showing that it was the white plume of exhaust and water vapor trailing behind a distant missile. The camera shook and shuddered, but that was merely vibration picked up via extreme zoom.

Lyons knew the behavior of video cameras, thanks to his association with Hermann Schwarz.

The zoom pulled back and the missile trail disappeared to the size of a speck.

"Don't blink or you'll miss the whole show," Jinan said, his voice deep, like a psychotic game-show host.

The actual missile's path was a mere blur as suddenly a freighter in the harbor took the bolt from the blue and cracked in two. The roar and screech of distant, tortured metal rolled quickly to the microphone, but that was soon drowned out by the sonic boom of a projectile going ten times the speed of sound arrived in the harbor. The ensuing shock wave of the sonic boom created a growing dish of water, air pressure slamming into the surface of the bay, waves pushed along on the back of it.

Small crafts were tossed by the wave from the thunderclap, overturned and swamped as inhabitants found themselves splashing and swimming for their lives. The wave front struck the ship that was filming, and the camera lurched violently.

The freighter in the middle, laden with containers, was snapped into two by the impact of the missile. A central bubble of fire spewed steam and light into the sky as the halves of the broken ship bobbed, the bow and aft clanging against each other before wheeling apart.

Secondary explosions erupted beneath the surface, smothering the blazing-hot ember at the center.

On the stage, bracketing Jinan, Lyons was close enough to the high-definition big screen to see sailors hurled into the air, their bodies twisted at unnatural angles, some of them having lost limbs by the subsurface detonations.

"Unfortunately, we didn't have a military-style target at this moment, so the submunitions that would have penetrated a major warship or escort craft perforated the hull, exploding in a random manner," Jinan said. "However, I believe the display of these explosions should satisfy your curiosity about the potential yield of damage capable of the Feng."

Hands shot up, questions coming from the crowd of buyers, even as Lyons watched men and women dying in Victoria Harbour, a tragedy whose sound track was the voice of the long-haired "businessman" hyping the murderous effects like a proud father.

Lyons turned from the screen and looked at Jinan, realizing that it was long past time to start reaping Abalisah minions by the boatload.

CHAPTER NINETEEN

This was the part that Barbara Price hated. Even though T. J. Hawkins had informed the Farm about the launch, even though the United States had rushed through back channels to relay the intelligence that a high-speed weapon had been fired toward their area, there was nothing the People's Republic of China could do to prepare for the impact. No one had a clue as to what the actual target of the missile would be, only that it had been fired by a third party and within the territorial waters of Hawaii.

"...the death toll in Victoria Harbour has reached nearly two hundred so far, but there are still over three thousand people missing," the BBC announcer said, her voice clipped, tense, concerned.

"Mach 10," Kurtzman said. "There was very little time to provide warning."

"Forty minutes to be exact," Price added. "Forty minutes, which didn't give the ships in Victoria Harbour time to move."

"Satellite observation of the missile impact showed dozens of submunitions penetrated out of the freighter's hull and into the surrounding waters," Hunt Wethers noted.

"They fired on an international freighter," Carmen Delahunt mentioned. "Not a Chinese national craft, but with Liberian registry."

"Making it one of ours," Price translated. "Something that keeps this from becoming an act of war by the United States of America and the red Chinese."

Her voice showed signs of a crack. Two hundred dead, and rising. It wasn't simply the freighter that had been destroyed, split in two by the initial, armor-shredding detonation, but other crafts, smaller ships being piloted to and fro. Looking at the replay of the missile strike on satellite, she could see one Hong Kong fishing boat literally disintegrate when a submunition came into contact with it.

Even with the replay of the missile attack slowed to one hundredth of normal time, the incoming missile was swift. Measuring its progress proved that the Naval Weapon Testing Ground's estimates of Mach 10 were on target. It came in at 7700 miles per hour. It didn't have to do anything other than touch the deck of the freighter to burst into the depths of the ship as if it were a soap bubble.

The blaze in the water, the shining sun of super-heated flame that burned, even beneath the surface, told Price that it was a rather conventional armor-piercing warhead, if wrought on a grand scale. Measurements from the cyber team informed her that it was 200 pounds of liquid copper, more than enough to tear through the deck or hull of an aircraft carrier, punching a hole the size of a basketball through heavy armor meant to absorb cannon and missile fire.

Two hundred people dead? Barbara asked mentally. Anyone on board the freighter was crushed if not incinerated by the copper jet.

The death toll would keep rising, as infrared cameras noted warm bodies rapidly cooling in the waters of the harbor. Some were floating, while others disappeared below the waves, hidden from the surface forever.

"Do we have software recording where those bodies are going down?" Price asked.

"We do. That information will go to recovery divers," Kurtzman told her. "Families will have something to bury, to say goodbye."

Price nodded. It wouldn't be saving their lives, the reason why they had broken radio and intelligence silence by contacting Hong Kong, but it would do something for the spirits of murdered families. There were hundreds of pinpoints where the Stony Man computers registered dying, fading heat sources from orbit. Some of them were classified as submunitions or the central blob of superheated copper that chilled and hardened. The copper kept the temperatures of the harbor high enough that people swimming within a hundred yards of it would suffer health problems caused by subboiling waters. A minute ago, it would have been outright lethal to be in that vicinity.

Hal Brognola, the director of the Sensitive Operations Group, contacted Price on her tablet. She brought him up on the video chat.

"Any word on our people?" Brognola asked.

"Phoenix is almost to Sri Lanka. We have our satellites over the island, and they've narrowed the search parameters for Gadgets," Price stated.

"Any more news from Carl and T.J.?"

Price shook her head. "Just that they were promoted from bidders to new muscle for Abalisah."

"Their mistake," Brognola stated. "Abalisah's, I mean."

"I know," Price answered.

"You look like hell. How much sleep have you gotten?" the head Fed asked her.

Price shrugged. "Enough that my head is clear. How're things at the White House?"

"The President is talking with Beijing," Brognola said. "Things are tense, but he's being diplomatic."

"We're keeping up to date on what the regular news says," Price returned. "Popular opinion in the United States is all about a blond girl gone missing in Mexico."

"Not even showing up on the radar?" Brognola asked.

Price shook her head. "Some of the fringe groups are making noise, but the death of a few hundred people in Hong Kong, even with such a spectacular explosion, isn't making much of a dent in the latest celebrity marriage or pretty-white-chick disappearance."

"Just when my faith in humanity was feeling a little better," Brognola mumbled. "What about Chinese military and police response?"

"Rescue units are in full force. They're busy dealing with the recovered scientists from their own testing grounds, as well," Price said. "No mention made of our boys, just a group of masked, faceless ninjas who struck like a storm."

"That's poetic," Brognola mused.

"The techs were quite grateful," Price stated.

"What's the situation in Sri Lanka?"

"Team is safe on ground in Colombo. They're driving to the facility where Gadgets is being held. Right now, their mission is just to watch," Price told him. "We're waiting for nightfall to give them cover, and for them to get some more high-definition maps of the grounds so they know how to make their approaches."

Brognola nodded. "Have you contacted Gadgets?"

"Not yet, but we're trying," Price said. "He might have a hint that things are all right, because he's taking a tour of the facility. His abductors have left him with his personal sidearm, which has small transceivers in the magazine base pads."

"So, he knows we'll be looking for him," Brognola said. "And he's drawing an outline?"

"More like a detailed plan," Price returned.

Brognola nodded. "Sounds like him."

"We're feeding David and the boys as soon as we get anything," Price added.

"Let me know so the President can give word to the Chinese PM that this mess is resolved," Brognola requested.

"As soon as things happen, we'll let you know."

Brognola signed off and Price set down the tablet, watching the screen.

"Just as soon as we get our own info," she added. "Come on, guys. Work some magic and put these bastards away!"

BEATRICE CHANDLER SAT overlooking the workshop where men were putting together the propulsion drives, but she looked at her tablet, watching the video display of destruction in Victoria Harbour. The missile strike on the freighter—an American ship shot at from American waters—was a resounding success and a display of exactly how much power Robert Baxter's design could bring to bear. She smiled, feeling vindicated by the test's outcome. But that was merely a small part of the experiment.

"What's the information on the alteration of water

temperature so far?" Chandler asked one of her assistants.

"Nothing yet, but if the proper amount of harbor water were converted to steam, we should be getting the humidity rise we were looking for," the man said. "Oh, by the way, the new brain, sent over by Jinan, is coming in."

Chandler looked up from her tablet. "Right. Herman Shore. He was the tweaker sent from Hawaii."

The man nodded. "He may tweak, but the man knows how to improvise devices. He turned a television into a laser capable of burning through walls, and turned his radio into an electrical emission device."

"A Taser?" Chandler asked. "Anyone can use the wires for that…"

"No. This actually projects an arc of electricity five feet," the assistant told her. "There, he's coming in now."

Chandler looked down at the man. He was clean for a biker, at least in terms of hair and dress, though, much of that came from being issued a uniform by the Abalisah staff. Still, his hair was not greasy, and his gear belt, while well worn, was not ratty. Indeed, he seemed to take good care of his tools and sidearm.

"You made certain to go through his equipment, scanning for tracers and other devices, correct?" Chandler asked.

The man nodded. "We went through everything. Shore is actually pretty good. He sandwiched electronic components between layers of leather in his boots."

Chandler went to his records on her tablet device.

"You're the boss, eh?" the newcomer asked as he was brought to her.

"Yeah," Chandler answered. "You seem surprised."

Schwarz looked around. "Nah. Kind of would have needed to be an inside job if they were going to start auctioning off missiles. What kind of production are you going to need from us?"

"'Us'?" Chandler repeated.

"You didn't hire me for my good looks and enormous dick," Schwarz answered, falling into the role of filthy biker. "You'll be wanting me to be out there, making engines for you."

Chandler shook her head. "You're quality control."

Now it was Schwarz's turn to repeat what was said. "'Quality control'?"

"If quality isn't good enough, you control the process by removing the snag," Chandler said. "This is a high-tech sweatshop, and sometimes, we're going to need a bullet in the head."

"And you wanted someone with the technical know-how who could see flaws and errors," Schwarz concluded. He nodded in appreciation of the idea, all the while realizing that he was going to have to give some very bad news to Robert Baxter.

"Right. Listen, I know you have a skill and knack for improvisation, but I don't quite trust your stability," Chandler said. "Tweakers tend to have jittery fingers and some of these components..."

Schwarz raised his hand. "Say no more. I'd get bored chained to a table riding a screwdriver. Especially without a hit of crank to smooth things over. When should I start?"

"We have things ready for now," Chandler told him. "How good are you at math?"

"How many places of pi do you want me to recite?" Schwarz asked.

"I was wondering if you could give me a double-check on some of my figures," Chandler said. "We introduced two hundred pounds of molten copper to Victoria Harbour, and I was wondering about the volume of steam given off."

"Two hundred pounds?" Schwarz asked.

She handed him a notebook and he looked at the equations she'd used.

"Do you have a chalk- or whiteboard handy?" Schwarz asked. She pointed the way for him, but even as he walked, looking over her initial calculations, he could see what she was attempting to put together. She was running the numbers to see if the introduction of superheated metal to a body of water could produce sufficient energy and humidity into the atmosphere to actually have an effect on the weather of Hong Kong.

The scientific theory was not exactly in Schwarz's field, but mathematics was mathematics, and he was aware of enough of the simple chemistry and physics involved that three-quarters of the walk to the chalkboard informed him her suppositions were accurate. The change to Victoria Harbour's average temperature and the infusion of steam into the atmosphere would be enough to create a new weather pattern over Hong Kong. It wouldn't be an apocalyptic storm front, but it would be raining regularly for two weeks following the detonation.

Fortunately, the numbers Schwarz was looking at would return back to average after the sudden influx of humidity was gone. No extra moisture entered the atmosphere, nothing that would have gone elevated, as in the case of a high-temperature event such as a subsurface nuclear detonation or a conventional explosion of similar thermal and pressure energy that would affect a much larger area and aerosolize greater amounts of water.

Schwarz stopped at the chalkboard and began killing time. He'd already "solved for X" but he wanted to buy some space. Even so, he could see Chandler out of the corner of his eye, nodding with approval at the start of Schwarz's equations and figures. She remained quiet, appreciating the squeak of dry-erase markers on the slick whiteboard. He set his multitasking mind to work.

He already knew his Beretta pistol base plates were working, simply because the magazines hadn't been disassembled. Most people would figure they were so disposable, and there would be such little room with a full 17 rounds and the spring in place, that even an undercover operative wouldn't risk discovery in them. In fact, Schwarz had been certain they might have thrown out the magazines, but a pass of a wand over them and the cartridges within gave a "good to go."

That meant Phoenix Force was likely en route to come get him. In the meantime, Lyons and Hawkins were stuck in Hawaii, waiting to make their move. He'd left them sufficient goodies in his duffel to assist them in that task, including a spare communicator for Sanay. If not, there was also a small beacon that could be activated to bring a group of Force Recon Marines to the site. That was a last-ditch plan on the part of Stony Man Farm, however.

The marines would be good. They would be deadly and they would be efficient, but they would not be so thorough in killing every single mobster and terrorist on the resort's grounds as the furious Carl Lyons while he was storing up a charge of primal rage, which Schwarz had not seen in a long time. The things Lyons had been forced to say while undercover, the people he'd been dealing with... Schwarz had seen that etching, scoring marks on his surface armor, his self-control.

The Able Team leader was a man of morals, a person of great compassion, a warrior of utmost discipline. But there was something dark, deadly and scary at his depths: a boundless rage, tinted by cruelty and a willingness to be the devil to devils, to be the terror of terrorists, to be a living horror. Lyons was not a man to torture, or to kill for pleasure, but when pushed, he had been known to leave the few survivors among opposing forces in trauma and shock at his passage.

"What were you hoping for?" Schwarz asked Chandler, stepping back from the board. "Because, unless your intent was to ruin a lot of picnics..."

"It was a scale test for the kind of thermal moisture transfer I want to bring to the forefront with the stolen Chinese weather manipulation technology," Chandler said. "What numbers are you getting?"

"It won't be monsoon season, but it'll be rainy for a couple of weeks," Schwarz said. He was double-checking the numbers as a matter of rote. Repeatable results were a scientist's stock and trade, and the math seemed to work out right.

"How about the missile strike?" Schwarz asked her.

"Obliterated the ship it hit and submunitions made the harbor inhospitable for water traffic," Chandler confirmed. She had a smile of satisfaction on her lips, a cold and soulless look that made Schwarz want to shoot her right then and there. Unfortunately he was currently outnumbered and out in the open. There were no clear lines of retreat and very little in way of solid cover for him to slip out. He'd take care of the murderous witch, but only when he was certain he could do maximum damage to the Abalisah organization.

"At least you got that much. This wasn't for the Dong-Feng, was it?" Schwarz asked. "That was a piece of work, but I don't see that thing holding an armor-piercing warhead."

"No," Chandler answered. "This was what I was working on with that weakling Baxter."

Schwarz nodded. "He asked me to keep an eye out for you, if you're Beatrice Chandler."

Chandler tilted her head. "He's worried enough to ask you for help?"

Schwarz was able to make his snort of laughter feel absolutely real only by focusing on the irony of Baxter's concern for a heartless murderess. "Yeah. Me. That's a hoot."

"I almost want to pop in and look in on him. He's folded like laundry, giving me the bits and pieces I didn't quite understand to get the rest of these engines up and running," Chandler said. "We warned him that if he didn't, terrible things would happen to me."

"Yeah. You wouldn't get a sale," Schwarz added.

Chandler laughed. She looked Schwarz over, a lustful eye tracing his fit, trim figure. Her gaze settled on his tattooed arms. "Not bad. Not bad."

"Trust me, lady. I'm very bad," Schwarz said, his voice dropping an octave.

"With a brain for numbers, and a great body, I certainly hope you're very bad for me." Chandler practically purred.

Schwarz felt his stomach start to turn, but he put his

loathing for her aside, stuffing it deep down. It wasn't often that he'd get a chance alone with a trove of information like her, or so close to an unprotected enemy asset.

Schwarz smiled exactly the kind of smile he imagined would cross the fangs of the raging, vengeance-drinking creature that existed in the heart of Carl Lyons.

Chandler's fingers brushed his arm, her touch electric and stimulating. "What do you say I finish this tour with a proper and thorough debriefing?"

Schwarz nodded, the evil thing's smile spreading across his face.

Chandler walked away from him, her slacks hugging her hips, and Schwarz followed them as they swayed back and forth. Her strut was full of confidence and allure. Even the Abalisah guards took note of her passage, nodding with appreciation.

"And if you think you can get a better job by strangling me after we're done panting and sweating, just know, everyone has seen you walk off with me," the traitor told Schwarz. She looked back over her shoulder. "That is, if you can get the drop on me."

Challenge accepted, Schwarz thought. "Never would've dreamed of it. Sex and death are Long's bag, not mine."

Chandler tittered, almost as if she were getting a thrill out of the possibility that Schwarz would try something. Then again, this woman had betrayed an American military installation, and was responsible for more than two hundred murdered during that act of sabotage and theft. All of that was for a payoff bought with the blood of coworkers.

Schwarz didn't need to confirm that Robert Baxter had undergone at least psychological torture under her demands, as well. That also didn't count the number murdered in Victoria Harbour, all just as a test of her weapon design and to provide a sense of scale for future weather manipulation attacks if the antiaircraft carrier missiles weren't enough of a seller.

They made their way to Chandler's quarters. It was a small house that didn't look prefab but had plenty of open air so that she could enjoy the warmth of the tropical Sri Lankan days, with screens to keep out the biting insects. She had fine furniture for her patio, and a tray with the makings of some good stiff drinks that she passed by. She was too busy unbuttoning her blouse, letting it slide from her freckled shoulders. She glanced back at him, a wry grin turning up the corners of her mouth.

She was not wearing anything beneath her blouse, her breasts rolling free and loose.

Schwarz clenched his fists as she led him through the small house toward her bed.

He was raised not to strike a lady, but this woman had already showed that she was as much of a demon as the rest of the Abalisah organization.

And then he turned the corner, looking down the muzzle of Bea Chandler's pistol. She bit her lower lip, eyes alight with fatal glee.

CHAPTER TWENTY

Traitorous rocket scientist Bea Chandler did not seem too interested in seduction, not when she leveled a SIG Sauer P-230 automatic at Hermann Schwarz. Whether it was because she suspected he was some form of infiltrator or she simply had a homicidal streak was unknown to the Able Team undercover operative. However, Schwarz's reflexes were in nearly flawless condition.

He brought up his forearm under her wrist, jamming the small handgun's muzzle up toward the ceiling of Chandler's boudoir. She didn't pull the trigger with that sudden deflection, which bought Schwarz a moment's more time as he folded his hand over the slide of the SIG Sauer, trapping it tightly in his grip.

Chandler's momentary thrill at having gotten the drop on Schwarz disappeared and her lips peeled back from her teeth, eyes going dark and brutal like a thwarted jackal's. She was about to lash out, her fingers curved like talons to slash at his eyes.

Schwarz kicked her in the ankle, knocking her off balance and deflecting the lash of those fingers. Now, she clutched at Schwarz's forearm, holding on to him to maintain her footing, which gave him the advantage he needed. With a powerful twist, he yanked her off her feet and hurled her to her bed. The impact knocked the gun from her grasp.

Schwarz snapped his arm straight, bringing the hard edge of his hand against the side of her jaw, a lightning-quick karate chop rendering her unconscious within the space of a moment.

He went back, grabbed up her blouse and tossed it over her exposed breasts. She'd been halfway to disrobing; maybe this might have all been a game, an element of danger while she took her latest male conquest by force. This could have been a jolt of a thrill, taking a man with a gun to his temple, denying him the pleasure of being in control of sex.

Either way, she was a criminal and a traitor to the country with which she'd sworn her allegiance. And because of her betrayal, hundreds of her fellow Americans were dead or injured, and countless more were suffering from a missile strike in Hong Kong, a missile that she had designed and now intended to sell to the highest bidder.

Too many people had died for Schwarz to want to look at her, even if she was half-naked. The blouse would keep her from being a distraction. He took the cords from the drapes on the window and bound her wrists and ankles to keep her out of trouble. He also tore a pillowcase to shreds and formed a gag to keep her from shouting and raising the alarm to her fellow Abalisah thugs.

He then went through her effects and found her personal phone. Schwarz turned it on and dialed one of Stony Man Farm's secure lines.

"I take it you found Ms. Chandler," Barbara Price said immediately upon answering on her end. There was very little chance of someone bursting in on the line. Once Schwarz had made the connection, all manner of monitors and defense encryption had been brought into play.

"Sadly, yeah," Schwarz answered. "How many did this bitch kill with her Hong Kong hit?"

"We've got death toll nearing three hundred," Price told him. "You have my permission to put two in the back of her head, just like any other thug."

"Unfortunately, she tried to hold me at gunpoint, so now she's tied up," Schwarz said. "I might not have the whole arrest thing straight in my head, but I sure as hell don't shoot unarmed, helpless prisoners."

"Too bad," Price murmured. "There's always hope that she gets caught in a cross fire, though."

"Yeah," Schwarz agreed, glumly. "What's the ETA on the rest of my boys?"

"They're on-site, checking the perimeter," Price returned. "Just give the signal and we'll put that place out of commission."

"No need to delay or wait for Ironman and T.J.?"

"He's getting ready for dinner," Price explained.

"I can just guess the menu," Schwarz answered.

He gave the Beretta a quick check and knew he'd need something a little more. "Does Pol come bearing gifts?"

"Yes. He knew you might need something more than your little nine," Price told him.

Schwarz smirked to himself.

"What numbers are we looking at? And are there any bystanders on base?" Price asked.

"They've got a sweatshop operating with two dozen workers. They don't look like they'd want a piece of any violent action," Schwarz said, looking through Chandler's home for more evidence that he could upload to the Farm. Even as he was speaking with Price, the cyber team was already hard at work raiding the traitor's phone for its contact lists and any stored notes or data. The auction and this production facility were two major assemblages of manpower and the illicitly gotten goods of the organization. However, there was little doubt that there would be more trails leading out to other coconspirators or those who would do business with arms dealers and other menaces.

Again, Schwarz's brain was multitasking, giving the information from his observation of this islet's defenses, manpower and such, even as he discovered that Chandler had a gun safe in her closet. The safe required an electronic code to enter it, but Schwarz managed to spoof that within the space of a minute.

The woman had been assigned an M-4 style carbine, one that had a full-auto chambering. After a few moments of observation, Schwarz internally pronounced that it was of quality manufacture. He was not one to look a gift horse in the mouth, not when Chandler also had a half dozen loaded 30-round magazines on hand, already in an over-the-shoulder bandolier.

Schwarz took a few moments every minute to peer through a nearby window to see if any alarm had been raised. Mosquito netting around Chandler's bed provided a screen of privacy for the traitor and her conquests, but there was still the possibility of Chandler's activity drawing out pervs and creeps. Looking at the surroundings of the house was one way that Schwarz could keep ahead of the curve, if he wasn't put into a hostage situation.

Something banged in the bedroom behind him. Beatrice Chandler was awake and moving, likely getting loose from her bonds. He had to end this phone conversation, so made a simple announcement to Price. "Got to go. Leaving the phone on."

Chandler had been very busy while Schwarz had been flipping her house for gear and information. She'd managed to untie herself and had gotten to a gun. Bullets were now snapping through the thin walls of her little bungalow. Schwarz went from standing to on his belly on the floor, loading the M-4 from its empty, neutered state to a full mag and racking the bolt to put one in the pipe.

She'd gone upscale from a .380, or maybe it was just the hammering of the gun in the close quarters of the small house, but once there were ten holes in the wall, he knew she'd definitely gone for something bigger. Schwarz flicked the selector on his rifle to full-auto, aimed beneath the cluster of holes and opened fire. The 5.56 mm rounds tore through the drywall with far more authority than Chandler's weapon, and suddenly, Schwarz's lack of blood thirst had proved to be a tactical liability. If the handgun hadn't alerted the Abalisah guards to the fact there was trouble, there was nothing like the chatter of an assault rifle on full auto to wake the unwary.

Schwarz pushed off from the floor, not reloading since the initial burst was only six to eight rounds, spent nearly wildly as he couldn't see his target drop. He still had enough to deal with anyone coming to the building, but he swung back around to the bedroom.

What was left of Beatrice Chandler was on the floor, upper torso replaced by a gory crater where Schwarz's burst had smashed into it. Near her hand was a Caracal 9 mm pistol. She tried to blink at him, but her eyelids wouldn't close around her distended orbs, lips moving as if to speak, but her lungs were gone, hopelessly deflated by the high-velocity passage of several 5.56 mm rounds.

Schwarz flicked the selector switch to semiauto and shot her through the face to end her suffering. That might not have been what she was asking for, but he couldn't bear to look at the crushed figure on the ground, trying to talk, eyes bugged out as intense hydrostatic pressure had bulged and popped them from their sockets.

The front door kicked open and Schwarz swung around. From his memory of the bungalow's layout, he opened fire, cutting through walls with the chattering assault rifle. He expended another ten rounds, blowing drywall to dust, and was rewarded by the grunts of dismay and pain as the assault team took fire.

On the heels of that burst of rifle fire, Schwarz suddenly heard the explosions of 40 mm grenades around the base.

That would be Phoenix Force and Rosario Blancanales, using their man-portable artillery as a means of softening up the Abalisah base. While the three grenadiers went to work, Schwarz readily imagined that Gary Manning was pumping precision shots into those who would prove the most dangerous to the assault teams, McCarter either as spotter or simply moving into the perimeter to work his close-quarters mayhem.

Either way, Schwarz swapped out his nearly spent magazine for a fresh one, stepping out of the path of return fire, just in case his opposition in the bungalow was intent on learning from his example of simply blazing through intervening barriers. Schwarz, thinking ahead of the enemy, kept his movements to dashes between supporting structures of the small house, and as he reached his new position, he was rewarded with distant gun bursts that tore through Sheetrock, but were off to one side, another salvo of bullets bracketing Schwarz as they struck a support stud he'd situated himself behind.

Schwarz squatted and aimed at the one avenue by which the opposition could approach him. As soon as the first of the Abalisah guards popped into view, Schwarz let him have it with a short burst of fire, a trio of M-4 slugs ripping through the guy's hip and pelvis, dumping him unceremoniously onto the ground in an uncoordinated heap. The man let out a shriek, but Schwarz ignored him for the moment as two more figures followed on his heels. Given these men didn't look as if they were wearing body armor, he took them at chest level.

High-velocity, copper-jacketed lead slashed through hearts and lungs with deadly accuracy, tearing the lives from the two guards. They flopped insensate, crashing atop their injured ally. Schwarz heard the ping of a grenade spoon being released and looked at the section of wall where he'd traded gunfire with Chandler.

It had been sufficiently weakened by their exchange and Schwarz lunged through, bursting apart drywall and tumbling onto the floor in the bedroom, looking at the guard who had lobbed a grenade into the room where his friend had been cut down. The man's hands were not on his weapon, and he was caught flat-footed, gawking at the Able Team commando. Schwarz triggered the M-4 and slashed the man from knees to throat with a long burst of auto-fire.

Schwarz got up and took cover behind a dresser. The dresser, against the drywall, wouldn't be much more in terms of protection against incoming gunfire, but at least he had something keeping him farther out of sight of the enemy. The phone still sat where he'd left it and he scooped it off the table.

"Still listening?" Schwarz asked Price.

"It was illuminating," she answered. "It also pointed out where your battle went on. The Force picked its targets. You've got Pol coming up with your gear under cover."

Schwarz grinned, then went to the window looking toward the perimeter. He watched as a couple of the Abalisah protective detail went down, one smacked by a powerful rifle cartridge, the other toppling with a crossbow bolt sticking from between his eyes like a macabre unicorn. Rosario Blancanales, his brother in arms from Able Team, rushed up bearing a package of gear across his shoulders. Schwarz smashed open the window, giving Blancanales an easier entry that wasn't exposed to incoming fire from deeper within the camp.

Already, guard towers were smoldering torches, lit aflame by the detonations of grenades in their centers. From the sizzling flames, Schwarz could tell that part of the initial wave of 40 mm shells were incendiary. Blancanales didn't come in, but did push Schwarz's gear through the window.

"I wanted this in thirty minutes or less with the free liter of diet soda," Schwarz complained.

Blancanales rolled his eyes. "You'd better give me a

good tip. Otherwise the next big sausage pizza is going to be laid there by a horse."

Schwarz tore out of the Abalisah uniform top, sliding on a long-sleeved compression shirt that would allow him better mobility and agility, as well as protection from minor knocks and the chafing from the armored load-bearing vest that came with it. He slid into the vest, enjoying the familiar, reassuring weight of his battle gear. He kept the spare magazines he'd taken from Chandler's gun safe, but discarded her rifle for one set up to his preferences. In essence, it was an update of an old classic, the CAR-15/XM-177 with a 10-inch barrel with a flash suppressor to keep the act of firing the weapon from searing all the hair off his face and forearms, as well as making him a beacon for enemy shooters. It was an M-4 with the shortened barrel, and a full-automatic trigger package instead of burst fire.

It was far from a long-range engagement weapon, though it still possessed considerable punch out to 200 yards. This was more meant for getting through doorways swiftly. The load-bearing vest had the usual Able Team-favored chain mail sandwiched between Kevlar pads. It had helped the team stay in the fight during desperate battles with maniacal opponents. He did a quick check, and many of his usual combat accoutrements were placed in their pouches. The CAR-15 he carried had all of his accessories in place on its forearm guard.

"Really, you guys made it all right?" Schwarz asked.

"McCarter took a few bumps and poundings, and I was in a car crash myself," Blancanales returned.

"That sounds exciting," Schwarz said, slipping through the window to join his brother on the ground.

"It was," Blancanales replied, letting his eyes grow wide. "I hear tomorrow we get to go to the zoo."

"Yippy. Can I come, too?" Schwarz asked.

And just like that, all the discomfort, the distaste with his false tattoos, his hatred of being undercover shattered and sloughed off his skin with just a little bit of grab-ass talk with his Able Team partner. It felt good. He wasn't quite complete, because Lyons was thousands of miles away in Hawaii, but this was much better than he'd been in countless hours. No more deceit, no more lies, just the brutal honesty of a rifle blazing away at 800 rounds per minute, punctuated by grenades and other explosions.

"Which way now?" Blancanales asked him.

"Sweatshop is that way," Schwarz answered. He removed a set of wired buds from the shoulders of his vest, inserting them into his ears, providing both hearing protection and communication capabilities. By putting the bulk of the electronics inside the armored vests, he was able to keep the ear wear low-profile, as well as having provision for a microphone in both earpieces, rather than in just the one.

It was a bit of trickery he'd parlayed into the body armor for both Able Team and Phoenix Force. With the chain mail sandwiched inside the armor, it also provided a far more extensive surface area for the antenna array, enabling communications even in the worst of conditions.

"Welcome to the party, Hermann," McCarter called.

"Nice work with the crossbow, David," Schwarz returned.

"Ah, you saw that," McCarter said with a chuckle. "Nice that our little touches are appreciated."

"Guys, hate to break up this happy little reunion, but I'm picking up movement on the road leading to the facility," Barbara Price called over their hands-free radio link. "Looks like there is a Tamil separatist militia set up about two miles north of your current location."

"Tamil separatists," Blancanales repeated.

Schwarz took his Combat PDA from its pocket on his armor. "Let me have the map. Gary, I'm sending it to you, too."

"Either a sniper or explosives to seal off that approach," Manning returned. "Right."

"I'll take over the long-range rifle," McCarter offered.

Blancanales stepped to the corner of the bungalow, scanning for threats even as both Schwarz and Manning received their satellite view of the approaching militia.

Schwarz ignored the nearby blaze of M-16 fire, which was just Blancanales "negotiating" on auto burn, cutting down Abalisah troops trying to protect their facility. More grenades hammered, but were fortunately not close to the bungalow structure.

"Gary, do you have something that can put down the lead vehicle? We snarl it up, we'll buy ourselves time to extract."

"Only if David lets me take his crossbow," Manning returned.

"All yours, mate," McCarter answered.

"Good. What was the way we're exfiltrating?" Schwarz asked.

"I've got a Blackhawk coming in, belly to the waves so we don't alert the Sri Lankan government," Price said.

Schwarz nodded. "I don't think they'd like our presence here. But if the military does show up..."

"Nah, that way of thinking won't work," Blancanales said. "You've got the Sri Lankan military, which has not won any awards for civil rights protection."

"So we can't count on them to pick up and protect the sweatshop employees," McCarter added.

Schwarz shook his head. "Nope. All right, screw that plan. We need to block the Tamil traffic coming in. And then pick up Baxter and Ling Fu."

"May Ling Fu is there?" Price asked. "We noted that she'd dropped off the grid, but we didn't think that she'd been abducted."

"She was snatched," Schwarz told her. "So, she's part of the exfiltration."

"And Chandler?" Price asked.

Schwarz's answer was studiously lacking in his current chipper mood. "That problem resolved itself."

With that, the men of Able Team and Phoenix Force set to work on destroying the missile production facility.

CHAPTER TWENTY-ONE

Carl Lyons and T. J. Hawkins bracketed the man they knew only as Jinan as he stood upon the stage. Behind them, on a large display screen, was a split image. One half displayed the awesome, awful power of an anti-ship missile shredding a freighter under an American and Liberian flag in Hong Kong's Victoria Harbour. The other half was a low-detail, almost cartoony schematic of that lethal weapon.

In the ballroom in front of them, there were more than a score of top-ranking mobsters or those who would be procurers of weaponry for paramilitary and terrorist groups, accompanied by their bodyguards. There were also others, people that Carl Lyons only recognized because he'd covertly taken digital photographs of them. These were international bankers, including one man from the Global Financial Conference whose rank and influence would create a worldwide scandal if his name was released. This same piece of human garbage didn't require photo-recognition software. Lyons knew his face from how he skated away from a rape charge in the middle of Paris a few years ago.

Jinan spoke, extending a telescoping pointer, aiming it toward the schematic of the missile.

"This was intended to destroy an American aircraft carrier, one of the most physically powerful and imposing displays of international diplomatic enforcement on this globe. It moves at Mach 10, so fast that even radar and computer-guided Vulcan cannon cannot track or destroy it. It is agile enough to thread between the masts of a flotilla of destroyers acting as the carrier's shield."

Jinan tapped the nose cone of the missile with the end of the pointer, and the drawing zoomed in to focus on the layout of the warhead. "This cone-shaped hunk of metal behind the nose cone is hundreds of pounds of copper. Behind that is a brutal shaped charge that turns all of that metal into liquid so hot that it cuts through five feet of armor, carving a hole through which the secondary payload can enter the belly of the ship."

Jinan pointed down, and the next section, a cylinder with multiple circles on it, appeared. That melted away, revealing a cross section with the drawings of dozens of pointed shells, facing away from a core of high explosives. "That secondary payload is a rapid-dispersion pack of submunitions which are launched by a fragmentation charge. In the freighter, the launch velocity was too much for the puny hull to withstand, so two-thirds of the submunitions dispersed into the waters of the harbor. Fortunately, these munitions have timed fuses, activated by the detonation of this explosive core.

"And as you can see, the dispersal radius was nearly 800 meters, causing damage to other watercrafts," Jinan said. He smiled to the assemblage gathered to view this big prize. "Naturally, this is not akin to the Dong-Feng, which we have mocked up in the display. That can utilize either a fuel-air explosive or a nuclear warhead, which can destroy a substantial fleet of crafts.

However, imagine the plausible deniability of putting a
Mach 10 bullet into a single building, and then dispers-
ing five hundred 'grenades' in a mile circle."

Lyons looked at eyes lighting up.

"A nonnuclear act of terrorism, with a stealthy, elusive weapon, yet capable of coring a modern metropo-
lis," Jinan offered. "As you can see, we have some big
ideas on hand. And we want to do more than merely sell
to you. We want to unite you. To give you the means of
global blackmail."

Jinan turned and pointed to Lyons. "Here you see
Karl Long. He is a former member of the Reich Low
Riders. He's put in his dues, breaking heads, serving
jail sentences. He was sent as a representative of a
minor league operation, one of many who have been
brought to this little resort, this slice of paradise."

Lyons remained impassive, despite feeling like the
star of a circus sideshow.

"Long is big and powerful. He's skilled with firearms and his bare hands. I have video footage of him
crushing a man's face with a single punch, destroying
his brain," Jinan said. He smiled. "And he is smart.
He has been snowing one of the Russian groups hired
on for security at this meeting. He's gotten in good
with them, so much so that he was able to murder one
of their own and get them to fake the death of one of
his allies."

Lyons didn't move his head, but his eyes swiveled
to Grigori, whose face began to twist in anger.

"Mr. Long had been given money and the authority to throw in with Abalisah, so his concerns over
Moscow 88, a street-level bunch of neo-Nazi thugs,
was only to keep them distracted by others," Jinan

stated. "When I offered him a place at our table, he jumped at it."

Bodyguards began moving their masters aside, putting themselves between Grigori and their money tickets. Lyons wished that he had gone with a more precision instrument than the Benelli M-4, but knew at the ranges in this ballroom, the buckshot spread would only be about six inches by the time it brought down Grigori.

Then again, he had the Taurus in a low-hanging quick-draw holster. And he hadn't personally had the chance to test out Schwarz's .410 rockets.

Lyons would give the Moscow 88 thug five steps, or five paces, whichever came first.

And Grigori did not disappoint. His first step was a lunge, his face turned into a mask of hatred, lips peeled back from his grit teeth, fingers extended like claws. On Grigori's second step, he'd passed the five-pace mark, and Lyons tore the big Judge from its holster, bringing it swiftly up to eye level, finger already taking up the slack on its double-action trigger.

He steadied the front sight on the tip of Grigori's nose, pulled the trigger and the subsequent disappearance of Grigori's head riveted everyone in the room.

The other men looked at their boss, decapitated and flopped on the ground. Blood spattered everywhere in a ten-foot ring around the Moscow 88 leader. Some people were splattered with gore.

"Also, for a nominal fee, we'll give you a kick-ass .410 shot shell," Lyons said.

Jinan smiled as Lyons reholstered.

Masters ushered their bodyguards out of the way,

walking closer to the Abalisah representative, even as Jinan gave Lyons a healthy clap on the shoulder.

HAWKINS AND LYONS were now on full alert. Moscow 88 knew that the two warriors were responsible for the deaths of two of their own, one of them executed right in front of their lies.

"Did you need to throw in a quip after killing Grigori?" Hawkins asked him.

Lyons shrugged. "They were already furious. Might as well prod them into full-on stupid."

Hawkins nodded with that assessment. Unfortunately that did nothing for their standing with the Russian neo-Nazi group or their security among the Abalisah organization. It was one thing to be hired on, but Jinan absolutely seemed interested in seeing how the two former bikers would handle themselves when they were openly on the line.

In a way, though, Hawkins could see Lyons settle into a more relaxed pose. With Sanay out of the line of fire, hidden away in the forest, he didn't have to worry much about a noncombatant. He also did not have to lie any longer, did not have to pretend to be friendly and cordial toward the Moscow 88 thugs. It also gave the two Stony Man operatives an excuse to walk around with major firepower, rather than sit in a hotel room, expecting an attack.

"We are still glorified rent-a-cops," Hawkins mentioned. "Except now, we're the ugly faces that the rest of the assembled scumbags see."

"Who're we calling ugly again?" Lyons asked. "Don't worry about it. My mind is aglow with whirling, transient nodes of thought careening through a cosmic vapor of invention."

Hawkins looked at Lyons blankly.

"What, you're not going to say 'ditto'?" Lyons asked him.

Hawkins rolled his eyes. "You're quoting movies when we're human skeet."

"Hermann would have been all over that," Lyons murmured. "All right. My cosmic vapor of invention is pretty damned simple. We load up on ammo…"

"We've got the ammo," Hawkins said.

"We go find Moscow 88," Lyons continued.

"Yes."

"And we shoot the hell out of them," Lyons concluded.

Hawkins blinked. "That's the plan?"

"Yes," Lyons returned.

Hawkins took a deep breath and relented. "God darn it, Mr. Long, you use your tongue prettier than a twenty-dollar whore."

"Damned right I do," Lyons answered.

With that, the two men went as if to enact Lyons's plan.

They could not simply go and empty shotguns into unsuspecting Moscow 88 guards, which Hawkins admitted was an okay plan, since the whole of their conversation had not been for their own benefit. No, as long as Jinan had the resort under audio surveillance, nothing that Lyons or Hawkins said out loud was going to be unscripted or elusive in nature, at least as long as they were unclear of their surroundings.

Avoiding members of Moscow 88, or any of the other rank-and-file guards was a matter of stealth, something both Lyons and Hawkins were well versed in. When it wasn't their former so-called Russian counterparts on the scene, the pair walked with purpose. When they did see the tattooed bigots, Lyons and Hawkins moved with purpose and menace, cold glares inspiring the lone men or pairs to stay clear, rather than risk a confrontation.

Even as the pair made their way to Jinan's reception and dinner with the big boys, the two Stony Man operatives took a careful inventory of their weaponry and gear. Sanay was in on making certain that nonessential and noncombat personnel were to stay clear of the ballroom, which had been recently reconfigured for the purposes of feasting and business discussion.

The Taurus .410 grenades were quite effective and devastating, capable of turning a human's head or torso into an aerosol mist, but Lyons wanted something more. And prior to Grigori's demise, the Russian had managed to arrange for his new comrade to have sixteen rounds of FRAG-12 shotgun grenade shells. Though only 19 mm in size, less than half of the usual M-203 cartridges, the fin-stabilized grenades were capable of punching inch-wide holes in steel.

In the dimming of sunset, Hawkins manned the FRAG-12-dedicated Benelli shotgun. As Lyons intended for them to go close quarters immediately, and the FRAG-12 shells were designed only to arm three meters from the muzzle, having an explosives-only shotgun was necessary.

Lyons aimed at the window of the ballroom, he and Hawkins both hidden in the foliage. Any tracing mechanisms had been discarded. He broke radio silence, even though he knew the network he had Sanay and Hawkins on was well encrypted and secure.

"All clear?" he asked.

Sanay answered quickly. "I've got the ballroom clear."

"Just remember to keep your head low and stick to cover once things start going boom," Lyons warned her. He felt the need to keep reminding her, simply because she was not a trained professional as he or Hawkins were.

"Gotcha," Sanay answered.

Lyons nodded for Hawkins to open up. They could see Jinan standing at the center of the spread, looking for all the world like the star of an ersatz remake of Leonardo da Vinci's *The Last Supper*. Lyons had his AK-12 shouldered and lined up on Jinan personally. This crucifixion would be on steel-cored .30-caliber nails, spitting out at 650 rounds per minute. He could have set it to burst mode to fire more quickly, but Lyons wasn't going for precision, he was going for the destruction of the windows.

"Picking up movement," Hawkins murmured. "They're looking for trouble outside."

"Let's rain hell upon them," Lyons returned. He cut loose with the AK, sweeping a scythe of 123-grain steel-cored bullets across the glass, hammering it into a spider-web pattern of cracks. Armored glass, of course. But Hawkins didn't let that stop him.

The Texan triggered his shotgun and that first FRAG-12 belched from the muzzle, armed after 3 meters, and struck the bullet-resistant glass. The sharp crack of detonation was a slap in the face, even at five meters, but suddenly the window, which had held up to Lyons's hail of auto-fire, was gone. Hawkins continued cranking the trigger.

Not having to work the slide action of a pump allowed him to fire the remaining rounds as fast as he could aim and pull the trigger.

With the window gone, Hawkins chose to hammer the FRAG-12 minigrens into the bodies of men who turned in reaction to the window exploding behind them. One of the fat pigs sitting at this feast of death dealers erupted like a volcano, the FRAG-12 shell punching through his rib cage, then detonating as it was stopped by solid spine. The blast threw open the man's chest, skin holding sheets of rib together like the petals of a flower, but the hammer blow suddenly filled the air with a cloud of reddish-black blood. As others covered their eyes, and as Lyons rocked one magazine free from the empty AK-12 and fed in another 30-round curved banana box, Hawkins struck a bodyguard in the shoulder.

The finned explosive dart severed the man's arm in one hit and detonated inches behind him, bursting in a thunderclap that peppered the gunman and others around him. Arterial spray gushed from the severed limb, and the bodyguard would be dead in moments, while five more men dealt with shrapnel. Hawkins aimed at the conference table for his third and fourth grenades, planting the microsize blasters five feet apart from each other.

Each explosion created clouds of sawdust and waves of splinters around each impact. Jinan clutched his face, screaming in pain as he caught a blast of shrapnel. The long hair and beard may have looked good, but they did little to shield his features from the hellish ejecta of grenade and bursting table.

FRAG number five smacked a bald man in the back

of his hairless head. The collision with solid bone atop sturdy shoulders was similar to Grigori's demise, except this time when the head disappeared, it looked as if a gigantic predator had taken a bite between his two shoulders.

Lyons had the AK-12 reloaded and cut loose, chasing after Jinan with his front sight, but the fleeing Iblis had his eponymous devil's luck. Lyons didn't mind, as the men who caught bullets intended for Jinan were either armed bodyguards or pieces of human garbage that had profited from mass murder and death over the years. Bodies were hitting the floor, ripped apart by 7.62 mm x 39 mm Russian slugs.

Lyons realized that Hawkins's fire was redirected, three rapid-fire FRAG-12 shells spitting toward a group of gunmen who had rounded the corner. The rapid trio of explosive shells slammed into the Abalisah hired thugs and suddenly they were under explosive attack. Bodies ruptured like melons beneath sledgehammers thanks to the salvo of shotgun-launched grenades.

"That is some satisfaction," Hawkins murmured as Lyons swung his AK-12 around and tapped off short bursts, further scattering the reaction force while Hawkins swiftly thumbed fresh shells into his Benelli. Hawkins took a look and fired two quick shots into the ballroom, a double explosion resounding in the distance. From the Texan's curse, Lyons knew what was up.

"Jinan got away?"

Hawkins growled and turned back to the guard force and pumped out two more FRAG-12 shells before having to reload. Lyons reloaded his AK-12 one last time and gave Hawkins the cover fire necessary to buy him time to load the Benelli with the last three of the high-explosive shells.

So far, however, after the initial shock wave of five grenade blasts among their number, and four more cut down by precision rifle fire, the Abalisah sentries were pulling back to cover and no longer pressing the situation.

"I've got things here," Hawkins growled. "I blew a couple of holes in the wall trying to tag Jinan."

Lyons nodded. He left the spare ammo for his AK-12 with Hawkins and switched to his Benelli, loaded with buckshot. Inside the resort hotel, it would be the king of devastation.

He rushed to the large plate window that used to enclose the ballroom. With a leap, he was inside, the 12-gauge tracking a bodyguard who had managed to find cover and was still in healthy enough condition to offer resistance. The man rose, a big handgun locked in both of his hands. Lyons swiveled the shotgun at him and fired. Eight wound channels sliced through the man's rib cage, pellets bouncing off ribs and the thick, heavy spinal column, causing massive internal damage.

The gunman toppled, big hand cannon unfired. The representative from the Global Financial Conference was smeared with blood, and he looked bewildered at the carnage that had turned an otherwise normal meeting into an abattoir. Lyons paused just enough to acquire a target and put a charge of buckshot into the acquitted rapist's face. It was a quick, painless end for a man who seemed to be willing to throw in the power of one of the world's biggest banks with Abalisah. But unless someone went to the trouble of taking his fingerprints, no one would even be able to tell what color the bastard's hair was.

Lyons surged along, passing the wounded and the dying, heading for the doorway marked by an irate Hawkins. The fist-size holes in the wall were a sure sign that Hawkins hadn't let Jinan go willingly. He swiveled into the hall and saw a trickle of blood along the floor, the occasional crimson smear against the wall.

It might have been from the splinters of wood that had ravaged Jinan's face, or it could have been shrapnel he'd take from Hawkins's FRAG-12s. Either way, Lyons now had a trail. He charged on, thumbing in fresh shells on the run.

Jinan might not have been directly responsible for dropping a missile into the middle of Victoria Harbour and killing hundreds, but he sure as hell crowed enough about it. There was no way the long-haired man was going to escape his punishment.

CHAPTER TWENTY-TWO

Gary Manning ran all-out, Calvin James racing alongside him as they sought to intercept a convoy of trucks Stony Man's satellites showed racing toward the Abalisah compound on Sri Lanka. Considering how Abalisah managed to find support among various separatist groups, it was not a surprise that the Tamil separatists would come to the rescue of the organization's base. Fortunately, there was only one road between the two areas, which would allow the two Phoenix Force warriors to slow the Tamil militia.

Manning had turned over his designated marksman's rifle to McCarter, exchanging it for the Barnett Commando crossbow that the Briton favored. Alongside him, James still had his M-16/M-203 assault rifle and grenade launcher, but the badass from Chicago had expended most of the 40 mm grenades on softening up the Abalisah defenses. He had three HEDP shells left, and one of those had been borrowed from Rafael Encizo, who had been the second grenadier who hammered the compound.

The two men stopped at the road, both glad they had reached this juncture before the Tamils. Manning unscrewed the broad head tips from two of McCarter's crossbow bolts, retrieving a pair of charges from his combat vest and replacing them.

"Explosive crossbow bolts," James murmured.

"Don't knock the classics," Manning said.

James smirked. "I'm not knocking anything. If anyone can make an aerodynamic grenade arrow that doesn't involve comic-book physics..."

"Thanks," Manning said. He cocked the Barnett and went prone beside James. The two men managed to find a berm that allowed them both cover and a look down the road the separatists would be taking. James was aiming through the sights of his M-203, and Manning, too, was aiming a little high for his intended point of impact. As soon as the enemy vehicles appeared, they wouldn't have much time to stop the convoy.

Even if they crippled more than one of the vehicles, the distance covered could be crossed quickly on foot. Manning and James both had just proved that. Their purpose was to create a wall of wreckage and flames that would hopefully seal off the road, at least long enough for them to get back to their brothers in Phoenix Force and the two Able Team members at their side.

"Target sighted," James announced. "They've got two technicals. Looks like .50-calibers mounted on pickup trucks."

"Not going to leave much of a barrier," Manning murmured. "Not for the beast coming up behind them."

"That deuce-and-a-half will plow right through the wreckage," James added.

The two small pickups were seven thousand pounds, or three and a half tons, but a deuce-and-a-half was just the main vehicle, and could haul another five tons of bulk behind it. Larger wheels and stronger suspension also meant the cargo truck could crush even the modern steel frames of the twin pickups.

"I've got the first technical," James said. "If you want to take down..."

"Got it," Manning said, adjusting his aim. "Weapons free."

James pulled the trigger on his grenade launcher and the 40 mm shell whistled through the air after it made the whole combo weapon kick hard against his shoulder. The armor-piercing grenade spiraled in its arc, smashing into the grille of the technical and detonating. In an instant a lance of molten copper slashed the pickup's engine in two, crippling the vehicle.

Behind, the other technical swerved on the road, swinging around the injured truck. James knew he couldn't reload the M-203 in time, so he switched to the M-16 portion of his weapon and fired bursts into the windshield of the rolling gun truck. Even as he fired, big bullets roared over the heads of the two Stony Man ambushers. Both trucks still had their guns working.

Manning loosed his crossbow bolt and quickly cocked the medieval weapon again. He didn't look to see if his explosive-tipped bolt had done its job. He heard the violent thunderclap, almost as an echo of James's grenade, and just ahead of the rumbling bellow of the two truck-mounted heavy machine guns.

Even as he rose and looked through the scope at the road, Manning could see the cab of the big cargo truck. It was an inferno, flames fading and being replaced by thick, choking billows of smoke that poured through the shattered windshield and the sides. Whoever was driving was either covered with burns or had been mercifully killed instantly. He saw the second technical swing closer to their position, but the enemy driver realized that getting too close would make him too vulnerable to James's chattering M-16.

Two big steel plates served as great shields for the gunner on top, and through the crossbow's scope, Manning could see that James had paid plenty of attention to him, trying to keep him from shooting back. Smears where 5.56 mm rounds struck the plates showed that the heavy machine gun provided too much protection to its shooter.

Manning aimed and fired the crossbow bolt with the second of the explosive tips.

The machine gun kept hammering away, the berm rocking as .50-caliber slugs smashed against the thick wall of dirt. However, the blast of the bolt was confirmation his aim had been true.

James held up a small pocket mirror to view over their cover.

"The pickup's a wreck, but the gunner isn't hurt. He's got too much metal between him and the cab," James announced. "The other gunner can't shoot because he'd take out his own man."

Manning pulled his mirror to survey the scene. It was just as James described, but now he could gauge the distances involved. "We can probably try to fall back, but the rest of the convoy will just keep coming on foot."

"Yeah. Plus, that fifty is making my teeth rattle," James growled. Since they were out of the line of fire, he was able to reload the 40 mm grenade launcher with his second-to-last shell. "What's the range?"

"I give it twenty-five yards," Manning told him.

James slid farther back down the berm, adjusted his aim, from below, then popped up and triggered a quick shot before diving down. The enemy gunner's bursts of fire had paused just for a moment, and James leaped upon that second of reprise. Thanks to the mirror and Manning's calculation, he was able to fire the 40 mm shell from his M-203 with certainty. It was a blind, Hail Mary shot, but in the end, the crash of the high-explosive egg caused the enemy's big gun to stop cold.

Unfortunately, with the end of the closer gunner's existence, the other pickup's heavy machine gun could pick up the slack. That fifty, however, still needed to walk its rounds to start hitting the berm.

"A hundred twenty yards isn't quite so bad. At this range, it'll take more effort for that fifty to cut through this berm," James said.

"Still going to make things tough for us," Manning returned. He raised the mirror again, hoping to gauge the distance to the heavy weapon down the line.

If they didn't do something about that big blaster—the thing had a lethal range of two miles—nothing short of several feet of packed dirt or multiple layers of reinforced concrete could slow the deadly slugs it hurled downrange.

James crawled back to try the same thing, except with an adjustment for the longer range and windage, but one of those big .50-caliber slugs sliced through the top of the berm and struck the M-16/M-203 in the forearm furniture. Only pure luck and happenstance kept James from losing fingers or whole hands due to the passage of the slug, but now, the combination weapon was a mangled mess, thrown thirty yards from the two Phoenix Force commandos.

James crawled back to Manning's side. "That sucked."

"No. It just is inconvenient," Manning returned. "Sucking would involve me trying to keep the team's medic from bleeding to death due to a severed arm."

James nodded. "There's that."

"And we're still in contact with the rest of the team," Manning added. "David, you've got my DMR. Can you get a bead on that heavy machine gunner in the busted technical?"

"We wrecked everything with enough elevation to get that," McCarter returned over the hands-free radio.

"We might have something," Blancanales said.

WHILE GARY MANNING and Calvin James rushed to intercept the convoy of Tamil separatists racing to the Abalisah base, David McCarter and Rafael Encizo launched their attack on the facility where Robert Baxter and May Ling Fu were being held. The two members of Able Team moved on to arrange the destruction of the missile engine assembly line.

Whereas Bea Chandler had been given a bungalow with comfort and amenities, the other two scientists were housed in a prefab steel building with heavy doors and minimal windows. Encizo had one last 40 mm shell in the breech of his grenade launcher, but it was a buckshot grenade, intended to make the launcher a gigantic shotgun. If anything could open up the entrance of the steel building, it would be a fist-size cluster of buckshot pellets.

Just to make certain, even as the Cuban warrior blasted the lock and handle section of the door, McCarter popped the hinges with shots from the AR-10 he'd borrowed from Manning. NATO rounds readily mangled the other supports on the doorway and the big, armored panel fell free.

Encizo let his grenade launcher drop on its sling, drawing his backup for the big-barreled cannon, the extremely compact Heckler & Koch MP-7 machine pistol. No larger than a big handgun, it could extend its stock to make it an accurate carbine, and held forty rounds of 4.6 mm high-velocity ammunition. Granted, an .18-caliber bullet wasn't going to have a lot of surface area to cause tissue disruption, but the 4.6 mm relied on two factors to increase its lethal impact. The first was an extreme velocity out of the muzzle, capable of driving the small-caliber projectile to penetrate through body-armor plates or military helmets. The second was the tendency for the bullet, upon meeting the fluid mass of the human body, to disrupt its course and tumble, cartwheeling end over end and churning up much larger channels of destroyed tissue in its wake.

Phoenix Force had been utilizing the MP-7 and the similar 5.7 mm P-90 submachine guns to good effect, and in room-to-room fighting, they excelled.

Encizo demonstrated the efficiency of the tiny bullets on an Abalisah guard who brought up his own shotgun to ward off the intruders. Faster on the draw, Encizo riddled the man with a quartet of 4.6 mm rounds that cut into his torso and mangled internal organs with ruthless efficiency.

The sentry was nailed down with a burst heart and lacerated aorta, dying before he could even pull the trigger. The rate of fire was so great that all three rounds struck within an inch of each other, but the vagrancies of rib cage construction and fluid interaction with a supersonic projectile meant the bullets veered wildly off course of one another, extending the damage and hastening the sentry's demise.

McCarter was on Encizo's heels, his locked and cocked 9 mm Browning Hi-Power in his grasp, a living extension of his arm. Holding thirteen rounds in the magazine and one in the pipe, it was a design that originated in 1935, and yet, after nearly eighty years, was still one of the world's premiere fighting handguns, accurate, easy to fire and possessing substantial payload and punch for nearly every purpose.

As a former handgun marksmanship champion, McCarter and his Hi-Power were essentially one contiguous living weapons system. He was as capable with the sleek pistol and turned to greet a new pair of Abalisah guardsmen, each carrying a machine pistol.

McCarter pumped one bullet into the bridge of one Abalisah guard's nose, coring a 9 mm jacketed hollowpoint directly through his brain. The terrorist gunman still managed to run four steps because the rest of his body hadn't realized it was dead, but that was merely momentum. The destroyed brain was unable to send the commands necessary to return fire, so the limp figure simply flopped against the wall then crashed to the floor. The messy exit wound at the back of his skull was mute testimony to the lethality of the Briton with his beloved sidearm.

The other guard jerked as he saw his friend reduced to a grisly, tumbling carcass, but with his attention divided, he was easy pickings for McCarter, who put a bullet through the Abalisah thug's left ear.

"Two for two," Encizo said. "Making up for your less than perfect shooting of Gary's marksman rifle?"

McCarter shrugged. "Maybe. Or it could be just getting reacquainted with my baby after handling that blocky thing."

Encizo smirked. The two men had their preferences in sidearms, but that was simply a side effect of familiarity and proficiency with different models. McCarter seemingly had been born teething on the GP-35 Hi-Power by Browning, just as Encizo had become enamored of the firearms produced by Heckler & Koch. Of course, a psychological comfort and prejudice toward one gun over another did tend to translate into superior ability with that chosen firearm.

McCarter and Encizo kept moving, discovering that there was one more gunman, busy trying to push his way into a room, cursing and punching the door in an effort to get at whoever was fighting for his or her own life by the use of their weight on the other side. It had to be Baxter and Ling Fu.

As soon as they saw the guard, weapon clenched in fist, they both peppered him, the combined salvo of bullets swatting the guy off the door and to the ground in a lifeless heap.

"Robert Baxter! May Ling Fu!" McCarter called out at the top of his lungs. "We're getting you out of this hole!"

Encizo rapped his knuckles on the door, which had slammed tightly when they'd killed the last guard. "The door's locked from their side."

"I know, but we don't need to hurt those two if they jump us," McCarter countered.

Encizo nodded. He used the guard's keys and opened the door. Inside, Baxter stood in front of Ling Fu, and though he was unarmed, he would stand as a shield, ready to give himself up for his fellow prisoner.

"Anybody need a ride to America?" Encizo asked.

Baxter relaxed. "Wait, what about Beatrice Chandler?"

McCarter and Encizo shared a quiet glance before the Cuban spoke up. "We have other members of our team looking for her. If she's here, and she's alive, we'll recover her, as well."

Baxter let out a relieved breath and the two Phoenix Force warriors escorted them out of their former prison and out onto the grounds. That was when Gary Manning asked for assistance over the radio.

SCHWARZ AND BLANCANALES found very little in way of resistance, despite the fact that James, Blancanales and Encizo had avoided hammering the factory with their grenades. Then again, neither James nor Blancanales let his M-16 with its twenty-inch barrel sit idly. Precision 5.56 mm fire at a distance was just as devastating and morale-destroying as a rain of high explosives.

Even so, there were still some guards who were glad to utilize the building as solid cover. Those survivors realized that either the attacking force didn't want to harm the sweatshop workers or they wanted to take back the engines intact.

Blancanales blew the door off its hinges with a buckshot round fired from a distance and Schwarz cut loose with his CAR-15 mini. They blazed away at the guards suddenly left without a steel barrier between themselves and the outside.

Though slowed by only having ten inches to accelerate in the barrel, riding that wave of expanding gases, the stubby rifle in Schwarz's fists put those 5.56 mm rounds through flesh and bone, crossing the few yards between shooter and target in nanoseconds. When they suddenly decelerated from more than twice the speed of sound on contact with flesh and bone, the carbine bullets produced massive trauma, ending any hope of their resistance or escape.

The Abalisah gunmen were no angels, and when warriors of Stony Man unleashed their vengeance, there was going to be a bloody toll paid. After a few moments Blancanales was certain that the commando teams had wrought sufficient carnage among the complex that they were no longer outnumbered or outgunned

However, no matter the situation, he still stood guard, observant and grim as Schwarz went to work, letting the workers loose from their tables and guiding them to freedom. Blancanales and Schwarz both watched over the former slaves, and they ran to the perimeter that they had blown holes through. The way the Stony Man assault force had entered was most logically cleared of mines or antipersonnel traps and would lead to safety.

Schwarz explained as best as he could that that was the case; it didn't look as if he needed a translator to confirm their understanding. They took off, disappearing into the forest.

"Hopefully they will find a way back to their home villages," Schwarz said.

"And that we're not going to be blasting their families to hell if they're related to the Tamils," Blancanales added.

Schwarz moved back into the assembly line. "I doubt the Tamils would sell their own people into slavery. And if they did, then those folks won't weep too hard if we blew Uncle Bastard to pieces."

"There you go again, using that strange thing called logic," Blancanales said.

Schwarz chuckled. "You don't believe in logic?"

"I know it exists, but I use diplomacy, so my personal experience with logic is fleeting at best," Blancanales returned.

Schwarz nodded. "Oh, right. You know, if we spread this thing called logic, a lot of the world's problems would disappear."

"But then people would have to actually deal with things they didn't like, rather than settle into angry camps trying to prove they're right by being louder than their opposition," Blancanales pointed out.

As warriors in the field, people who spent their time interacting with different cultures and actually battling toe to toe with those involved in heinous violence, they knew far more than any person left behind, be they political pundits or self-appointed intellectuals. They saw the world in far more than black-and-white, or even shades of gray. To them, the acknowledgment of facts and the actual causes of evil were very plain and obvious, despite the hyperbole and bile of one political party or the other. To them, most news was simply opinion, cherry-picked from the whole cloth of the world.

The two men looked to see what materials they had with which to turn this assembly line when they heard the situation and dilemma on the radio link, as well as the distant thunder of the .50-caliber machine gun.

Schwarz immediately began gathering parts together.

"We might have something." Blancanales spoke up, watching Schwarz rapidly assemble a rocket.

CHAPTER TWENTY-THREE

Jinan's breath was ragged in his lungs as he dashed through the back hallways of the hotel. His arm bled, but it was a mere flesh wound, even though it made his cream-colored blazer soak through pink. The injury came when one of those two maniacs—who should have been killing Moscow 88 goons—opened fire on the big committee.

They'd been firing explosive shells into the conference. They weren't even just utilizing rifles; they'd been throwing grenades or something. After the fourth or fifth body exploded, Jinan was in full flight. During the lull of bodies detonating in the conference room, he'd noted that others in the room were falling to automatic rifle fire, but that was nothing in comparison to the horror of watching men he'd been talking to coming apart.

It had been a neat, interesting end to that racist goon Grigori, watching Long fire a single shot and the man's head disappearing in a burst of crimson.

Standing much closer to such detonations was not something he wanted to experience ever again. And yet Jinan realized that if he couldn't keep up his pace, he would personally experience such an explosion inside his own body. Long and Presley had repaid him for their new position by engaging in an act of outright terrorism.

What the hell was wrong with them? Jinan thought

as he skidded and grabbed on to a door frame to change course. The impact with the doorjamb knocked the breath from him, and he scanned back down the hallway. Something lurched into view in the distance, but he didn't stick around to get a good look.

Even as he ducked through the door into the next room, he heard the thundering boom of a shotgun and the snap of drywall and wood framing as buckshot tore into it. Long, or whoever he was, had tried to core him with that weapon.

At least it's not a grenade, Jinan told himself, driving forward and toward the lobby.

And as soon as he reached the open lobby, he saw some of the survivors of the Russian neo-Nazis standing there, armed as they should be, but none of them casting their gaze toward him with anything resembling compassion. Why should they? He'd served up their commander to Long, let the man execute Grigori right in front of them after humiliating the group.

And now, with a cut on his arm, sweat matting long strands of his hair down his face, he was like blood in the water for sharks. One of them had a grin cross his face as he started walking toward Jinan. The Abalisah representative glanced around to see if anyone else, someone more trustworthy, was present.

Then again, he *had* deemed Long and Presley trustworthy. He turned and raced away from the Moscow 88 gunman, but heard the grinning man stomp after him. Jinan's legs felt like lead, but he struggled to keep one foot moving in front of the other. To give up now was to offer himself up as a meal to the scavengers hungry for vengeance. He thrust himself forward, breathing in dry, raspy gasps of air.

Long wasn't acting like a biker, but he sure as hell wasn't a cop. No policeman would scar himself with that many tattoos, nor would he commit cold-blooded murder. And if he was trying to infiltrate Abalisah to destroy it, why hadn't he waited until after the auction? Why would he take everything and throw all the good information away? Why would he gun down a big-time banker like that?

Jinan's thoughts raced through his mind even as he pushed himself forward. This was madness. He couldn't find a single motive that would make Long go on a killing spree like this. If he was a rival, then he wouldn't have killed half of those men in the conference room; he would have tried to woo them. If he was an antiterrorist operative or a spy, he would have had much better luck keeping them happy and healthy, alive so that he could tap them for even more information.

No, Long is out for blood, Jinan decided.

He didn't believe there was any good reason for Long to go so maniacal. He'd killed recklessly, doing things that would never allow him to make a proper prosecution, and he'd acted in ways that subjected him to too much risk that a good espionage agent would never be able to win trust except on the wildest of risks.

If Long was a criminal, or had other mercenary motives at heart, then he would have kept in a position to further himself, to actually get paid rather than blow the first potential paycheck. Hired by a rival gang, he would have remained calm and quiet, seeking acceptance and the opportunity to be paid by both sides, working one side against another.

This was murder. This was blood for blood, killing rival bikers, killing people not even related to him.

And yet, Abalisah hadn't done anything to the Reich Low Riders or the Aryan Right Coalition to warrant such reprisal.

Jinan's reverie was interrupted by the sudden thunder of gunfire in the lobby behind him. Shotguns and handguns blazed, screams filling the air. Groups exchanged fire and Jinan paused only to see the Moscow 88 goon who'd begun chasing him fall over, a smoldering pillar of steam rising from the small of his back. Jinan locked eyes with Long, who let his shotgun drop on its sling, bringing out one of his handguns.

Jinan leaped, finding just that little bit more energy as a slug whizzed desperately close to his head.

"Screw figuring out who this bastard is," Jinan rasped. "Just get the hell away from him."

LYONS BARRELED ALONG the hallway after Jinan. An external police raid, or even a commando hit, would have been an ideal means of dealing with this group. Even better would have been an unmanned drone loaded with air-to-ground missiles. That was how the United States had started inflicting terror upon terrorist groups over the past several years. Precision, laser-guided munitions were one clear message that it was time for diplomacy to take a backseat.

Unfortunately, foreign policy by guided missile that might have supplied the results desired in most military instances—dead terrorists lying in multiple pieces—had also been seen as a sign of weakness, an unwillingness to send men in to get even for horrors. Lyons never minded going into harm's way to kill a maniac, no matter how many protectors they had on their payroll.

He'd tapped off a shot or two after Jinan, but the mastermind of this auction was just running too quickly to be caught by anything but a close-range hit. Whether it was luck or speed, Jinan would not go down. Lyons realized that long-range removal would not be as satisfactory for him.

Nothing less than a hands-on strangulation or a neck break would let him think that he'd accomplished his mission.

Now Lyons was out in the open, in the lobby of the hotel, noticing a squad of Moscow 88 gunmen as they watched one of their own tear off, rage in his eyes. The Russians turned their attention toward Lyons, who had his Benelli shotgun out and ready to rock.

"This can go peacefully," Lyons growled.

Thankfully for the gene pool of Moscow, the neo-Nazis decided to react in a violent manner, guns rising and pulled from holsters and off slings. Lyons already had the Colt Python aimed and braced, so he pulled the trigger, launching a fist of flying lead into the chest of the foremost gunman. The thug's breastbone erupted in splinters, and lungs, aorta and heart were pulverized in a brutal rampage of murder and destruction. The gunman crashed backward into one of his allies even as hastily fired shots erupted from unaimed handguns.

Bullets thwacked against the wall off Lyons's right shoulder as he let the slack out on the Benelli's trigger. The semiautomatic shotgun cycled quickly, a fresh shot shell loaded into the breech within instants. All he needed to do was to pivot slightly and fire again. This time the Able Team leader smashed the forearm and elbow of a second gunman, bursting bones and severing the man's hand. Paw and weapon cartwheeled through the air, severed by the shotgun blast, gravity and momentum pulling them apart in the air.

The empty case ejected and the swift gas operation loaded another payload of mayhem into the breech. Lyons adjusted his aim a little higher and to his left. His third shot struck one of the Russians in the face. Most of the pellets entered the screaming bigot's open mouth, tearing bone and flesh out the back of his skull and neck. The projectiles that didn't go into his roaring piehole made .32-caliber holes in his cheeks, turning one of his eyeballs into a deflated sac of ruptured jelly.

The shot that had gone in deformed as it struck bone and flesh, flattening and growing in diameter, tearing ugly channels. The man was not decapitated, but one could see through the ragged hole ripped by the blast.

Two dead, one disarmed, almost literally.

Lyons swung toward the fourth member of the group who was in the middle of blazing away with his own shotgun, even though his aim had been disrupted by the falling form of Lyons's first target. The Able Team commander decided to give him a double tap, blasting him at gut level, then shooting higher.

The first load of buck tore out the belly of the man. The next salvo of pellets smashed his shoulder into a pulp filled with bone fragments and splinters. Both shots were less than perfect kill shots, but the split between their impacts, the fact that the Russian caught sixteen rounds—fully the equal of half a magazine from most rifles or submachine guns—and the spread of carnage as the individual projectiles tore through flesh and bone spared the man's suffering. As well, when his shoulder had been smashed, the compression of the man's clavicle dislodged vertebrae, scissoring his spinal column instantly.

Three dead and in pieces. The fourth man had only a stump of an arm, and gaped wide-eyed at Lyons, who raced around the corner.

The Able Team leader spotted the last of the Russians who was in full pursuit of Jinan. Lyons didn't need the impediment or competition, so he loosed round six from the Benelli, catching the Russian between the shoulder blades. The blast lifted the Russian off his feet and hurled him to the ground in a tangle of uncontrolled limbs.

Rather than use up the last of his shotgun ammo, and because Jinan was just a little far outside of the range where he could get a clean shot, Lyons drew his Colt, aimed and fired his shot at the fleeing figure in one smooth, rapid movement. Lyons's bullet struck the doorjamb just short of taking off Jinan's head, once more reinforcing Lyons's opinion that the only way to put him down forever was to crush him to death with his bare hands.

Lyons flicked the safety on his pistol and continued on, racing at full speed, long strides eating up ground as he sought to cut the distance between him and the fleeing devil. Jinan had taken off like a bat out of hell, but even as he'd ducked out of the path of that last bullet, he had lost several steps. The criminal didn't have enough cardio in his life, while Lyons continued pushing himself and his endurance, keeping himself in top condition.

So even with a head start, Lyons was catching up.

Behind him, in the lobby he'd just blazed through with his shotgun, he heard the crash and thunder of dozens of weapons suddenly opening up. The resort was hearing the storm of war in the distance, and all veneer of civilization stripped away as the semblance of Abalisah's control vanished. Naturally, Lyons expected this sort of thing to start much sooner. Of course, there were several bodies already made before now, some of them not even the fault of the undercover Stony Man operatives.

The auction, for all of its claims of equality among the bidders, and then later a recruiting drive for Abalisah, was nothing more than a prison complex. The illusion of power, given by the allowance of sidearms, by the treats to appease the varied appetites of the visitors, were all obfuscation for the true nature of this particular hellhole. The setup was nothing more than a glorified penitentiary full of gangs, and competing gangs at that.

Now that Lyons had seen that the Abalisah organization was trying to set up a survival-of-the-fittest set of trials, and had gone so far as to have Lyons execute Grigori of Moscow 88, he knew that the stopper in the dam of civility was gone. The floodgates holding back a storm of violence crumbled, and Lyons's obliteration of several men in the lobby was the wake-up alarm.

Guns now blazed, petty rivalries and old scores coming to the forefront.

"Good," Lyons growled on the run, thumbing shells into the feed ramp. "Do our jobs for us."

Elsewhere, Hawkins was cleaning up the summit that Jinan ran away from. When he was finished, his job was to fight his way to Sanay and her hiding spot. Exfiltration was the next part of this mission. Abalisah's abandoned fortress resort was drenched in blood, their efforts at making peace with prospective allies or hiring on potential troops turned to carnage and bloodshed.

Lyons wondered how Hawkins was doing as he closed in on the fleeing Jinan.

THOMAS JEFFERSON HAWKINS, the youngest and newest member of Phoenix Force, was not a man who often felt as if he were out of his element. The Texan had served active tours of duty with the Rangers and with Delta Force, where he'd honed the skills and knowledge that made him a valuable addition to the Stony Man action team. Across dozens of missions with Phoenix, he'd risen to every challenge.

Hawkins was on his own as he cleared up the last of the troops who had rushed to the scene of the conference room slaughter, AK-12 sputtering 1000 rpm bursts that snuffed out enemy gunmen with a single trigger pull.

He fed the hungry AK, scanning for more threats. So far, except for the group they'd devastated with FRAG-12 shells and precision rifle fire, not much had showed up. Even so, that was still a group of more than a dozen that had managed to hang on for half a minute after Lyons left in hot pursuit of Jinan.

Hawkins knew that the plan was to split up anyway. That way they could cover more ground, clear out some of the targets of opportunity who would be on the run once the bodies started to hit the floor. In the distance, he could hear the crack and bark of weaponry, battles raging between a group of very dangerous people who had been sitting on old grudges up until now. Hawkins swung wide toward the front of the resort.

One of the things that had been done under the cover of darkness was a mining of the drive. Selectable Lightweight Attack Munitions—SLAMs—had been secreted in the growth along the driveway leading toward the main road, away from the resort. Part of the "magic" of the SLAMs was their ability to be utilized in multiple fashions, either as timed, motion-sensor activated, remote-detonated or pressure-detonated—as in rolled over. Since the SLAM was a shaped-charge explosive that could spit out a cone of liquefied copper more than four meters, it had the ability to cripple a tank or take out lightly armored vehicles and people walking by on foot.

Since the SLAMs were easy to hide, being very low profile, and with shielded transceivers to avoid detection by sophisticated enemy forces, Hawkins and Schwarz had been more than capable to get placement accomplished. With a properly encrypted set of signals, they could make the system live in a two-part harmony. He hit the transmitter just before they went loud with the Benelli and its grenade rounds.

That signal activated the SLAMs and their motion sensors.

He recognized the distant pop of one of those SLAMs now, instants before the crash and screech of tortured metal. One of the vehicles on the resort had just broken a magnetic detector beam and had been blown to a brutal mess. Other SLAMs were tuned to passive infrared, the tiny packages of death mixed and dispersed to turn the whole of the driveway into an impassible hell zone.

People running on foot would activate the passive infrared beams, and the SLAMs' shaped charge would produce a sheet of force and shrapnel that would sever legs, crush pelvises and shatter spines. The magnetically keyed SLAMs would hurl that screeching hot jet of explosive force through a van or car's thin metal shell, turning the interior into a rolling crematorium, killing all within.

The first mine would get people wondering. Efforts to circumvent the explosive deathtraps would receive other bits of lethal trickery.

Hawkins was glad that Schwarz was not an enemy of mankind, because the booby traps and horrors he'd set aside for those trying to avoid or defuse the mines were wicked and brutal. Another crash in the distance informed him that someone thought he'd discovered a live mine.

Hawkins was at the lobby, looking up the road to see smoke billowing through the trees. He clutched the AK-12, scanning around as panicked criminals saw the blockage caused by the destroyed, escaping car. He watched a pathetic figure, holding out the stumps of arms blown off at the elbow, stagger into view. Screams of horror filled the air.

Thai and Kyrgyz separatist security staff suddenly cut loose, their AKs and shotguns blasting into the group assembled in the lobby, handguns barking from inside the building. Hawkins turned his AK to the shattered glass doors of the lobby and kicked in his talents. He was still wearing the uniform given to him by Jinan and the Abalisah organization, and a couple of the gunmen gave him a thumbs-up.

Hawkins tagged bodyguards and scrambling kingpins as they rushed for cover or tried to blast their way to the entrance. A couple of them had gotten hold of long arms, and Hawkins didn't need much to realize that Lyons might have already cut through some of the "many devils" on his pursuit of Jinan. The presence of big guns, however, was no guarantee of survival, as the Texan schooled the escaping buyers of murder.

For all their journey, for all their efforts, everything came down to a face full of bullets or a heart torn asunder by lead.

The Asian security forces were doing well when Hawkins noticed there were others moving away behind them. They were tearing off their uniform shirts and he could see the tans of Colombian FARC goons brought in to round out the security forces. Hawkins took cover behind a pillar as he watched some of the "skins" sweep in behind the guards doing their job in containing the riot inside the hotel.

In an instant the Colombians had flanked and ambushed the Kyrgyz and the Thai, unleashing the contents of their assault rifles and shotguns on the unsuspecting sentries.

Hawkins reloaded his AK-12 and then carefully chose his targets for maximum effect. The AK-12 began to chatter and the head of the nearest Colombian gunner vanished, spattering the man next to him with gore.

Hawkins took aim at a second gunman and his well-timed burst chopped the FARC soldier down just before the enemy gunner could aim his shotgun. The downed Colombian squeezed the trigger and the shotgun blast slammed into the lower spine of a Kyrgyz trying to run from the ambush. The young man crashed to the ground.

Hawkins didn't feel any pity for the separatist. His brothers had engaged in multiple acts of horror across

China, and the Kyrgyz thug had been firing at other people in the lobby. One way or another, Lyons and Hawkins were going to have to give these jackbooted hired killers more than a taste of why engaging in terror was a bad idea. That it was a Colombian gun that ended him rather than the Phoenix commando's own weaponry was incidental. Death was being spread.

These guns for hire, if they somehow survived, were going to look over their shoulders for the rest of their lives. Hawkins was tempted to leave them something to be frightened of, but such was the nature of Phoenix Force and Able Team that they couldn't let their enemies know exactly who or what was responsible for their failure. It would compromise the very secrecy that had made Stony Man Farm's action squads so deadly and effective.

Instead of shouting a battle cry, Hawkins opted for the anonymous, lethal tactics that bore the Stony Man signature.

The snap and crack of gunfire exchanges informed him that this was far from over.

CHAPTER TWENTY-FOUR

"How much longer is your special little gift going to take?" Calvin James asked over the hands-free radio. He and Gary Manning were huddled behind a berm that was receiving a volley of distant heavy machine-gun fire. They had managed to hold up the convoy of Tamil insurgents, coming to cover and protect the slave labor camp.

Neither the Tamil separatist forces nor the government of Sri Lanka could be considered friends or allies, or even benevolent forces in regard to the population of the island nation. The convoy, however, was on the rampage due to a mutual protection pact, likely one where they would receive top-of-the-line weaponry from Abalisah. With Phoenix Force and Able Team destroying the arms-building facility, the Tamils were out of the kind of firepower that would have put them at an advantage over the Sri Lankan government.

Right now, thanks to the use of some 40 mm grenades and explosive crossbow bolts, the Tamil convoy had been slowed to a halt. One wrecked jeep had a gunner on it, utilizing a .50-caliber machine gun of some sort. And sooner or later the packed berm of dirt Manning and James were using for cover would give out under bullets that struck with the force of a six-ton jackhammer and were coming at them at a rate of 650 rounds per minute. Only rocky soil ten feet thick had enough substance to stop those bullets.

Even while pinned down by the big fifty, James and Manning still managed to keep the Tamils from approaching too closely. Manning had his plastic explosive disks, which he could sail into a group of enemy gunmen, and James had the more traditional fragmentation grenades and smoke canisters to provide cover. The smoke enabled them to rise and pop off single rounds at Tamil troopers attempting to push up on the pair. Manning was using his .357 Magnum revolver, while James, his rifle destroyed by a .50-caliber round, was relying on his Beretta 92-FS.

It wasn't hard to make long-distance shots with the big 9 mm pistol. Its nearly five-inch barrel, excellent sights and supercrisp single-action trigger, as well as the size to smother almost all of the recoil of the Parabellum bullet, made hits at a hundred yards easy for James.

The only trouble was that with every single shot made by the Phoenix pair, the muzzle flashes, even with the suppressors attached to their weapons, gave away their positions. Manning took to putting crossbow bolts through Tamil gunmen, but without the deadly crack of a weapon, the separatist troops kept pressing forward, necessitating a blast from the big Magnum.

"Listen, Cal, do I stand over your shoulder and tell you what stitches to use when you're doing your medic thing?" Schwarz said on the other end of the radio line.

Even as the electronics genius gave up his sarcastic remark, James could hear him moving parts around, quickly assembling an improvised missile.

If there was a person alive who could take disjointed

pieces off an assembly line and throw them together as an artillery missile, it was the man Able Team called Gadgets. Still, James was feeling the heat as that fifty down the road kept hammering at their only cover.

David McCarter was helping as much as he could, utilizing Manning's Designated Marksman Rifle to snipe at individual troops, but the Briton could not get a good angle to hit the man at the vehicle-mounted gun. The only saving grace was that the gun was too heavy to move off the wrecked pickup it was mounted on, and Manning had destroyed the vehicle's engine with an explosive crossbow bolt. What could have been so much worse—a mobile gun platform—was now merely a gun emplacement, but one that could provide cover fire for the army of Tamil rebels being held at bay.

"Any time you guys feel like firing that missile would be nice," Manning offered. "I know…"

Suddenly, in the middle of their own crisis, the two men of Phoenix Force were listening to the grunts and gurgles of Schwarz and his partner Blancanales, as well as the exertions of fellow Phoenix warrior Rafael Encizo.

Things were happening.

Whether it was good or bad, it still would be precious seconds as, suddenly, James and Manning were helpless observers far from the sidelines of their brethren's current situation.

MANJUN AND JUNUN had waited long enough. They watched the man that they had known as Herman Shore, the tweaker biker genius they had kidnapped from the resort summit in Hawaii. They had taken the right man to this place, at least in terms of technical skill. Utilizing parts not intended to go together, he had constructed a pair of miniature artillery rockets loaded with submunitions, intended to be utilized at short range. They were clumsy, ugly devices, and seemed held together by nothing more than spit and bailing wire, but Shore seemed confident in the construction.

"Listen, Cal, do I stand over your shoulder and tell you what stitches to use when you're doing your medic thing?" he said, applying a blast of soldering to keep one of the canister shells of the improvised rockets together.

Manjun and Junun looked at each other. Though they had lost the assembly line and most of the slave labor provided to them by the Tamil separatists, if they could capture him again, they could salvage this crashing situation.

Sure, the loss of Abalisah manpower was horrendous, more than thirty trained guards now dead, their remains strewed across the facility, and Beatrice Chandler was nothing more than a gory, lumpy stain on the floor of her bungalow. But Shore, or whoever he was, would be a prize with which Abalisah could recover. He'd be the ideal genius to provide them with weapons as yet undreamed of.

As an added bonus, Manjun had retrieved the portable stun gun Shore had crafted from a clock radio, a device that actually fired a lance of electrical energy across several feet without need of Taser tines or wires.

All the better to hoist this Shore by his own petard, and then to deal with his allies while they were busy hauling the missiles into a firing position.

"ALL RIGHT, GET these outside," Schwarz told Blancanales and Encizo. "It's heavy lifting…"

"I got this one," the stocky Cuban said. Though he did not have the height or bulk of Manning or Lyons, Encizo had been a swimmer all of his life, and life on the sea had forged his body into a compact wedge of muscle made for slicing through the water with his own form or pulling the oars on a boat. The swarthy Phoenix Force veteran grabbed up one of the missiles, giving a grunt at its weight.

Blancanales watched Encizo take off, moving to the door that Schwarz had indicated.

"How heavy was that?" Blancanales asked.

"Just shy of three hundred pounds with the fuel and submunitions on board," Schwarz answered. "Don't worry, I'll help you with lifting the other missile."

They heard Manning begin to say something over the radio when two figures—big, mahogany-skinned Indians by their facial features and complexion—stepped into the open. One of them aimed a small hand device at Blancanales, while the other lunged, his long limbs reaching out for Schwarz.

Rosario Blancanales knew his brother in arms, Schwarz, and the kind of devices that he put together. They were not necessarily the prettiest of objects when first assembled in the field, but they worked. He recognized the electrical gun in Manjun's hand and leaped backward over the table as the air hummed and smelled of ozone from the zapper's discharge. Blancanales could tell by the stench that the weapon had been tuned to maximum output, more than sufficient amperage to kill a human being.

Getting his feet into the air was a lifesaving maneuver that kept him from making a circuit to the ground, so even if Manjun had somehow struck him, the current would not go through his body and seek out the ground. Electricity sought the quickest path to the ground, and air was not a particularly ideal medium for that purpose. That was why lightning struck tall structures and why lightning rods were placed on roofs. Given a metal conduit, the lightning would strike the tip and ride between those atoms to the earth. People were fine conduits in comparison to air, given that the human body had sufficient iron and the nervous system was already electrically conductive to deal with its own neurological processes. Unfortunately the body, being a fine road for lightning to choose, was not built for handling that kind of current, or the heat energy inherent in a lightning bolt.

Schwarz's electric gun didn't produce the same heat of a lightning plasma discharge, which would take enormous amounts of electricity and such a blast would be hotter than the surface of the sun and melt the device in Manjun's hand. Blancanales dropped to the dirt, keeping himself out of a straight line with the blaster.

In the meantime, Schwarz had dived into a somersault, rolling beneath the grasping arms of Junun and coming up to his feet behind his adversary. Schwarz's preferred martial art was "Monkey Style" kung fu, a Shaolin method that had been developed hundreds of years ago when a monk studied the motions of monkeys as they fought off trespassers and predators such as snakes and eagles. Schwarz felt at home with the natural, free-flowing style of kung fu. His diving roll toward and then behind Junun's attack was a perfect example of that kind of maneuver.

Even before Junun could turn to face Schwarz, he was fully erect in a Tall Monkey stance, knowing that he would have to deal with the Indian who had a height advantage on him. Even so, the Tall Monkey stance would give Schwarz an even better advantage against the long, lean-limbed opponent. Junun pushed forward, a tree-branch-strong arm lashing out to connect a brutal punch to Schwarz's shoulder and collarbone.

Schwarz snapped both hands on Junun's forearm in monkey claw fists, pulling his opponent toward him and off balance, adding his weight to his opponent's forward momentum. Schwarz released the monkey claws from Junun's forearm and snapped forward, hooking them around the back of his neck.

Pulling down hard, Schwarz brought both of his knees up into Junin's chest. Using his foe's weight in addition to his own, he dragged the kidnapper to the ground, the knees to the ribs knocking the wind from his lungs. Suddenly caught breathless and upended, the Abalisah operative was helpless as Schwarz rolled and kicked out.

Junun sailed over Schwarz's prone form, arms spread wide in surprise. He tried to take in a breath, but he crashed against assembly line tables. Metal clanged and clattered as his tall form slammed through the furniture and the components spread about. As the tables themselves were heavy, solid wood, Junun suffered and lost his breath again as the edge chopped into his back.

Schwarz scurried to all fours and spun to face Junun as he rolled down prone on the table. The Indian man pulled his knees up to his chest in an effort to shield himself, to coax his lungs into taking a deep breath, but in true Drunken Monkey style, Schwarz brought

his clawed hands down on Junun's throat. It was seemingly just a mistake, grabbing on to his foe's windpipe
to help steady him or to bring him to full height, but
the true intent was to close off the man's breathing.

The Abalisah operative gagged, trying to suck in
a breath, but as Schwarz was leaning on him, squat-
ting low, Junun couldn't swat at him or bat him off his
throat. Panic began to take hold of the kidnapper. This
was the man who had been so distracted that he'd gone
to sleep within moments of the chloroform placed over
his mouth. How could such an absentminded tweaker
have suddenly gone to complete, deadly focus, strangling the life from him?

The answer came to Junun too late as Schwarz suddenly somersaulted, rolling along the length of the Indian's chest. The Able Team genius's weight squeezed
even more breath out of his lungs.

The tall Abalisah operative reached out to snatch
at Schwarz's shoulder, to do something offensively
against this tattoo-covered tweaker. Instead of a handful of Schwarz's shirt, a monkey claw clamped on to
Junun's wrist, dragging him until he was sitting up.
Then the commando seemed to slip and topple off the
table, still clutching Junun's wrist.

Once again, what seemed like clumsiness was brutally efficient cruelty. Schwarz was totally in control
of the situation, using his own weight to lever the tall
man after him. Before Junun could catch himself, he
flew face-first into the next table along the assembly
line with all of his weight and Schwarz's leverage.

The nasty crunch and crackle of facial bones im-
ploding against heavy oak was mercifully the last thing
the kidnapper ever would feel. He would have died

eventually from all the crushing his windpipe had taken, but when his face struck the edge of the assembly table, it was like a guillotine blade, except it was the head falling upon the immovable blade.

Face bones were mangled, splinters driven into Junun's brain, and all the while his own weight drove vertebrae up into the base of his skull, crushing his medulla oblongata and shearing his spinal cord.

Schwarz rose from between the tables, turning the brain-dead man around and shattering his collarbone with two powerful downward stabs of his clawed fingers. The impact on already-battered ribs and lungs collapsed the internal organs, producing a sputtering rasp.

BLANCANALES REALIZED THE two Abalisah men had stolen in here to take Schwarz, likely to go back to wherever the group called home. They had also wanted to do it silently, hence the use of the quiet electrical projector Schwarz had invented and the attempts at martial arts on the part of the other man. With Phoenix Force distracted by the Tamil separatist convoy, they would have gotten away with it, if only the two devils hadn't tried to capture Able Team warriors by surprise.

Even so, Manjun had given up after the third shot from the electrical device. It was a powerful weapon, but even so, the laws of physics, chemistry and thermodynamics would not allow for more stun charges to be held in the commercial batteries of the clock radio. Manjun hurled the zap rod at Blancanales, who snatched it out of the air.

Manjun sneered, and saw that his partner was currently dragging Schwarz across several tables, or so it seemed. He decided that the stealthy plan was not going to work. He reached for the Pindad Browning Hi-Power knockoff pistol from his hip.

Blancanales judged the weight of Schwarz's improvised stun prod, and was impressed that it was well-balanced enough to be used as a missile on its own. With a sharp toss, the former clock radio disintegrated against Manjun's jaw, bowling him backward and interrupting the draw of his pistol.

Blancanales hurled himself up onto the assembly line table, grabbing a length of conduit for his own bit of improvisation.

Manjun clutched his clawed-up face, lacerated by metal and plastic splintering and tearing the skin across his jaw and cheek. Distracted and stunned by the hurled invention, when he did notice Blancanales, it was far too late for him to do anything except an impression of a golf ball on a tee. The fatter end of Blancanales's conduit pipe caught Manjun's jaw on the unmarked side of his face and the mandible crunched with the sound of breaking glass.

A riot of nerve signals blazed through Manjun's brain as he staggered along the table. Jolts of misfiring nerves from the juncture smashed by the dislocated jawbone left the Indian blinded, dazed and reeling. One arm tried to clutch at anything for support on the assembly table, and the pistol he'd drawn halfway out of its holster toppled from numb fingers to the ground at his feet.

Manjun brought both hands around to stabilize himself. Thick, bloody spittle drooled over his lower lip and his legs felt like rubber. Unfortunately, he didn't have any more time to evaluate his physical condition.

His right kidney suddenly blazed with its own trauma signals as Blancanales stabbed the conduit into his side with enough force to rupture dozens of blood vessels within the organ.

Renal shock turned into paralyzing pain and Manjun hurt so bad that he tore the tips of his fingers off, clawing at the assembly table.

Those rubber knees finally buckled and he slumped to the ground, gasping and gurgling. Manjun swiveled his eyes over to see that his adversary wasn't slowing down. He caught the glimpse of silvery metal gleaming and then everything turned to crimson, then black.

Rosario Blancanales stepped back after lashing the improvised *jo* stick across Manjun's eyes. Both orbs were ruptured, blood and creamy white spilling through deflated eyelids.

Blancanales swallowed. "Okay, that was a little bit much. Sorry."

Manjun sputtered, but with a shattered jaw, there weren't any words that he could form. However, it did seem that the Abalisah thug did acknowledge the apology.

Off to the side, Blancanales heard Junun's skull and neck shatter against the table.

Blancanales sighed. "I never meant to be so cruel."

Those were the final words that Manjun ever heard as the conduit came down one final time, the lead pipe bursting his brain like overripened fruit.

RAFAEL ENCIZO HEARD the crashing behind him and the grunts of Schwarz and Blancanales over his hands-free radio. Someone had waited until the two Able Team members were alone, but right now, Encizo knew that if guns weren't blazing, then his Stony Man counterparts were going to be all right for long enough to accomplish his mission with this improvised missile.

Schwarz was an engineer, and even though the missile was heavy, it was no heavier than it had to be, and only seemed to have enough fuel to deal with the convoy, as long as Encizo reached the spot that Schwarz told him to put it down. The Cuban set the missile on a flat piece of stone that had been chosen for the task, setting it upright on a clamped baseplate tilted at a slight angle.

Encizo recalled the directions. Set missile down. Unlock baseplate clamps. Flip switch and step back. All that was necessary was to maneuver the three-hundred-pound chunk of death into position. Encizo followed the instructions and stepped back quickly.

"Of course, Gadgets would give me a second to get away from the rocket blast," he muttered.

The engine fired and suddenly the missile, laden with submunitions, burst into the sky. There was a sharp pop and the next thing Encizo knew, a pillar of cottony smoke stretched upward into the sky.

Please, don't let this be a ranging shot, Encizo prayed, making a sign of the cross. He wasn't a devout Catholic, but at times like this, a little bit of faith and a request for help never could hurt.

Instants later he saw that the trail of smoke had made a hairpin, turning at the apex of its flight and falling. Hot gases sloughed off the exhaust nozzles as the falling warhead came down a couple of hundred yards away.

"Don't be a ranging…" Encizo repeated his prayer out loud.

The missile suddenly popped, a hundred yards above the ground. The Cuban squinted, fearing the warhead had come apart, rattled to pieces due to the violence of its launch and the harsh pull of gravity.

That's when Encizo noticed that the ground began shuddering under his feet. It couldn't have been an earthquake or a volcano, as they were too far from a seismic fault for that. It had to be the detonation of the dozens of bomblets Schwarz had stuffed into the missile. The roar of the blasts reached his ears moments after the vibrations through the earth. Like lightning passed more swiftly through metal than through air, sound traveled quicker through the ground.

And the multiple booms sounded like an assault rifle going off at close range.

"Gary? Cal?" Encizo asked over the headset.

"Rafe, remind me never to enter a bet over the biggest boom with Gadgets," Manning said aloud.

"Gadgets! Pol! You two okay?" James called over the com.

"Easy, dude," Schwarz returned. "We have radios. You don't have to shout loud enough to be heard a hundred yards away."

"We heard some scuffling and struggling," Manning said.

"A couple of pieces of trash needed to be swept aside. The convoy is toast?" Schwarz asked.

"Blown to perdition," Manning answered.

"Great. Come over here and help Rafe point the Mark Two version at the Tamil camp," Schwarz said.

"Mark Two?" Manning asked.

"Probably another fifty pounds of bomblets," Encizo said, heading back to the missile factory.

"Another hundred and fifty," Schwarz corrected. "Barb said there're no civilians in the area, and I'm getting sick of trouble here on the island. Maybe with a few hundred less Tigers, the government might ease up on its 'counterinsurgency.'"

"And what if I doesn't?" McCarter asked.

There was a brief pause.

"There's always the Mark Three variant," Schwarz stated with grim resolve.

CHAPTER TWENTY-FIVE

The beautiful thing about an Able Team infiltration mission was that you only had to stay undercover long enough to get everybody in a position where they were at their cockiest feeling and their most comfortable, when guards were lowered and enough trust had been gained to enable the members to simply cut loose.

That had already happened and dozens of enemies on hand were already dead. Carl Lyons couldn't count the actual bodies, especially since some of the security forces stayed far away and dragged their wounded out of sight. Nor could he tell how many had been slain while crossing the minefield of SLAMs set up along the access road to the resort.

But bodies were hitting the floor and blood flowed like cheap wine. The only thing that Lyons really felt the urge to do was catch up to Jinan, the boss running this meeting of the damned, and personally send him screaming all the way to Hell. Merely arresting Jinan was never going to be in the cards for him, not when he was involved in murderous attacks on at least two continents and making deals to unify several criminal and terrorist organizations.

No, Stony Man wasn't called in to handle the jobs that could be done by even the most elite of the Special Operations community. Able Team and Phoenix

Force were the last resort when it came to law breakers, espionage or military action.

Jinan had finally left the building and was now out on the grounds, Lyons loping along with smooth, ground-eating strides. Jinan was slowing down, feet stumbling and tripping over each other.

The Abalisah representative didn't have the kind of physical conditioning Lyons possessed; in fact, it was here in Hawaii that the Able Team leader had taken part in his first Ironman Triathlon. He'd had the title of Ironman from his tour of duty as a cop without taking a day off, but a race with his name on it was just the thing that drew his attention. Since he'd been in the race to protect a high-level official from a kidnapping attempt, he hadn't tried to win or actually compete. However, that bit of marathon running had made him far more than a match for any European pretty boy who seemed to have the physical toning of a fifteen-year-old boy.

"Jinan! Just stop running, you'll only die puking!" Lyons called after him.

It was a bit of cruelty that he punctuated the taunt with a blast of buckshot that kicked up a clod of dirt at Jinan's heels, but that shotgun boom finally made the sleazy businessman trip over his tired feet and crash to the path through the woods.

And yet, for all the comedy of that stumble, Jinan still clawed his way to all fours.

Lyons skidded to a halt just behind him, still three yards between the two of them.

"Jinan!"

"Karl! No!" the long-haired Abalisah rep called back. He raised one hand, as if to magically ward off the bone-crushing, flesh-rupturing power of a 12-gauge loaded with 00 buck.

Lyons rested the gun on his shoulder, looking him over. When Jinan was back in the conference room, seemingly hours prior, his cream-colored suit was neat and impeccable. Now one sleeve was soaked with dried blood, tears were on the knees and the shoulder seams of his jacket had popped to reveal his black silk shirt beneath. Grass and bushes ground off their emerald blood, while mud had dug into the fibers of the once sharp-looking outfit.

Jinan's shiny, flowing hair was no longer a fluid brown, but wiry, dingy black sticking to the sides of his face. His breaths were ragged and rough as he wheezed.

"You have anything to say?" Lyons asked.

"Why? Why are you doing this?" Jinan asked. "Whoever is paying you, we can offer you more money."

Lyons chuckled. "I'm getting a salary. This isn't a mercenary mission, sleazeball."

Jinan's shoulders drooped at the sound of that. "What?"

"I said that I haven't been hired to take you and the rest of these goons down. Well, in a way, a long time ago someone took me on to his cause, and I've stuck with the team he's given me," Lyons told him. "The cause of eradicating forces of corruption like you and the bastards you were going to supply weapons."

"Are you a Fed?"

"Call it a pest-removal expert. Vermin extermination," Lyons told him, walking closer.

Jinan shook his head. "That's insane."

"Part of why we've lasted so long. We do shit that

makes extreme sports look like Tuesday-night bingo," Lyons said. "And me? I'm the craziest bastard in the whole chicken coop. I live for situations where I'm out-numbered and surrounded. It means I've got plenty of targets to shoot, and can fire in any direction I damn well please."

Jinan took a step backward as Lyons reached out. He snarled a fist full of Jinan's black silk shirt, halt-ing his retreat.

"In fact, thanks for taking my buddy Gadgets away from here," Lyons told him. "One less friendly I had to worry about accidentally blowing away. The new guy, he's not usually with my squad, so I wouldn't worry about clipping him."

Jinan lashed out, slapping Lyons across the cheek. The Eurotrash must have been more exhausted than he seemed, because while the slap stung, it had no weight or strength behind it. Lyons shoved Jinan away from him.

The Abalisah leader tried to right himself, to keep his balance and to stand, but after three wobbly steps, he crashed down onto his ass. Dark eyes were wide with horror.

"So, who are you meeting out here?" Lyons asked.

Movement through the woods ahead and the distant throb of a helicopter's rotors gave the Able Team com-mander everything he needed to know, but Lyons was in no hurry to betray his knowledge. He'd been play-ing Jinan with his cards close to the vest and wasn't about to give the long-haired sleazeball an inkling of just how truly doomed he was.

On the other hand, he did bring the stock of the Benelli shotgun to his shoulder, ready to greet the security guards from the helipad. Lyons sidestepped off the game trail, taking refuge behind the thick trunk of a tree.

"Be careful! He's going to ambush you!" Jinan croaked, but he'd been running too hard, too long, and the volume of his words was barely above a harsh whisper.

"Sir!" someone called from up the path.

Lyons followed the movement of the figure with the front sight of his shotgun, and there he was, another dressed in a guard uniform similar to the one Jinan had given Hawkins and him. This man had on a helmet and goggles, body armor tugged over his torso to increase his odds of surviving in combat.

The guy also had a brand-new, black and sleek AK-12 full automatic rifle, a weapon Lyons had already utilized minutes earlier to shoot up a conference room and a responding sentry team. Loaded with thirty rounds in the magazine, and firing them out at rates of 1000 rpm in bursts, it was deadly, efficient and had all the charm of the original AK-47, except with tactical black furniture, rails and that new gun smell. Abalisah had handed them out to whoever wanted to work for the organization.

The body armor also looked new and quite capable, which meant that Lyons had to shift weapons in his hiding spot. He let the big Benelli shotgun hang on its sling, pulling out the Taurus Judge, loaded with a quintet of Schwarz's high-explosive rocket shells.

Jinan waved, pointing desperately toward Lyons's position, even as the armored trooper drew closer to him, distracted by the disheveled Abalisah officer and not paying attention to his surroundings. There were others appearing just at the next turn in the path, similarly armed and armored. Lyons moved his attention and the aim of his Taurus pistol toward them, thumbing back the hammer with a soft click.

Any hopes for stealth disappeared when the Judge roared and a sabot-driven tungsten tip riding atop a core of shaped plastic explosive, propelled along by a stiffer than normal charge, leaped through the woods and struck one of the black polycarbonate helmets in the distance. The thunderclap of the rocket round's impact was a loud, distinct pop echoing the muzzle blast of his revolver.

In an instant the armored goon next to Jinan dove off the trail, abandoning the man he'd been so interested in moments before.

Lyons moved as soon as he touched off the shot. While the .410 shells kept the Judge from being an overly large .45 Colt revolver, the gun was still big, loud and ungainly. From a standing position, he'd gone to the ground, skidding prone and turning his attention toward the Abalisah trooper's position, cutting loose with the AK-12.

The chatter and muzzle flash of the assault rifle was just the thing Lyons needed to locate the gunman, even through long grasses and fern bushes. Lyons fired at about waist height, wondering what the .410 sabots would do against body armor.

Turns out, the rifle-armed gunman let out a grunt and fell backward, the explosive bursting as it struck a ceramic trauma plate in the vest. Even without penetrating, the impact knocked him over. But the enemy shooter now had Lyons's location and again triggered the AK-12. Bullets churned up the ground as the Able

Team commander rolled, squirming to get out of the way of incoming fire.

Lyons fired again, the big Taurus bucking in both fists. The third shell detonated high in the air, deflecting off the Abalisah gunman's helmet. The bouncing rocket round and continued bursts of AK-12 fire convinced him to let go of the Judge and drop it in the dirt. He rolled onto his knees, pulling out the Benelli shotgun.

From up the path, two more weapons roared, muzzle flashes tracking Lyons's movement. Lyons chose to continue dealing with the closer opponent. Since his foe was too well armored in the torso for shotgun fire, he decided to utilize the general destructive capabilities of the Benelli, triggering three rapid shots. The gunman shrieked. His vest and helmet might have protected his vital organs, but buckshot slashed through his forearms, tearing muscle and breaking bone, rendering the AK-12 in his hands utterly useless.

Lyons turned and put out three more rounds, rushing across the path, leaping over Jinan's huddled form along the way. His goal was the injured trooper and the assault rifle he had. While Lyons wasn't much of a fan of the 5.56 mm NATO, it still possessed armor-defeating capabilities at close range, much better than the 12-gauge buckshot that was great against unarmored foes.

Lyons slowed a few steps in front of the fallen trooper and kicked him in the face with all of his might. Through the uniform boots and all up his leg, Lyons felt the man's neck breaking on impact. He wasn't one to leave a foe to suffer, and since this guy was already crippled and bleeding profusely, he wouldn't last long.

Lyons reached down, scooped up the AK-12 and hit the magazine release. The partially spent mag tumbled from the receiver and he reached into the corpse's magazine pouch, bringing out a full one. He paused, checking the ammunition within. He could see that this one was in 5.56 mm NATO, but just by eyeballing the tips of the bullets, he could tell they were likely heavier for the caliber, increasing their horsepower and penetrative capabilities.

Lyons slammed the magazine home and secured it in one swift, smooth movement. The stock rose to his shoulder and he got a view of the two gunmen in the distance over the sights. One of them also saw him in return, pivoting to target him.

Lyons gave the AK-12's trigger a short stroke, a trio of high-velocity bullets punching into the gunman's face. Eye protection goggles were good for dealing with slivers of brass or for burned gunpowder, but when it came to a 72-grain slug blistering along at just under 3000 feet per second, they were useless. The trio of projectiles shattered the polymer goggle lens, crushed the orbit of the eye socket and burrowed deep into the soft, spongy brain deep beneath. The gunman was dead so quickly, his body didn't get the signal to fall, muscles still locked in place. The destruction of his central nervous system was an instant neutralization.

Lyons turned toward the other Abalisah soldier.

Panicked by the sudden collapse of his partner, the rifleman jerked the trigger, sizzling a swath of slugs over Lyons's head.

The projectiles came so close, he could feel the wind parting his hair.

Lyons opened fire, but the other man was moving too quickly. His rounds hit the opponent, but they were center-mass shots, striking ballistic armor that had similarly blunted his shotgun blasts. Lyons adjusted, pushed the muzzle lower and cut loose with a trio of tribursts.

Very few armored soldiers had significant protection to their thighs and calves. They had hard knee protection, but Lyons swept around thigh height. There would be a good chance that one of the projectiles could rupture the femoral artery, or at least cause major muscle damage. The slugs did not possess the weight or momentum capable of shattering a femur, at least reliably.

The gunner suddenly toppled out of sight, falling to the ground. Lyons jogged closer, keeping the rifle ready to fire, his sights locked on the trooper's last known position, though the savvy ex-cop kept his attention spread out, searching for signs of trouble in his peripheral vision. He didn't want to come this far, only to be brought down by carelessness and inattention to his surroundings.

Sure enough, the enemy rifleman had crawled away, his rifle discarded, leaving a trail of blood. The bullets had hit, but Lyons could tell by the color of the blood that he hadn't struck an artery. It wasn't bright enough, so that meant his opponent was still alive and kicking, at least with injured legs. Lyons swept around the back of a tree, using it for cover as he scanned the forest floor.

Almost instantly he caught a flash of movement. Lyons jerked back reflexively, the crack of a 9 mm pistol filling the air as the wounded enemy opened fire. He swung around the other side of the tree, dropping to one knee. The change of height and position meant that he caught the other soldier off guard. Lyons had flipped the selector from burst-mode to full automatic. Instead of putting out rounds at 1000 per minute, it was at a more sedate 600 rpm.

This allowed Lyons to hose down the fallen opponent with seventeen shots. Some struck body armor, others struck limbs, but one of them hit hard enough for the enemy to flop onto his back, his gun silent. Lyons tossed aside the empty rifle and scooped up the fallen one from the bloody trail, closing in on the presumed dead man.

He needn't have worried about finishing the job with this armored gunman. Three of Lyons's bullets had shattered his jaw and opened up his throat. Lifeless eyes stared up through safety glasses, no breath escaping the large, ragged holes in his windpipe and face.

Lyons let out a relaxing breath when he heard a shout in the distance.

"My turn to torment you, Karl!"

Lyons threw himself to the ground just as one of those rocket rounds burst against a tree trunk. He hissed as splinters peppered his face and shoulder from the nearby detonation. Jinan had rushed to pick up the Taurus, and he likely had one more of those .410 rocket shells on hand.

The gunshot that struck the tree was close enough to show that Jinan was either a good shot or he'd gotten his breath back enough to steady his aim. Unfortunately, the terrorist leader was nowhere to be seen. The guy likely had taken hints from Lyons's own fire and maneuvering, disappearing like a ghost in the trees.

"You have one shot left, Jinan!" Lyons called out. "And I've got another gun in addition to this rifle."

Absently, Lyons plucked two magazines from the pouches of the dead armored trooper. He wasn't going to end up with a useless weapon a second time this fight. He pocketed both in his borrowed uniform vest.

There was movement, and Lyons already could see that Jinan was heading toward the Benelli shotgun that he'd dropped next to the first gunman. He cursed under his breath. He fired off a couple of quick bursts in the direction of where that body lay in the forest.

"Goddamn it!" Jinan swore.

A shotgun blast echoed between the trees and Lyons grimaced, buckshot pellets plucking at the back of his shirt. He'd ducked, but already he could feel his shoulder blade grow hot with the blood and lacerations of a near miss from a 12-gauge payload of death. Lyons opened fire in the direction of the shotgun's muzzle blast.

Again, there were curses filling the air, punctuated by the thunderbolt response of the Benelli shotgun. Lyons, staying low and holding his fire, scurried through the foliage on the forest floor, allowing ferns and long grasses to conceal his passage. They could exchange shots all day long, or Lyons could take the initiative and finish this accursed mess.

And the Able Team leader was not going to sit back idly.

Jinan fired the shotgun into the woods, having lost track of the stealthy Lyons.

"You hurt, you tattooed freak?" Jinan asked. "Did I finally put a dent in your armor?"

Lyons padded along with lithe agility belying his two-hundred-pound bulk. His arm hurt, and he felt his uniform shirt becoming drenched with blood seeping from his shoulder wound. But he stayed quiet, approaching Jinan from downwind, in his blind spot.

Some bit of devil's luck was still with the death dealer, however. Jinan whirled, maybe noticing Lyons out of the corner of his eye. In a flash, the Abalisah representative pulled the Judge, still with that last .410 explosive sabot in its cylinder. The big muzzle of the handgun whirled ever closer to Lyons's eyeline when he reached up with his uninjured hand, seizing Jinan by the wrist.

There was a brief moment where the two men pitted the strength of their arms against the other, the big revolver trembling as Jinan tried to stuff the muzzle into Lyons's face and Lyons trying to aim the gun away from himself.

"You're right-handed, and you're fighting me with your left," Jinan said through gritted teeth. His rictus turned slightly upward into a smile, confidence starting to fill him. "You'll die covered with Nazi tattoos, you know that?"

Lyons locked his cold blue eyes with Jinan's. Instead of the inside-out arm wrestling contest, he changed the rules and suddenly yanked the revolver closer, the muzzle sweeping past his head. Off balance, Jinan fired the big hand cannon too late. Hot gases peppered Lyons's cheeks and eyelids, but he'd blinked against the flare, protecting his eyes.

"No. Because the ink will break down in a few days," Lyons returned. He let go of Jinan's wrist, snapping his knee up and into the frame of his shotgun, jarring it aside.

Jinan spit and brought his left hand around, fingers hooked and ready to claw at Lyons's eyes. Lyons straightened his left arm, a single knuckle forming the point of a fist-spear that crashed into his opponent's windpipe. The unmistakable feel of cartilage collapsing under the throat punch rewarded Lyons as Jinan stumbled backward, clawed fingers swiping at empty air.

"My skin won't be covered with hate speech when I die," Lyons said, stepping closer to the stumbling figure of Jinan. He flattened his hand and slashed down hard, crashing the edge against the side of the death dealer's neck. The karate chop was an old, tried and true maneuver, one that might have seemed passé in an era of Krav Maga and mixed martial arts.

Even so, the force of Lyons's chop was more than sufficient to shatter Jinan's collarbone and dislocate his neck bones. The Abalisah leader's dark brown eyes lost the spark of life long before he would have choked to death, thanks to his crushed windpipe. His spine severed, he flopped to the ground in a lifeless, boneless heap.

There was no need to check, no need to make sure, but Lyons lifted his boot and brought it down, stamping Jinan's face mercilessly until he'd literally stomped a mud hole in the place of his head.

"Carl!"

Lyons turned at the sound of Hawkins's voice. The Texan was approaching, Sanay in tow. He had a few small cuts and scrapes on him, but looked otherwise in good health.

Hawkins and Sanay approached Lyons and the head-less corpse of Jinan, looking down at the red-tinged mud.

"Jinan?" Hawkins asked.

"Yeah," Lyons answered.

Sanay put her hand over her mouth at the grisly display.

"Just got a call from Barb. They're sending a helicopter to pick us up," Hawkins said. "You don't have your PDA on?"

"Didn't notice any incoming calls," Lyons returned. "What about the rest of the noncombat hotel staff?"

Sanay's eyes were still locked on the lifeless form on the ground.

Lyons snapped his fingers.

"They…they got out. And they didn't take the main access road," she said.

"Won't matter," Lyons noted. "T.J., send the signal to pop whatever's still live on the driveway. I don't want Hawaiian cops hurt by our mines."

Hawkins nodded. "I got you."

There was only one distant pop. Apparently other criminals and terrorists escaping the resort had set the rest off, likely dying in the attempt.

"Want me to take care of your back?" Sanay asked, turning away, studiously ignoring the evidence of Lyons's true rage and murderous intent.

Lyons nodded. His rage was spent. Those thugs who weren't dead were on the run, frightened, wounded and scared.

He was right about the tattoos; in time the blueberry extract would fade from his skin. Even before then, he would be back together with Schwarz and Blancanales. His scored back would heal, but the sight and presence of his brothers in Able Team would do far more to heal the grim demeanor that had weighed so heavily upon him over the past days of this deadly mission.

Sanay would never get a chance to thank the big blond warrior who had protected her on that Hawaiian resort, however. It was not a Stony Man soldier's place to stick around, to receive praise. Getting out of her life would allow her a far greater measure of safety than if Lyons stuck around with her. Too many former lovers were in graves for Lyons to want her to live with that specter of doom hanging over her.

For now, the many devils of Abalisah had been exorcised, banished from the face of the Earth.

And when they, or their ilk, rose to continue their damned ways, the Stony Man cyber crew, Phoenix Force and Able Team would be there to put them down, and keep putting them down, until none rose in their place again.

* * * * *

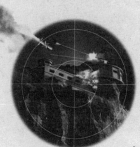

The Executioner

Don Pendleton's®

SAVAGE DEADLOCK

No Man's Land

A missing US nuclear scientist resurfaces as a member of a guerrilla women's rights organization in Pakistan, raising all kinds of alarms in Washington and gaining the attention of rebel fighters.

Mack Bolan is tasked with extracting the woman and getting her Stateside, even if she doesn't want to go. But as the rebels close in and the guerrilla group realizes it's weaker than the trained fighters, Bolan and a handful of allies are forced to join the battle. Their team might be small, but the Executioner has might on his side.

GOLD EAGLE®

Available January 2015
wherever books and ebooks are sold.

Don Pendleton's Mack Bolan®

CRITICAL EXPOSURE

Classified Annihilation

Across the globe, undercover US military missions
are compromised when double agents begin
identifying and killing covert personnel. The
situation threatens to devastate national security,
so the White House calls in Mack Bolan.

Posing as a spy in Istanbul, Bolan infiltrates
the realm of black market arms dealers and
intelligence brokers determined to expose the true
enemy of the state. Faced with an expansive and
extremely dangerous operation, the Executioner's
strategy is simple and hard: strike at the heart,
and don't let up until it stops beating.

Available January 2015
wherever books and ebooks are sold.

JAMES AXLER

DEATH LANDS®

HIVE INVASION

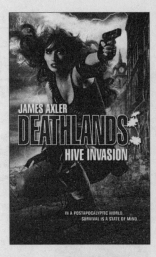

HARNESSED MINDS

Desperate to find water and shelter on the barren plains of former Oklahoma, Ryan and his team come upon a community that appears, at first, to be peaceful. Then the ville is attacked by a group of its own inhabitants— people infected with a parasite that has turned them into slave warriors for an unknown overlord. The companions try to help fend off the enemy and protect the remaining population, but when Ryan is captured during a second ambush, all hope seems lost. Especially when he launches an assault against his own crew.

Available January 2015 wherever books and ebooks are sold.

James Axler
Outlanders®

TERMINAL WHITE

The old order has a new plan to enslave humanity

The Cerberus rebels remain vigilant, defending mankind's sovereignty against the alien forces. Now a dark and deadly intelligence plots to eradicate what it means to be human: free will.

In the northern wilderness, an experimental testing ground—where computers have replaced independent choice—is turning citizens into docile, obedient sheep. The brainchild of a dedicated Magistrate of the old order, Terminal White promises to achieve the subjugation of the human race. As the Cerberus warriors infiltrate and get trapped in this mechanized web, humanity's only salvation may be lost in a blinding white doom.

Available February 2015